D1600941

SANCTUARY

A FAN FICTION COLLECTION

SHERI-LYNN MAREAN   RACHEL HAILEY

NICKI NANCE   KRISTA KELLN

KIMBERLY FORREST   T. ELIZABETH GUTHRIE

MARY E. JUNG   CARRIE HUMPHREY

L.J. SEALEY   SAM BRETON   JENNIFER FORIST

JENNIFER BECKER   CATHY GRAHAM

KIM MAY

Foreword by SHERRILYN KENYON

Edited by CAROL SHAUGHNESSY

Foreword by SHERRILYN KENYON

OLIVER
HEBER
BOOKS

All rights reserved.

No part of this publication may be sold, copied, distributed, reproduced or transmitted in any form or by any means, mechanical or digital, including photocopying and recording or by any information storage and retrieval system without the prior written permission of both the publisher, Oliver Heber Books and the authors, except in the case of brief quotations embodied in critical articles and reviews.

PUBLISHER'S NOTE: This is a work of fiction. Names, characters, places, and incidents either are the product of the author's imagination or are used fictitiously. Any resemblance to actual persons, living or dead, business establishments, events, or locales is entirely coincidental.

Dragon Heart Awakened Copyright © Sheri-Lynn Marean

Brave Copyright © Rachel Hailey

Mourning Shadows Copyright © Nicki Nance

Dreaming of New Orleans Copyright © Krista Kelln

Hot Wings and Howlers Copyright © Kimberly Forrest

The Fugitive Jackal Copyright © T.Elizabeth Guthrie

Ravaged Angel Copyright © Mary E. Jung

Sanctuary Copyright © Carrie Humphrey

One Fated Night Copyright © L.J. Sealy

Valentine's Day at Sanctuary Copyright © Sam Breton

New Beginnings Copyright © Jennifer Forist

From her Darkest Dreams Copyright © Jennifer Becker

Falcon's Delight Copyright © Cathy Graham

A Fox With New Fur Copyright © Kim May

Cover Design: Dar Albert

Published by Oliver-Heber Books

0 9 8 7 6 5 4 3 2 1

THE LEGEND OF SANCTUARY

SHERRILYN KENYON

You can take my life, but you'll never break me.
   So bring me your worse...
   And I will definitely give you mine.

Those words, written in French, still remained on the top of Nicolette Peltier's desk where she'd carved them with her bear's claw after the death of two of her sons. It wasn't just a motto, it was her angry declaration to the world that had taken her sons from her. A ruthless tragedy that had spurred her on to create the most renowned of the shapeshifter havens.

Sanctuary.

For over a century, she'd owned the famed Sanctuary bar and restaurant that rested on the corner of Ursulines and Chartres in New Orleans.

There, she'd reigned as the queen of her kingdom. The mother bear of her remaining twelve cubs who struggled hard every day with the grief over the ones they'd buried.

Not a day had passed that she hadn't mourned them.

Until the day war had come to their door. True to her nature and the words she'd carved as a permanent reminder of her spirit, she had done her worst and she'd protected her children with everything she had.

But that love for them had cost her her life. When her enemies moved to kill her daughter's mate, she'd protected the lycanthrope with the last of her strength and she'd given her life to save her daughter Aimee the agony of burying the wolfwere she loved.

The tragedy of her loss was felt throughout the entire Were-Hunter counsel. Nicolette Peltier had been as much a legend as the club she'd owned. A club that had welcomed all creatures and promised them safety and protection so long as they obeyed her one simple rule:

Come in peace.

Or leave in pieces.

Since the night of her death, her cubs have sought to carry on without her support and guidance.

Any fan of Dark-Hunters knows the legend of Sanctuary, as well as the Were-Hunters who frequent and populate it.

It's the cornerstone and stands as a sentinel against outside ills.

A true Sanctuary for anyone who needs it.

My idea for it spun out of the clubs I frequented as a teen and young woman. Those were my refuge from the evil in my real life, so when I was building the Hunterverse, it was only natural that the very thing I relied on for my relief would be brought into my fictional world.

I had no idea just how popular it would become.

The idea behind Sanctuary was to be a meeting

ground for people of all walks of life and from widely different backgrounds.

All accepted.

All equally loved.

Therefore, I could think of no better title for this anthology as it represents the breadth and depth of Dark-Hunters fandom. A safe meeting place where they can let their own ideas flourish.

I am thrilled that so many fans turned out for the project and honored that so many have embraced my series for so long.

And I have a special thank you to Carol who took time from her own writing to spearhead this project.

Thank you all!

I hope you enjoy this foray into my universe as explored by the fans who have made it what it is.

And I will leave everyone with one small reminder. These are fan stories, written by fans. While I gave them the ability to write in my world, what they have done isn't necessarily Dark-Hunter canon.

This book exists outside of the time line of the Dark-Hunters.

And I hope all of you enjoy our little side adventure.

Hugs!

DRAGON HEART AWAKENED

SHERI-LYNN MAREAN

1

THREE YEARS AGO

A figure dressed all in black, with glimmering chestnut hair that hung past her shoulders, hurried into the lab. Sawyer got to his feet. He crossed to the bars of his cell. "What's going on?"

Evany rarely came here unless it was time for an injection, though sometimes she'd sneak in and visit with Sawyer. She was the daughter to the scientist who kept him here and an Ilyium witch and mortal enemy to his kind, but Sawyer liked her. He lived for the moments he'd get to see her. "What are you doing here?"

"Freeing you." She unlocked his cell then reached up to remove his collar. A collar that prevented him from accessing his teleportation ability.

"Why?"

"I shouldn't like you, but for some reason I do," she said.

She did? "You do?"

"I've shocked you." She grinned.

"Yes." Sometimes Evany seemed like two different people. One day she'd sneak a smile his way, other times her eyes would be full of hatred. "Your father will be furious."

Guilt followed by resignation crossed her face. "I know, but I can't leave you here any longer."

Despite the fact she often confused him, he didn't want to leave her. "Come with me."

"We're enemies."

"You don't feel like my enemy," he said.

"I can't. If I go, my father will know it was I who released you. But if I'm here I can tell him you escaped, and get on the team sent to retrieve you, and attempt to keep you safe," she said.

Sawyer had forgotten she was also an Ilyium soldier, trained from a young age to fight his kind. "Evany—"

"No. Now go before I put this collar back on you!"

Sawyer left, but as he teleported away, a part of his heart remained with Evany.

2

THREE YEARS LATER

A rustle outside the hut jarred Sawyer's sleep. Heart racing, he opened his eyes. Had they found him? He shoved the threadbare blanket away and sat up. He inhaled mildew and rotting wood—the structure he'd been sleeping in for the past few weeks.

The Ilyium had been relentless in their goal to re-capture Sawyer, and it was beginning to wear him down. He sighed inwardly and his eyes started to slide closed.

"No!" Sawyer mentally shook himself. What the —? No matter how fatigued he'd been lately, now was not the time to slack off. Those following him certainly wouldn't.

He listened and caught another whisper that didn't belong to the night. Though the Ilyium were well trained, he always knew when they were near.

Time to go.

Sawyer reached for his knife, wincing as pain stabbed his skull. As it dissipated, he slid the blade into its sheath. Then with a longing glance at his pallet, he teleported away.

He hated running, but his fighting skills ended at

age fourteen when the Ilyium first captured him. He could possibly take one of their soldiers, but not more.

They'd follow. They had his blood and even if they didn't, they'd probably conjure a spell to find him. That didn't mean he had to make it easy.

Sawyer materialized in the alley of a city not far away, then teleported to a town on the other side of Lavellas before jumping to another realm. Then another, and another.

He lost track of the time and places as a throbbing drummed at his head. Out of breath, he gazed around. Whatever town this was, the noon-day market was in full swing.

He grimaced when he caught a glimpse of his reflection in a shop window. His long brown hair was a mess, and his golden eyes were dull and bloodshot. He desperately needed rest along with a meal.

Sawyer gazed around, looking for an establishment that might be willing to trade work for food and a place to sleep, when someone grabbed his arm.

Sawyer tried to teleport away, but nothing happened. Then he realized it was an elderly woman with salt and pepper hair and pale blue eyes in a wrinkled face. "Can I help you?"

Her eyes paled to milky white. "Hurry! Go to Sanctuary on Earth. It's in New Orleans. You must get there before sundown."

"Earth? Are you an oracle?"

She nodded. "Go, or you'll be done, young man."

Her words sent prickles down Sawyer's spine. "What do you mean?"

She turned back to the market.

"Wait, tell me why?"

But she'd already melted into the crowd.

Sawyer didn't know the oracle's motives, but her

words stirred a deep sense of foreboding. "New Orleans, huh?" He'd been there, but honestly, would being done be so bad? He was tired of running and looking over his shoulder.

Except, while he might want nothing more than to sleep for a year, was he ready to give up?

Sawyer envisioned the lively city in Louisiana. Why not? It was as good a place as any, and it was always warm.

Only as he drew on his ability, it sizzled, then sent him on his way with a burst of power.

3

S awyer landed in a swamp. As he sank under the
water, sharp needles bit into his leg. Sawyer
grabbed hold of the snout of whatever creature had
him and fought his way to air. The beast came with
him and as they surfaced, he found himself staring
into cold reptilian eyes.

Crap. He'd teleported onto the mouth of a freaking
alligator?

He grabbed both sides of the powerful jaws, but as
he tried to pry its mouth open, it started to pull him
back under.

A piercing whistle rang out. "Release him!"

The teeth embedded in Sawyer's leg let go.

As the creature dove under the water, Sawyer
swam to shore and dragged himself up the bank.
What the heck was up with his ability, he wondered,
as he stared up at a large blond-haired male.

"Are you alright?" the guy asked.

Sawyer nodded, unable to speak as he tried to
catch his breath.

"Not sure what you're doing way out here, but I'm
headed to town if you need a ride," the guy offered.

"I'm good, thanks."

"Okay, well, try not to feed anymore alligators then," the guy said as he left.

A FEW HOURS later Sawyer wanted to kick himself. Why hadn't he accepted the ride? Cause he was a grade-A idiot, that's why. Sure, he'd grown leery of strangers over the years, even apparently ones who saved him from scary water monsters, but the truth was he'd been shaken, and thinking didn't seem to be his strong suit today.

Now, as he entered the French Quarter, Sawyer found himself racing the sun.

His leg had healed, but the throbbing in his brain, along with the lethargy that had plagued him for days grew even worse at the cacophony of music and humans laughing and talking.

Even the aroma of food made his stomach cramp.

A skinny man with shifty eyes approached. "Dude, you look like roadkill. I got something'll make you feel better if you get my drift?"

Sawyer kept going. Roadkill sounded appropriate —what was wrong with him? He never got sick and always recovered from injury fast. Not that he didn't feel pain. He did, and it had been beating his ass all day.

Never in all Sawyer's twenty-one years—including the ones he'd spent in a cage—had he ever felt quite this horrible.

Sawyer passed a happy couple walking hand-in-hand, and envy flared. What would it be like to have a mate to love and who'd care for him in return?

In his mind Sawyer saw Evany smiling and talking to him in the lab. He'd have liked the chance to know her better, but that would never happen now.

· · ·

THE SUN SANK EVEN LOWER, and a warm breeze caressed his skin, bringing with it the scent of salt water. Despite his screw-up, Sawyer finally found himself in front of a three-story rust-colored structure. A sign —a full moon rising over a hill with a motorcycle underneath—hung above the door. Sanctuary.

As waves of dizziness assaulted Sawyer, he braced himself against the warm brick of the building. He needed to go another few feet. Sawyer closed his eyes and let the sounds of the city soothe him as he waited for the spell to subside.

When it was over, he pushed off and as the last rays of the sun splashed a warm haze over everything, he made it to the door, where a male and female stood talking.

"Not so fast," the male said, as he blocked Sawyer from entering.

4

F rom their scent, Sawyer realized they were bear
shifters. "I seek sanctuary."

The female smiled at Sawyer, her blonde hair
shining in the fading light.

But the male, a muscular guy with long blond hair
tied back, wrinkled his nose. "I see the day upchucked
another stray wanting shelter, only this one reeks of
Talon's bog."

"Sorry," Sawyer said, hoping his smell wouldn't
stop them from letting him in.

The female nudged the male. "Let him in, Dev, he
looks half dead."

"He reeks. Besides, I haven't read him his rights
yet."

"I don't think he's in any shape to harm anyone, do
you?" she asked.

Dev crossed his arms over his chest. "Looking like
something your wolf drug in doesn't mean he ain't a
powder keg ready to blow demon boogers all over us."

"True." The female focused on Sawyer. "I'm
Aimee, what's your name, and do you plan to harm
anyone here?"

"I'm Sawyer, and no, I don't want any trouble."

"Why are you seeking sanctuary?" Dev asked.

"I'm not sure, an oracle told me to come," Sawyer said, desperate to sit down.

"An oracle?" Dev repeated.

"Sawyer, you alright?" Aimee asked.

"Sorry," Sawyer said, humbled at her concern. Not many strangers cared what happened to people they didn't know. "I'm tired and haven't eaten in a while." He looked at Dev. "All I know is I met an oracle who told me to get here before dark tonight—why, or what will happen if I don't, I've no idea."

The bears exchanged a look.

"I must warn you though, I am hunted," Sawyer added.

"Aren't we all?" Dev muttered.

"Please," he said. "I'd love a glass of water, and who do I talk to about working off a meal and place to rest?"

"You talk to me," Aimee said. "I came out to get some fresh air, but I'm ready to go back in. Follow me and we'll get you that water and something to eat."

"Don't break your word, Sawyer, or I'll eat you," Dev said as he moved aside.

"Dev, leave him be." Aimee rolled her eyes.

"I'm not kidding," Dev responded.

The place was filled with the scent of humans and supes, along with food and drink. Sawyer's stomach cramped again, then a weird vibration shook him.

"You don't want something stronger than water?" Aimee asked, leading him to a table.

"No, thank you."

"All right, I'll be back.".

When she returned, Aimee handed him a clean white t-shirt. "Figured this would fit."

"Thank you," he said, changing as she set a large

jug of water and a meal that smelled divine in front of Sawyer.

"You're welcome." Aimee sat across from him. "So, where are you from, and what's your talent?"

"I'm from Tartaria, and the only thing I'm any good at is singing."

"Tartaria?"

"It's another realm," he answered, eager to dig into his meal, but afraid of looking like a starved pig, though he had the feeling Aimee might already know.

"I see." Aimee said. "It just happens tonight's entertainment cancelled. How about you eat, sing a few, then I'll show you to a room for the night?"

"Sounds wonderful," Sawyer said.

"Good." Aimee stood up. "I've got to get back to work, let me know if you need anything else."

"Thank you."

Sawyer devoured half the meal, then his stomach cramped so hard he feared he'd throw everything up. Headache worse than ever, he struggled to his feet. He needed to sleep, but first he had to earn the right to lay his head down in this place.

Sawyer got up on stage; then, since Evany had been on his mind earlier, he picked a song he'd written for her. The ability to make up songs in his head had been the only thing that kept him sane the last three years.

As the words flowed from his mouth—words of love, loss, and unbearable loneliness—the place fell quiet.

Maybe, for once, everything would be all right.

Maybe not. A hooded figure dressed all in black moved through the crowd.

Sawyer froze. How had they found him so quickly? He should be safe, this was Sanctuary, but what's to stop him from being taken? Yeah, he'd rather die than let that happen again.

As the figure got closer, Sawyer attempted to teleport. Nothing.

Then everything went black.

5

Terror flooded Evany as Sawyer's eyes rolled back and he dropped to the floor. No! After all this time trying to keep him safe, she couldn't lose him now. As she went toward him a stunning blonde blocked her.

"Who are you?" the female asked.

"Evany, now let me pass," she snapped.

When the blonde didn't move, Evany feinted left, then right, zipping past her.

As she dropped to her knees beside Sawyer, the female was right beside her. "Get away from him."

"Make me," Evany snarled. Though she'd likely die if she harmed anyone, Evany wouldn't hesitate to burn the place down if they tried to make her leave Sawyer.

"If you hurt him, you won't walk out of here alive," the blonde warned.

"I'm not here to hurt him." Evany pressed fingers to Sawyer's neck. Please be alive.

"I'm Aimee, one of the owners of this bar. I saw Sawyer's fear when he spotted you. He said he's hunted, so tell me why I shouldn't have you removed."

Relieved when she felt Sawyer's heartbeat, Evany

glanced at Aimee. The answer wasn't simple, and nothing she wanted to discuss with a stranger. It was clear Aimee cared about Sawyer even though she couldn't have known him long.

"I'm his enemy," she answered, soul weeping at the sad truth.

"He was starving and dehydrated when he came in. We gave him food and water, so there's something else wrong. Any idea what?" Aimee asked.

Evany swallowed hard. "It's his awakening."

"His what?"

"I know what that is." One of the curious onlookers, a young woman with long black hair and horns perched atop her head came over. "I'm Simi. He's a dracones, right?"

Evany nodded.

"What's a dracones?" Aimee asked.

"A dracones is someone with a dragon inside, but it can't come out until they awaken." Simi frowned at Evany. "But you don't seem happy about it, why? Don't you want his dragon to come out?"

"I do," Evany said. "But not all dracones survive their awakening."

"My friend Genna didn't tell me that," Simi said.

"Is she a dracones?" Evany asked.

"Yes."

"Do you think she might help us?" Evany was afraid to get her hopes up, but what else could she do? Even if she got Sawyer to Tartaria or another realm where other dracones resided, she'd have to locate them. Most would kill her on sight. Not that she could blame them. Still, if that was what it took to save Sawyer's life, she'd chance it.

"I sent Genna a text," Simi said as her phone dinged. "She's on her way."

"Thank you." Evany gritted her teeth as Sawyer's pain swept through her.

"Evany, what are you doing?" Aimee asked.

"She's taking Sawyer's pain into herself," Simi said.

"You're a healer?" Aimee asked.

"No, I'm a druid witch from another realm. Most of us don't have a lot of magic anymore, but... well, let's just say I'm a conduit, and right now I'm trying to lessen his pain." Shame flooded Evany—she wasn't born with magic or any abilities. But she had them now, thanks to her father and the blood of an unwilling recipient.

Evany hated the work her father did for the Ilyium, but what could she do? She'd learned early in life that to defy her sire earned swift repercussions. But seeing her father hurt Sawyer bothered Evany, so she'd released him.

Except he wasn't really free, was he?

Evany pushed the niggling thought away for the moment, because with it came the knowledge that to gain him real freedom, she'd have to end the ones who were after him.

6

"Evany," Aimee said. "We're drawing too much of a crowd, let's move Sawyer upstairs."

"All right."

Aimee waved over a big male, who picked Sawyer up and carried him to a room.

"Thank you," Evany said, after Sawyer was settled on a bed.

The male glanced at Aimee. "You need anything else?"

"Not right now, thanks," Aimee said, and the guy left.

Evany started to draw Sawyer's pain into herself again when a knock sounded at the door. A petite female with long black hair and bright blue eyes entered.

Simi squealed. "Genna, you came!"

"Hi Simi," Genna said. "Your text say emergency, so I bring backup." Genna indicated two large males out in the hall.

"Oh, it's not that kind of emergency." As Simi drew Genna into the room and closed the door, she introduced everyone.

Genna eyed Evany. "You be Ilyium, yet you be taking his pain."

"Yes," Evany replied.

"Not many you witches be good peoples who help us."

"No, and I'm sorry about that," Evany said. "Sawyer is going through his awakening and needs another dracones to get through it, Simi said you're one —can you help him?"

"I can," Genna said. "But you can help him more."

"I don't understand," Evany said.

"You likes him, like lots, right?" Genna asked.

"I have no idea how you know that, but yes. How does that help though? I thought only another dracones could help," Evany said as a wave of pain too strong for her rolled through Sawyer. He arched up, then fell back to the bed, whole body shaking. Then his pulse slowed even more. "He's going to die if we don't do something."

"Another dracones help, or it can be someone who gots a connection to him, likes what I see in your head. You can do this yourself, but I be here, so I show you how. Lay beside him," Genna instructed, then placed her hand on Evany's shoulder. "I get you inside his head, but you be the one that gots to take away pain and make him wanna stay."

Before Evany could question her, the room disappeared and she found herself in the middle of a storm. Booms of thunder and whips of lightning struck a lonely figure shrouded in black fog. "Sawyer?"

No answer.

"Genna, what do I do?"

"Talk to him and take his pain like you been doing."

As Evany waded through the stinging fog, she

drew it into herself. "Sawyer?"

He turned. "Evany?"

"Hi." She smiled and continued to pull his pain into her. The thunder and lightning eased up. In her mind, Genna waved and left.

"I've dreamed of you for years, but this feels so real," Sawyer said.

"Because it is." Evany took his hands, siphoning more of his pain.

"Even if it's not, I'm glad you're here. I'm dying," Sawyer said.

"Trust me, I'm really here, and I'm not going to let you die. You're going through your awakening."

"I couldn't think, my head was full of fog, and I thought I was sick. But now I realize what's happening," he said.

"I'm going to help you through it," Evany said.

"I've missed you."

"Oh Sawyer, I missed you as well."

Sawyer gazed at Evany. "How did you find me?"

"You do know what my father was injecting into me all those years, right?" Evany asked.

"I figured it was my blood, but—"

"It was, and thanks to you, I heal really fast and can now teleport as well. It also helps me track you, although today I'm a little slow," she said.

Sawyer's eyes shone. "I didn't want to leave you, but honestly, I'm glad I did. I'd have hated seeing you spend your life running like I've been."

"I have a confession," Evany said, as guilt filled her. "I've kept an eye on you."

"You have?"

Evany nodded.

"There were times I felt like you were close, but then I told myself it was all in my head," he said.

"Not in your head. I cast a blood spell to let me know when you were in trouble or when any of my people were close to you."

Sawyer laughed. "I thought it was my dracones senses warning me each time they arrived."

"No, I made sure I made noise to alert you. I'm sorry I couldn't do more—"

"You've nothing to be sorry about," he said, caressing her cheek with the back of his fingers. "But why didn't you tell me, let me know you where there?"

"My very presence put you at risk, though if I'm honest, I think I was scared that if you asked, I'd stay with you."

"That would have been terrible."

Evany laughed, savoring his humor. "I cared too much to put you in more danger. I hoped my father would stop looking for you and you could start a new life. You deserved to be happy. But with me in your life we'd be running forever. I betrayed the Ilyium—my father. He'd never let that go."

"I understand."

"I shouldn't even be here now. My father knows what I've done, but when I sensed you in trouble I had to come," Evany said. "I'm so sorry for what my people did to you, how you must hate us."

"I do hate what the Ilyium's done to my kind, but you? Never. I love you. My heart burns for you, always has."

Evany couldn't believe his words.

"I've stunned you," he said, throwing her words from so long ago back at her.

"You have, but can I tell you a secret?"

"Anything," he said.

"I love you as well." Evany cupped his face. "For a long time, I worried that I cared about you because I had your blood in my veins, but then I realized that I liked you before my father started injecting me."

"I've always felt a connection to you," Sawyer said.

"I promise, after we get you through your awakening, I'll do everything in my power to end my father's quest to capture you again."

"I want you safe, with me." Sawyer's lips brushed hers in the sweetest, most loving kiss ever, and suddenly they were lying on a bed in a meadow of flowers. Above them the sun pierced fluffy white clouds. "I want to keep kissing you," Sawyer said. "But I'm so tired..." His eyes closed.

Evany left Sawyer's mind, knowing she'd be able to get back if needed now.

"Genna left with Simi to go eat," Aimee said. "What about you—are you hungry? I can bring something up, so you don't have to leave."

"I'd love that," Evany said, feeling bad at how she'd acted earlier. "Aimee?"

The blonde paused at the door and looked back.

"Thank you, for everything. I was horrible earlier." Evany had always kept everything to herself, but she needed to open up for once. "I've spent my life safeguarding my thoughts, and years trying to keep Sawyer safe. I went against my family to help him, but when I saw him collapse tonight, I feared I might be too late. I know now that you were looking out for him, but at the time I saw you as someone else I had to fight, and I'm truly sorry."

Aimee smiled. "I understand, and apology accepted. Love makes us do things we normally wouldn't. How did this vendetta arise anyway?"

"It started when a crazy ancestor of mine cursed all of dragonkind."

Aimee shook her head. "No one can ever simply

get along, can they?"

"Not in my experience," Evany said.

"Well, we can only do our part. Now, let me go get you something to eat."

"Thank you." As the door closed, Evany settled back beside Sawyer. He looked so peaceful.

She started to close her eyes when a tingle rushed down her spine. Evany sat up, panic taking hold as a familiar presence flashed into the room.

"Hello, sister. Nice of you to lead me right to the prize. Daddy will be so happy."

"How did you get in here? This is Sanctuary, the place is protected." Evany leaped from the bed and faced the intruder. "I won't let you hurt Sawyer."

"You know I can do things others can't, Daddy saw to that. I go where I want and do what I want—nothing can stop me."

"You have a twin," Sawyer said, sitting up.

"An evil one," Evany muttered, then glanced at Sawyer. "Wait, why do you sound surprised? You saw her in the lab many times."

"I did, but I never saw you together. The only reason I knew your name was because you told me when I first arrived," Sawyer said. "Your father isn't one to talk much. I had no idea."

"Who cares," Evany's twin waved her dagger. "You, dear sister, have thwarted me far too long, and Daddy's getting impatient. If not for you, that beast would be back in his cage where he belongs."

"His name is Sawyer," Evany snarled.

"Whatever."

"I'll die before I let you take him." Evany had given up her weapons upon entry to Sanctuary, but that didn't mean she was helpless.

"I'm counting on it."

7

S awyer always thought there were two sides to
  Evany. How wrong he'd been, and he should've
seen it. They might look the same, but they were as
different as night and day.

Evany tensed to fight, and then her evil twin froze
her with a bolt of magic.

"No." Evany had protected him for so long, now it
was his turn. He darted in front of her and ran straight
into her evil twin's blade.

As it pierced his heart, a howling shriek filled his
head—Evany.

Sawyer's power rose, then began to flow from him
to Evany.

She broke free, rage gleaming in her eyes.

"Catch me if you can, dear pathetic sister," her
twin taunted, then teleported away.

"Evany?" Sawyer said.

The flow of power stopped.

"Sawyer?" Tears streaked Evany's face as she made
him sit on the bed. "I'm sorry I led her here to you. We
share a twin bond, and no matter what I do, she always finds me."

"Not your fault—you can't pick your family," he

said.

Evany hugged him tight. "I won't let this happen again. I must end it. I'll make sure you're free."

"What? No, wait. Evany!"

She was gone.

Aimee burst through the door. "What happened? Is that blood?"

Sawyer looked at his chest. "Yes, but I'm fine."

"Where's Evany?"

"Her twin attacked us. Evany went after her. I need to find her," he said.

"I bet Genna can help—she was talking to Simi about how good she is at tracking others. I'll go get her," Aimee said.

"All right, but hurry, please. I have a bad feeling," Sawyer said.

Moments later, Genna burst into the room. "Aimee filled me in and I gots Evany's mental signature, so I take you to her," Genna said.

"Thank y—"

Genna grabbed his arm and the room blurred.

Sawyer found himself in a blazing inferno. As he gazed around, he realized it was another lab. "Evany?"

He spotted a body in a white lab coat, and bile churned in his gut as he recognized the man.

"Evany be outside," Genna said, and teleported them out as the ceiling caved in.

The compound was a battlefield of chaos, with Ilyium soldiers fighting dracones warriors. Some were in their human bodies while others flew through the sky in dragon form.

Sawyer spotted a female lying on the ground, her chestnut hair soaking up blood.

"No!" As rage blinded him, the beast within Sawyer rose. He began to shift.

"Sawyer?"

Her soothing voice penetrated his brain. Sawyer turned. "Evany?"

"Yes."

His dragon retreated.

"My father was dead when I got here, but my sister..." Evany shuddered and dropped the blood-covered blade she'd been holding.

"I'm sorry." Sawyer pulled her close.

"I had to. She wasn't always full of hate. As we grew up, she changed. Our father favored me, and she hated that. When Father learned I was the one who'd set you free, she vowed to find me for him. She'd taunt me each time she located me, saying she'd torture you and make me watch before killing me." Evany sighed. "I never thought I'd feel this way..."

"She was your twin, you had a bond," he said.

"Yes, but though I was born into this family, they weren't my choice. You are."

"Let's get out of here," Sawyer said noting a group of males watching them. He looked for Genna, but she was gone.

"Together?" Evany asked.

Sawyer nodded and as their power combined, they zapped back to the bedroom in Sanctuary.

"Now that you're free for real, will you be my mate?" Evany asked.

"I'd love to—I love you. But never scare me like that again, please?"

Evany smiled. "You were shifting into your dragon. That means you survived your awakening."

"Thanks to you." As Sawyer lowered his lips to Evany's, claiming her, his soul surged with happiness.

"I love you, my dragon heart," Evany said, holding him tight.

BRAVE

RACHEL HAILEY

"Who the hell let New Orleans get so damned cold?" Hannah grumbled, as a bitter wind whipped through her hair, jerking strands free of her ponytail. The cinnamon-and-alcohol scented breeze tore at her clothes, penetrating her leather jacket like it was made of linen. Laughter and raised voices swirled over her. No matter how cold the night, Jackson Square was never empty.

Wincing, she resettled her backpack. Maybe coming to Louisiana was a mistake. Melpomene, the muse of tragedy, had warned her, and the gods knew the last few months had been disastrous.

Head lowered against the wind, Hannah picked up her pace, dodging puddles and pedestrians. She might love coffee, but the dark brews the busy cafe offered weren't enough of an incentive to brave the cold. It was the anonymity. Her parents and siblings always hesitated to check on her if she was in a crowd. With the dark thoughts buzzing inside her head, they were the very last people she wanted to see.

Or that's what she thought.

The tinny clang of a bell chimed above the hum of conversations as Hannah shoved the door open and slipped inside. She sighed, and her shoulders drooped when the aroma of fresh ground beans washed over her. Shaking her hands to get the circulation going, she joined the long line. Two college-aged girls waited ahead, chatting and giggling. Their winter-pale faces were chapped, eyes bright while they gossiped about some club. Envious, she slid a step closer, hoping she could absorb some of their happiness.

She couldn't remember the last time she'd had something to gossip about. Hell, she couldn't remember the last time she'd smiled.

Familiar laughter sliced through the chatter and clatter, making her body go rigid as she caught her breath.

Morris.

She should have turned and fled or squared her shoulders and raised her chin in defiance. Instead, she looked up, following the sound as if it were a careening train. And like a train wreck, everything happened in slow motion. Vivid green eyes met hers across the crowded room. Her heartbeat faltered, and her mouth went dry.

His tan had faded, the golden strands of his shaggy blond locks had grown brown, but he still made her insides lurch. Although this time, for a vastly different reason. The left side of his mouth quirked into a cruel smile before he leaned down and whispered into the ear of a girl seated beside him.

Her eyes lifted and automatically found Hannah. The girl's pink glossy lips rounded. "Her?" Disdain and laughter colored the word, twisting the single syllable into a dagger that slammed into Hannah's chest hilt deep.

Heat scalded her cheeks as she spun out of line, crossed the few steps to the entrance, and jerked open the door. Fleeing the sound of their laughter, Hannah ran. The cold air stung her face and pierced her lungs, while raised voices followed her mad dash. The streets and faces blurred around her until she stumbled. The rough ground scraped her palms, but the pain was a pleasant distraction from the ache in her heart.

Hannah stared at the ground seeing nothing as she struggled to rise. Once she managed to stand, she leaned against a storefront, wrestling with shame and pain.

She'd been stupid to have fallen for Morris. So excited to be on her own for the first time, desperate for connection, she'd bought every lie he'd sold, and it wasn't until too late she'd realized how costly they were.

Gradually, her silent tears slowed, and she looked around to get her bearings. Ursuline. Damn, her feet had carried her farther than she thought. It was too bad she couldn't get away from the past so easily.

Her phone vibrated. She pulled it from her pocket and groaned when her mom's name flashed on the display. Glaring, she hit 'end call' and shoved the device into her backpack, wishing she had the courage to toss the thing into the gutter and disappear.

She knew her family loved her, but damn, love could be suffocating.

A strangled scream echoed behind her. Hannah whipped around.

"Shut up, bitch," a voice growled from the shadows.

Fear slid through her veins, tightening her chest. Cold skittered down her spine, and her body turned, feet already pointed toward safety.

No.

She was tired of being afraid, tired of constantly

being a victim. There was someone down there who needed help. If she could keep them from suffering from the kind of nightmares that plagued her, maybe her life would find some equilibrium. Maybe, she could be the hero—for once.

Morris's smarmy smirk surfaced in her thoughts, sending a flash of anger sizzling through her veins.

"I am brave," she whispered, as she gathered her courage.

No more victims.

Hannah sprinted down the alley. "Hey," she yelled, pushing authority and confidence into her voice. "Everything okay?"

Low laughter filtered through the night. "Things are just fine."

Hannah's feet faltered, and she stifled a scream. A tall man with long, platinum-blond hair turned toward her and grinned. He was over a foot taller, and his biceps were as big as her waist, but those weren't the most unnerving attributes. That honor went to his exposed fangs and the crimson droplets staining his chin.

"Help me," a petite girl whispered from where he held her pinned against the bricks.

"Hush." His voice was as soft and tender as a lover's as he pulled the girl to his front. "We have a dinner guest."

Hannah gasped and took a step back on trembling legs. She'd known better than to confront someone in a dark alley. She just hadn't expected it would be this bad. "Daimon."

Her parents had warned her New Orleans was full of the soulless vampires who came to feed on tourists, but her mom Melpomene was full of dire predictions.

If she had her way, Hannah would never leave Olympus.

"That's right, little girl."

Little girl. Hannah straightened, and though her legs still resembled tubes of water, she forced her feet forward. She was not a little girl anymore. She was not a victim.

"Let her go." Hannah gestured at the girl he cradled.

The Daimon laughed. "Sure. It looks like you're much more fun to play with." He released the girl, and she hit the ground with a grunt.

"Run," Hannah yelled.

"Nah. I don't think so." He casually stomped on the girl's leg. The crack reverberated off the dirty bricks and echoed in her ears. The sound was so loud, so visceral, it drowned out the girl's anguished screams. "I don't like fast food. Don't you know, it's terrible for you?" He stepped over the prone girl, stalking closer. His lips curled away from his fangs.

"Stop," Hannah said, attempting to push power into her quavering voice.

"No." His bloodied hand traced her face.

Revulsion and terror curdled the contents of her stomach as she cringed from his touch. She could flash out of the alley. Her powers were weak, but she could always go home. Nothing a Daimon could do would prevent that.

Her gaze dropped to the human. If Hannah abandoned her, the poor girl would never see her home again.

No. The same anger that brought her down the alley resurfaced and rolled through her, pushing down the fear. It was time she stopped being pathetic.

She was a strong, independent female, and damn everything to Hades, she would be better than this.

Using techniques she'd learned from her aunts and uncles during their weekly self-defense classes, Hannah grabbed the Daimon's forearm and jerked him forward. He collided with her body, and she brought her knee up, slamming it straight into his crotch. Before he could recover, she headbutted him, busting his lips against his fangs. Pain slashed across her forehead. The anger and adrenaline pumping through her veins dulled everything except for the feeling of victory.

He stumbled back, and profanity blistered the air as he cursed her.

Laughing, she reached within, tugging on the feeble magic coiled there and manifested a fireball. "Stay away from me, or I'll roast your balls like marsh-mallows," she said, bringing up her hands.

The Daimon stalked to the right, eyes flashing and nostrils flaring. "Aw, don't be like that, sweet one. This won't hurt a bit," he growled. "For long."

She'd warned him. Hannah tossed the flames directly into his chest and knocked him flat. Glee ripped through her—she'd never felt more powerful. It was the first time she'd felt like a demigod. But before her laughter died, he bounced to his feet. Menace poured from his aura, and his eyes glinted with malice.

Oh, no. Hannah's eyes widened, and she scrambled back. Now what? She looked around the dark-ened alley, desperately searching for inspiration. The alley was empty except for the unconscious human girl. There wasn't even a trashcan. Weren't alleys supposed to be full of pointed wood and bits of metal? Something she could use as a weapon.

The Daimon darted forward with fangs that

gleamed in the scant light, his breath exploding from his lungs in a visible cloud. Hannah yelped and fell back, reaching again for her nebulous power.

Magic erupted from her palms. It shot across the distance, sizzling through the air in a bright white arc, striking him square in the chest, but too late. He barreled into Hannah and took them both to the ground.

She shrieked as she fell. Her ribs broke under his weight, and her wrist cracked as she landed wrong. Panic, astringent and sharp, coated her tongue in copper. She lost all sense of reason and decorum. Kicking and screaming, she summoned every ounce of power she could and lashed out. There was no thought, only survival.

Her vision ran with red streamers, and her head gave a furious throb while nausea turned her stomach contents molten. She lost track of what happened next. There were too many sensations and not enough sanity.

Suddenly, a soft, amber light permeated the alley, reminding her oxygen-starved brain of sunset. Pressure built in the air, and without warning, the Daimon exploded into a cloud of golden sparkles.

Hannah cried out and covered her face. What the hell happened? The seconds dragged into minutes as she lay there, too scared to move. The cold ground leached into her jeans and turned her skin icy. When nothing else happened, she shoved herself upright, ribs and wrist screaming in agony. Her heart rocketed around in her chest, rattling the broken bones.

The human girl still sprawled on the ground, blood leaking from her neck and head. Hannah wasn't sure how much blood a human could lose before they died, but she knew enough to be worried. She stumbled across the alley and placed her fingers on the girl's throat, searching for a pulse. Though it wasn't steady, there was a definite thump-thud.

Hannah's backpack lay on the ground, the contents scattered. Fumbling with her good hand, she searched the mess for her cell. When her fingers closed around the device, she wanted to cry. The screen wasn't cracked—it was shattered. The one time she would have willingly called her parents for assistance, she couldn't.

Looking up at the sky, she cursed the fates. Those awful bitches were going to pay for this one day. Hannah had to get help. There was only one option, and it meant breaking a promise to her mom. She had to get the girl to Sanctuary.

The bar was a rare haven in their world, where no one was allowed to fight. It attracted a lot of what Melpomene called 'unsavory sorts' she didn't want her youngest daughter exposed to and was one reason why she'd tried to make Hannah choose a college in another city.

Hannah wasted a moment to pray for forgiveness before climbing to her feet. Closing her eyes, she summoned her powers, masking them from sight. For once, her magic came easy, as if eager to do her bidding. She frowned, but she was in too much pain to question it. The girl didn't weigh much, and Hannah was stronger than she looked, but with her injuries, it was still all she could do to get them moving in the right direction.

Thank the gods the bar was close.

A few minutes later, Hannah stopped in front of Sanctuary's doors. A cold sweat covered her body, and her chest heaved. The human girl hadn't stirred, and Hannah was beginning to panic.

A cute blond guy stood with his arms crossed next

to a sign that read, 'Come in peace or leave in pieces.' His handsome face was impassive until she dropped the magic and became visible.

"Help," she gasped. Now that she was here, the adrenaline evaporated, leaving her legs weak.

"What the hell?"

"I found her being attacked by Daimons." Hannah's knees gave out, and she and the human slid to the ground. "I didn't know where else to go."

"Dammit," the guy snarled. His aura flared. Werehunter. He must be one of the bears. The guy scooped the human up and swung her around, dashing through a door that opened for him. "Yo, Dev. Little help here."

Another blond, identical to the doorman, popped up as if summoned by magic. Had he cloned himself? "What's up?"

"Daimon attack. I'll take this one. You see to the other girl."

"On it."

Hannah blinked as the doorman disappeared into the bar with the girl. "Wait, is she going to be okay?"

The second blond knelt beside Hannah. "She'll be fine. What about you? You doin' okay?"

"Why are there two of you?"

He grinned, blue eyes sparkling. "Brace yourself, there's four."

Four? "Oh," she murmured, then shook her head. "I think I might be in shock."

He gave her a kind smile. "I don't think you're wrong." He pulled her to her feet, and her head swam. The brick facade spun and merged with the sky.

"Whoa." The guy caught her against his chest. "Let's get you settled." He picked her up and carried her awkwardly to the bar.

Smiling faintly, she fought the wave of nausea the trek across the room inspired.

"Sorry, I usually carry people out, not in," he said as he deposited her on a stool, then walked around the counter.

She flexed her wrist with a wince. The bones had started to mend, but they'd be tender for another hour or so.

"Here, drink up." He pushed a glass of dark liquid toward her. "Soda. You need the sugar."

Her head bobbed on its own accord. "Thanks. I'm okay now." He arched his brows as he stared across the bar at her. "Really."

"All right. Have fun and remember the rules. No biting. We bite back, and my teeth are longer and sharper than yours," he said with a grin before he returned to the entrance.

The cold liquid felt good in her hands and even better in her mouth as she drained the glass. Her head was still spinning when she placed it on the polished counter with a clink, but now for an entirely different reason.

"I'm in Sanctuary," she whispered, shocked by her bravado.

She turned, resting her back against the counter. Men and women in leather clustered around pool tables and sat drinking and laughing at rustic tables. The furniture was all different but somehow managed to match. It was oddly beautiful and relaxing. She'd expected to feel intimidated, yet she felt at home in a way she hadn't since she was very young.

She was in Sanctuary. "My mom is going to kill me."

"Yeah, been there, done that, and bled on the t-shirt."

Hannah twisted around to find a tall guy with jet-black, wavy hair leaning against the bar. He regarded her with eyes of deep jade. "What?"

"I'm pretty sure my mom made attempted murder a holiday tradition. It's good to know my family isn't the only one that puts the fun in dysfunctional."

She shook her head with a light laugh. "Definitely can relate to that."

He sank to a stool next to her with a dazzling smile that displayed two deep dimples. "I'm Kearse."

"Hannah."

"First time in Noo'Awlins?" he asked, pronouncing the city like the locals.

She smiled. "Is it that obvious?"

His eyes twinkled. Halfway between green and blue, they were magnetic. "Very. I would remember seeing you. Beer?"

Lost in his eyes, she nodded.

He waved to the bartender and held up two fingers. "Hey, Justin."

The pain in her ribs faded while warmth unfurled in her center. Kearse's presence was even better than the atmosphere of Sanctuary. She should have been frightened of him, or at least cautious. He was a Were-Hunter, an animal, as Melpomene would say. Yet, Hannah felt safe with him. Something she wasn't likely to take for granted after the encounter with the Daimon.

The bartender grunted, pulled two long-necks, and shoved them over. She wrapped her fingers around the bottle and took a slow sip, watching Kearse warily. "So, I guess you hang out here a lot?"

"I pop in and out." He winked, leaning closer.

. . .

THREE DAYS AGO, Kearse had glimpsed Hannah in the square. It had only been a single smile as she offered to help an older woman with her bags, but it'd been enough. The jaguar inside him caught her scent, and it wouldn't be denied. Tonight, watching her engage the Daimon, his human heart was in complete agreement.

He wanted her.

She was an evocative blend of warrior and innocence. He wanted to challenge her, see her eyes glow with amber light, while guarding her delicate spark. Letting her engage the damned Daimon had gone against his instincts, but she needed her confidence back. Her spirit was wounded, and a deep sadness clung to her. That was why he'd waited to strike the Daimon until she could claim the credit.

Still, he yearned to touch her, check her for injuries. A darkening bruise discolored her tawny cheek, and her pale amber eyes that sparkled like cognac were red-rimmed. "Been a long night?" he asked.

"You have no idea."

He turned his head to hide his smile. Kearse wasn't sure what she'd think if she knew he'd been following her for days. He was confident it wouldn't be a positive revelation, so he held his tongue and savored the moment. Angling himself on the stool so their shoulders touched, they sat in companionable silence, listening to the music and people watching.

Hannah tilted her head to the side, identifying the various creatures who ate and danced. Laughed and played. The inside of Sanctuary was a microcosm, each species that haunted the New Orleans streets were represented. Some she could do without seeing. She flinched as she recognized two Daimons having a whispered conversation.

"So, what do you like to do? Dance? Play pool?"

She lifted a shoulder, sipping from her bottle. "I don't know. I've never done much of either." And by that, she meant ever. Entertainment options at home were limited, and Morris? Well, he hadn't been interested in showing her anything outside of a bedroom.

Kearse rose, holding out his hand. "We need to fix that."

She looked at his palm, hesitating. Melpomene's voice rang in Hannah's head, warning her about the creatures. His dark gaze sparkled with challenge. Daring her. Canting her chin, she took his hand.

What Mama didn't know wouldn't hurt her.

He tugged Hannah around the tables to the edge of the dance floor as the song changed. The bass thumped, drums boomed, both reverberated through her blood as Kearse's hands settled on her hips and pulled her close. His scent enveloped her, flavoring every breath. She sucked in a lungful of spicy air, savoring the rich aroma that held traces of cinnamon, tobacco, beer, leather, and a wildness she couldn't identify.

She placed her hands on his shoulders, relishing the way his muscles rolled beneath the thin t-shirt, the sensation of his hands on her bottom. They burned through her jeans as he pressed their bodies closer still. Chest to chest, his heartbeat pulsed under her cheek. He rolled his hips, stroking against her body in a way that wasn't suggestive. It was a promise. Shuddering, she tried to imitate his moves, but her feet couldn't find a rhythm in the unfamiliar music.

"I'm sorry," she said, face flaming. "I guess I'm not good at dancing."

"You're thinking too much," he said, tightening his grasp. "Don't think, feel."

She stifled a laugh. It seemed more like she wasn't thinking enough. How could she with his scent thick in her head? But she nodded and closed her eyes, focusing only on the feel of his body, the rich, lush aroma that rolled from him. The music became secondary. Soon, they were moving together. The music and Kearse's presence thrummed through her.

THE SWEET SCENT of her was a caress that made Kearse want to purr. Her curves were so warm, her skin soft. He desperately wanted to bury his face in her hair, scent mark her as his, but if he let his jaguar out even that much, he would lose all restraint.

He couldn't risk frightening her off. She wasn't a Were-Hunter. This was a recipe for disaster, yet he couldn't help himself. There was something powerful about Hannah that made his teeth ache with the desire to nip her, claim her.

The music's tempo increased, and he took the opportunity to roll his hips against hers again. Gods, this was exquisite torture. He lowered his head, intending to let his lips skim her throat—his teeth to graze.

Hannah's eyes opened to find his lips inches from hers. She hadn't kissed anyone since Morris, hadn't wanted to. But as his breath fell against her mouth and his body curved around hers, she couldn't think of anything else.

She closed the distance. His lips were soft, tender... until they weren't.

The kiss morphed, becoming harder, wilder. Kearse growled into her mouth, and Hannah groaned, surrendering her weight under the onslaught of sensation. His hands clenched, digging in until she knew he'd pierced the thick material. She didn't care. No, she needed more.

She rubbed against him, loving the feel of the erection pressed against her stomach.

This fierce kiss was nothing like the pale thing she'd experienced with Morris. This was fire and tornado. Desire and demand. As if whatever had transpired in his cramped dorm was a faded watercolor, and this was the real deal. The Starry Night. The Mona Lisa.

Kearse's mouth opened, and his tongue plunged between her lips, coiling over hers. There was no hesitation, only raw demand and need. Her hands slid across his shoulders, over the thick muscles that rolled and flexed.

Kearse broke the kiss on a growl and met her gaze with eyes that shone with passion. They stood still as people danced around them. "You are a very good dancer," he whispered.

"Yeah?" Breathless, she smiled.

He pressed his mouth against hers again. Heat spilled between them, burning in her veins as her body ached.

The music suddenly cut out, and Sweet Home Alabama blared from the speakers. Kearse pulled away. His face twisted into a grimace. Profanity erupted while several people hurried for an exit.

"What—"

Kearse gave her a quick kiss, cutting her off. "Sorry, doll. That's my cue to leave." He cupped her face. The feel of his rough palm against her chin, the sensation of his thumb stroking across her cheek drew a sigh from her and caused her eyelids to flutter. "But I'll see you again. Soon."

"Wait, why?" She opened her eyes, leaning into his touch.

"That's a story for another time." He pulled away, and instantly her entire body felt cold. She might as well have been back in the square pelted by the unseasonably cold wind.

"Kearse?" His long strides carried him away. The dark denim cupped his ass, and his broad shoulders strained the limits of his black tee.

"Soon," he called and grinned over his shoulder without slowing as he stalked away. She couldn't stop the smile that bloomed or the blush that colored her face when he winked.

Animal, vegetable, or mineral, the creature was special, and she hoped he was right.

A giant man with black hair dressed like a goth biker entered the bar. Her back went rigid. Acheron.

That explained the thinning of the establishment's clientele. The leader of the Dark-Hunters, Acheron was many things. At the very top of the list, right under sexy-as-hell, was terrifying.

Her breath hitched. Yeah, it was time to leave. She'd been brave enough for one night.

On unsteady legs, she headed for the restroom, making sure her steps were even. She would do nothing to draw his gaze. Yet, as she made it to the door, she couldn't keep herself from glancing back.

Though dark shades covered his eyes, there was no doubt he could see through the lenses and her.

Acheron inclined his head, his perfectly shaped lips curved into a sly smile.

With a squeak, she shoved the bathroom door open and flashed to her tiny apartment. It took several long minutes before her heart calmed and she could stop shaking.

Acheron had smiled at her.

THAT NIGHT as Hannah lay in bed, she couldn't stop thinking about her time at Sanctuary, but it wasn't the Dark-Hunter on her mind. It was Kearse and the memory of his touch she couldn't banish. What would it be like to do more than kiss him? To feel those calloused palms stroke across her bare skin...

She was certain he would blast the memories of Morris far away.

THE NEXT DAY, she wasted no time heading to Sanctuary. To hell with class, she needed to see Kearse again, and in the state she was in, she wouldn't be able to focus on anything else anyway. Her dreams had been filled with the dark-haired Were-Hunter, only heightening her need.

She was behaving like a silly, love-struck schoolgirl, but that was exactly what she was. And it didn't matter. She may be attending Tulane under the guise of getting an education, but what she was really after was experience, and there was nothing she wanted to experience more than Kearse.

This time the blond bouncer grinned as she approached. "Back again so soon?" he asked with a knowing smirk.

"I had fun yesterday." She feigned indifference.

"I noticed." He stepped back, holding the door open. "Kearse is waiting at the bar."

Her heart rate doubled, and a wide grin broke across her face. Almost running through the door, she came to an abrupt stop as Kearse turned and their gazes collided. Cobalt light flashed in his jade eyes. He rose, all feral grace and power, and prowled toward her. Her entire being shivered under his intense stare.

"You came back."

She nodded, unable to speak.

"Wanna pick up where we left off last night?" He held out his hand. Those seductive, kissable lips curled into a daring smile.

How could she resist?

Hannah took his hand. Relief crashed through her. It made no sense, but for the first time since they'd parted, she felt right. Air rushed into her lungs as if Kearse's presence truly allowed her to breathe easier.

"Yes." Her fingers curled over his, entwining. "More dancing?" She bit her lip and looked up through her lashes.

He tugged her forward, using her arm to spin her around so her back pressed against his chest. "That depends. How brave do you feel?" The whispered words fell against the side of her neck as he nuzzled her throat.

She shuddered, and heat bloomed deep inside her belly, rolling lower. "Brave. Very, very brave."

KEARSE'S entire being vibrated as Hannah's delicate floral scent washed over him. Today her hair was down, and the silky brown curls teased his skin. It was too much and far from enough. He wanted all of her bare and under his body.

"Good," he growled. "I'm going to need you to be very brave, doll." He claimed her mouth and groaned as her soft, luscious taste burst across his tongue like caramel. He couldn't wait another minute. She was his whether she knew it yet or not.

He pulled back, meeting her glassy gaze. "Come on, Hannah. Let me show you the rest of Sanctuary."

She frowned. "What?"

He stroked the wrinkle between her eyes. "It's a big place. A lot of people call Sanctuary home." Still, she looked at him in confusion. Her naivety made him chuckle. He leaned down, placing his lips against the shell of her ear. "I want to take you to my room."

"Oh." She tilted her chin, and an impish grin spread across her face. "Okay."

Heart light, he spun her around and dragged her through the kitchen to the door leading to Peltier House. He'd come here after a group of Katagaria attacked his clan, leaving him orphaned and alone. He never thought he'd fit in or find family, and he sure as hell hadn't expected to find Hannah. Now that he had, he wasn't going to let her go.

Her soul sang to his, quieted the darkness in his head. There were no matching marks on their palms, but it didn't matter. Before morning that would change.

This was his mate. He could feel it.

MOURNING SHADOWS

NICKI NANCE

"I won't miss that," Mar Greico said to no one as the shop's shrill doorbell jarred her out of a mind drift. Damn. Did I leave the door unlocked? "Welcome to Magique," she called out brightly. "I'll be right with you."

Shem chuckled. "It's just me, Boss. I brought boxes from Sanctuary. Aimee said to take as many as I could carry. We're tripping over them."

"Great," she said dryly. "We can trip over them here for a while." She was pacing and talking fast. "We have a lot to relocate. Let's put what goes to the new shop by the front door. Anything going to the house or the new office can go to the back room for now. Donations by the back door, trash in the alley, and us in an exhausted heap on the sidewalk."

"Sounds like a plan." In less than a minute Shem had dropped the boxes to the floor and was fitting books into a crate. Mar approached him unnoticed. She tugged on the crate, and he jumped, meeting honey-colored eyes.

"A plan where you do all of the heavy lifting?" She pointed at his chest.

"If you need me to, sure."

"What do you need, Shem?"

It took a moment for him to respond. *I need out of this eye lock. Does this woman ever blink?* "I'm not sure what you are asking."

"I'm asking how you would feel about a change."

His stomach rolled. *Is she firing me?*

His tremor of uncertainty went through Mar and she chastised herself for being cryptic with him. "I'm in a big transition here, Shem. There's an opportunity for you to have more hours, more money, and more flexibility. If you are interested, we'll need a conversation about what that would look like and where it might take you. You don't have to answer me this minute, you can—"

"I'm interested."

She hid her surprise at his quick response. "OK. Let's talk over lunch. We can grab more boxes while we're at Sanctuary. I have some errands to run first. Meet me there at 1:30."

MAGIQUE WAS DIRECTLY across the street from Sanctuary Bar and Grille. Mar conducted a lot of business in the last booth on the left. Today as she settled in, Aimee Peltier-Kattilakis, the owner, brought her usual sweet tea to the table. Blonde pigtails and a pink t-shirt belied her position at Sanctuary.

"Hey, Mar." Aimee smiled broadly. "Trying to miss the lunch rush?"

Mar shook her head. "Nope. I'm on a mission. I wanted to talk to you about something. Do you have a minute? I'll be quick."

Aimee glanced around, then dropped herself into the seat across from Mar. "We're not busy. The boys can handle it. What's up?"

Mar broke into a smile. "I'm moving Magique around the corner to Royal Street." Aimee furrowed her perfect brows. "You've been talking about a change, but I wasn't expecting that. I'm glad you're not going far. Sanctuary might be your office, but Magique is my sanctuary."

Mar appreciated the word play as much as the sentiment. "There's more. I closed my downtown office. Grace Alexander and I are going to share a suite upstairs from Magique Deux." She put two fingers up.

"Your French really sucks," she chided. Then she reached for the saltshaker and spun it around. "You really deserve this, Mar."

"I want to live, not just make a living," Mar said, putting her hand over her heart. She leaned in and lowered her voice. "What I want to talk to you about is Shem. I want to train him as a manager. I don't want to do anything that is going to cause a problem for you, Aim, but it's a perfect opportunity for him. He'll get business experience and I'll pay him enough to take more than one class a term. He's so gifted." She sighed. "It's a shame he doesn't know it."

Aimee let out a breath. "Oh, Mar, thank you for helping him. The kid is a gem. He's long overdue to get out of our kitchen." She jerked her head toward the kitchen door. "If I didn't have a pack of little brothers, I would have promoted him myself." She stopped spinning the saltshaker. "You know, he's had it rough," she almost whispered.

Mar nodded. "I sensed that, but he's never said anything about it."

"Seriously? I'm surprised that he hasn't opened up to you. He really likes you, Mar."

"You couldn't prove it by me. We joke around, but otherwise he doesn't initiate a lot of conversation. And you know how I am." She flung one palm up. "I only pry when I'm doing therapy."

Aimee cocked her head. "How about when you are free reading?"

"Free reading?"

"That's what we call it here when you go into our heads," Aimee put her hands by her head and wiggled her fingers, "and tidy up our thoughts and we don't even have to pay for it."

Mar's eyes widened. "We who?"

"Uh, almost all of us. I've seen you do it with customers you didn't even know. Don't get me wrong. No one wants you to stop. You're like a cranial cleaning service."

Mar dropped her head and shook it. "Apparently I'm not too subtle."

"The paralyzing gaze gives you away."

Mar bit the inside of her mouth and looked away until Aimee tapped her hand. "Mar, why don't you do readings at Magique for the big bucks?"

"I prefer to do psychotherapy for the big bucks. Reading was a gift to me, so I gift it whenever I can." She lifted a finger. "For the record, I do charge for readings at Magique occasionally. Some folks need to pay money before they pay attention."

"How did I not know that?"

Mar rolled her eyes. "Uh, you've been in an emotional tornado for six years. It sort of trumps noticing the habits of the not-so-rich-or-famous." Mar was Aimee's anchor during those years. Aimee had been devastated when her mother, Nicolette, disowned her because of her relationship with Fang Kattilakis. Ironically, in a fight at Sanctuary, Nicolette died protecting Fang. Aimee's father died beside her.

Mar looked at Aimee for a long moment. "Still feeling the pull, Sweetie?"

Aimee sighed, "So much."

Just then Shem burst through the kitchen door juggling a stack of boxes. He dropped them near the booth and went behind the bar to grab a soda. Mar ordered an appetizer of Scoobies, the hush puppies Shem liked. She got a salad for herself and told Aimee to take her time with the Cajun Burgers. She would take hers home for dinner. As Aimee stood up, Mar grabbed her hand. "Come see the new shop, Aimee. You'll like it there." She released her with a little shake.

"Hey, Shem," Aimee teased as he took the seat she vacated. "Aren't you getting enough free food from me?" She nodded at Mar. "You need your other boss to feed you here, too?"

"That's me. I'm in it for the perks," he flatly declared, but his eyes were playful.

"I'd give him perks from Magique, but bells, books, and candles aren't as tasty as your burgers, and he seems to have no interest in casting spells."

"Really? I thought the free magic was why he worked for you."

Mar replied without a glance to Shem. "I thought it was the convenient location."

"I'm right here," Shem reminded them.

"Don't worry, sweetheart." Mar assured him. "No more about you without you."

"What does that even mean?" he asked, palms up. His expression had both women laughing. He was a master of self-deprecating humor, and unaware of how his large brown eyes and dark shaggy hair powered his delivery.

Aimee left and Shem met that gaze he both welcomed and dreaded. Mar was ready to do business.

"I don't want to cross any boundaries, so stop me if I'm getting too personal." She sensed his internal shudder but went on. "You don't share a lot about yourself, but I see you. You've been running between Magique and Sanctuary since you graduated. You arrange your classes at LSU around work and you study on your breaks. I can't imagine where you squeeze in fun, or even sleep. I'm watching an excellent human being turn into a human *doing*."

Mar introduced the details of her plan to Shem while they waited for lunch. She raised her fingers one at a time as she listed her goals. "I want to do more psychotherapy, spend less time at Magique, develop some seminars, and have some time for real life." She raked her hand through her short hair. "I'm asking you to manage Magique, coordinate my professional activities, and infuse the whole operation with fresh ideas. I want you to schedule your work around your classes instead of scheduling your classes around work." He looked away.

Slow down. You're going to overwhelm him. She took a breath. "That's just the big picture. I know it's a lot. Need a break?"

He gave a small shrug. "Uh... Nah. I'm good."

"Then it must be me who needs the break." She took a deep breath.

Shem studied her for the few minutes she was quiet. The contrast of olive skin and light eyes captivated him. Her chestnut hair was unruly. He stopped himself from reaching out and fixing a stray lock. So beautiful.

Aimee brought their food, and Mar chuckled at Shem's unrestrained "mmm" when he ate the first Scooby.

"Love at first bite?"

"Every bite," he munched out. "We add cheese and pimento to the batter. No one else makes them like this." Over lunch, they chatted about Magique's upcoming move. When Aimee brought the check, Mar borrowed her pen.

"I'll have your go bag ready in a few minutes," Aimee called as she retreated.

Mar twisted in the booth and stretched out to pull a crumpled receipt from the pocket of her jeans. Shem stopped breathing to behold her sensuous moves. *Could you be any hotter?*

"We haven't talked money," she began, jerking him back to the conversation. "This is a salaried position. All you have to do is get the job done. If it takes you 30 hours or 50 hours, the pay is the same. If you are working too much, we can hire someone to cover the shop and run errands." Shem felt his throat getting tight.

She wrote on the back of the receipt as she spoke. "I'm calculating your starting salary using twice your current hourly rate for 40 hours a week." She slid the paper to him. Shem looked down at the number, but he never looked back up. When she saw a tear hit the paper, she got up and gave his shoulder a squeeze. "I'm going to return this pen and grab my doggy bag."

Shem's head was buzzing by the time that tear had escaped. *What the hell. Am I crying? Get your shit together.* A violent childhood had taught him to hide his emotions. He took deep breaths and was composed when Mar returned and stood by the booth.

"So, are you in at those terms?"

He looked up at her. "How could I not be? Mar, why would you do this for me?"

"I'm doing it for both of us. I trust you, we work

well together, and it just feels right."

He tapped on the crumpled paper. "This changes my whole life. I'll be able to get out on my own. I've been with Peltiers since my cousin Nick disappeared." He tapped the paper again. "This means I can stop being a pathetic charity case—I mean, as long as I'm not *your* charity case." He looked away.

Mar stepped in, put her hand on his shoulder, and gave him a little shake. She was serious. "Is that how you see yourself? Because I see a bright, attractive, hardworking guy trying to get ahead. I would have offered this job to you even if you were living large. You earned this." She stepped back to let him out of the booth. He slid out, stood, and stunned her by pulling her into a quick, tight hug.

"Thank you, Mar. I won't disappoint you." God, she feels so good. He let her go so she wouldn't feel him getting hard. In the odd silence that followed, he added, "You're really short." Did she say attractive?

"I am?" she tossed back. "That certainly clears up the mystery of the empty top shelves."

MAR SCHEDULED the big move for the week after Mardi Gras. Shem told the Peltier brothers Mar was moving, and they all showed up to help. Dev came last, stashing a cooler of beer in the back room. When the last box was in the door, the crew congregated in the alley. Shem passed on the beer. In response, Dev shook the can and sprayed him with it claiming, "It's tradition." Shem hated this kind of play, but the brothers would never find that out.

Mar was unpacking boxes in the back room when Shem came in. "They got you, huh?" He didn't answer. He's pissed. Rummaging through a box, she said, "The blue promo shirts are right here." When she turned to toss one to him, he was pulling off his wet shirt. She was immobilized by the sight of him. God, he's beautiful. She locked her eyes on his abs, trying not to explore the rest of him. When she finally tore her eyes away and looked up, he was staring at her. Damn. Caught.

"I'm sorry," she said, with all the sincerity she could muster. "You're gorgeous, Shem. I couldn't pull my eyes away." She reached forward and handed him the blue bundle she was now fisting, then she stepped back.

"Welcome to my world. I've been looking at you that way since I was 15." He took the shirt, shook it out, and pulled it on. Then, neither of them moved until Mar broke the silence.

"If I kiss you, will you report me for sexual harassment?"

He stepped forward in reply. She pulled him down to her by his shoulders and put her lips to his. He put one hand in her hair and the other around her waist to pull her closer. He kissed her tenderly, then passion swallowed them both. When they heard Dev come in, they pulled apart, both breathless. Mar pressed her cheek to his and whispered, "To be continued?"

She felt his smile. "I sure hope so."

IN LESS THAN A WEEK, Magique Deux was almost ready for a grand opening. Mar and Shem were working in the conference room and sipping sodas. Mar sighed and looked up from the computer screen. "We'll have more foot traffic here for sure, but I'm going to miss the Sanctuary walk-ins. They love those impulse items."

"Maybe the sign on the old shop isn't enough," Shem offered. "I put one on Sanctuary's bulletin board, too, but who drinks and reads?"

"I think you're on to something. Can we do a promo that would benefit us and Sanctuary? They could distribute Magique coupons for a giftlet of some kind. In return we could add a coupon for a soft drink at Sanctuary with every purchase. We could pre-pay Sanctuary or settle up weekly... if they are interested."

She could almost hear Shem thinking before he said. "Why don't I just hustle my buns on over there and talk to Aimee. I can take care of all of this, uh... what's the giftlet?"

"No clue." She answered. "Do we have a box of anything small that hasn't sold? What about the generic mojo bags?"

"We have enough of those to cover the first 8000 customers. Our surplus has surplus." Shem rolled his chair beside hers at the computer and nudged her out of the way. His fingers flew over the keyboard. When he stopped, he pulled her next to him. "I've been cataloguing everything on a spreadsheet as I unpack." He pointed to the screen. "A case and a half of mojo bags are on the 'M' shelf in the storage room. People like those little bags, but you need a hook for them to spend two bucks."

"We can add a charm buffet," she mused. "Anyone who buys a mojo bag can choose an item to add. We can label them by intentions or something. Put it on our bright ideas list."

BRIGHT IDEAS SEEMED to flourish in Shem's hands, and Magique Deux was soon thriving with a hearty flow of

Sanctuary customers, a busy tourist season, and a profitable internet store. The charm buffet was a hit.

Mar's next goal was orienting Shem to her clinical practice. As he looked around her office, he asked about her given name, Masciarina, on her framed license. Here it comes... the dreaded witch talk. "It's pronounced mah-sha-ree-nah. I'm a descendent of the Italian Masciare witches. The day I was born, my grandmother called me her Masciarina. It means little witch."

"Should I be afraid of you?" he asked, as he sank into the chair across from her.

Inside, she cringed.

"I practice with positive intentions. You're safe with me."

He met her disclosure with his own. "I hope so. You're the first person I've been close to since Nick left me." He lowered his head. "My parents were addicts. My brother is a thug. My life—" He choked on the words, whispering, "God, it's humiliating."

"Your parents failed you. That was their story, not yours. Your story is about an honorable guy with a kind heart." She reached out and put her hand on his chest. "Behind those feelings you hold on to so tightly, you have some little magics just waiting to be set free."

After a long moment he nodded, punctuating some private thought. "Sorry for the drama."

"Nothing to be sorry for." She pointed up and rotated her wrist. "Drama built this house."

He chuckled. "Yeah, I guess it did. Is there therapy in the walls or something?"

"Something like that." She started gathering papers. "Let's cover the rest of this over lunch."

Aimee's brother, Dev, met them at Sanctuary's

door. Like Aimee, he was blond and beautiful. "Hey, Mar, someone is waiting for you in your booth."

"I own the booth now?"

Dev laughed. "It's yours more than anyone's. No one wants to be that close to the kitchen."

When the booth came into sight Mar smiled broadly. "Menyara!"

"Masciarina! It's good to see you." They hugged, and when they pulled away Menyara stared at Shem.

"Menyara, do you know Shem?"

Shem answered for her. "Yes, she does. Hi, Miss Mennie."

Menyara's green eyes shimmered as she went to him and took his hands. "Child, I thought Nicky was standing there."

"I wish. I miss him so much." He glanced at Mar. "I was just telling Mar about him."

"Join us for lunch, Menyara." Mar ushered her into the booth. "You two catch up while I find Aimee."

Mar went off to pay Aimee for the soda coupons. When she returned, she slid in the booth next to Menyara. "You look sad, Menyara. What's wrong?"

"My heart hurts, Masciarina. Cherise has been gone a long ten years. She's as good as forgotten. I talk to her at the grave and take care of the flowers Acheron brings, but I don't feel her anymore. I miss her. I miss Nicky. I miss me. I am shriveling inside myself."

"Menyara, how can I help?"

Menyara shook her head. "I don't know, Masciarina. I just don't know."

They both looked up when Shem spoke decisively. "You do know, Miss Mennie. You both know. Mar, you have to eye lock her and do a cleanup." The women looked at each other then back at him. "It's like when the computer freezes because the memory is full of junk files. Miss Mennie, your sadness is taking up too much space. You don't have enough room to work."

Menyara patted Shem's hand. "Smart like Nicky, too."

Mar slid out of the booth. She went to Shem, leaned in and kissed his cheek. "Make that honorable, kind, and clever." Then she stood up and looked at Menyara.

"I think I can help. Menyara. Come to my charm buffet with me. Shem, would you mind ordering take out for us? We can eat at Magique."

Shem snapped up the menus. With a devilish grin and a wag of his eyebrows he said, "OK, but let me surprise you."

When the women arrived at Magique Deux, Menyara stood just inside the door and let her eyes roam over the shop.

"I can feel your power in here, Masciarina." Mar smiled proudly, then stepped forward and put her hands on Menyara's shoulders to pull her closer. She bent down until their foreheads touched.

"Borrow my power, Menyara. Banish your regrets with it."

In a moment, Menyara raised her head and smiled. "I'm ready to look for some treasures here. Where are those charms?"

Shem arrived whistling. He set up the conference room for dining and served Mar and Menyara as though they were the most important guests at the most exclusive restaurant in New Orleans. He remembered that Menyara liked Sanctuary's Jambalaya. He brought Nick's Cajun Burgers for himself and Mar, and three of Papa Bear's Cookies for dessert.

"You are a charmer like my Nicky, Master Shem,

and you won't be disappearing," Menyara patted his arm. "Thank you both for sharing this lovely space. It's time for me to take my treasures home. Walk me out, Masciarina."

They hugged at the door. "Thank you, sweet girl. You are a treasure, and you have a treasure. The boy is in love with you." Mar opened her mouth, but Menyara continued. "Don't think. Let time do its work."

AT LUNCH THE NEXT DAY, Shem asked, "What's our next project?" Mar smiled broadly.

"What?" he asked, returning the smile.

"Space is the final frontier," she answered holding her arms to the heavens.

"Meaning?" he asked, lifting his eyebrows.

"Meaning we need to breathe some life into two dead spaces. First, my duplex. The back unit used to be my office. Now it's a warehouse. I would give the right person a great deal just to have a live body in there. It needs updating, though. What do you think?"

"I think I want to know what's behind door number two."

"It's the old shop. I inherited it."

"From the Masciare?"

"Yes. You remembered that?"

"I liked your story. I Googled the town and the witches. Am I in trouble for stalking your ancestors?"

"Nah. I like my story, too. That's why I can't let go of the building. Any ideas?"

"I'll think about it while I'm handling door number one."

Shem and Mar chatted on their drive to the duplex, but Shem went quiet as she showed him around. He studied every corner. Maybe he's on overload. "If it's too much of a project we can contract it out. Door number two is—"

"I can do it," he blurted. He looked up at the ceiling, took a deep breath and said, "Mar, I love this place. Would you rent it to me?"

She grinned. "And forego that cumbersome application process? You bet!"

"I'll draw up a lease."

"OK, but I'm not accepting rent while you're fixing it up. I'll reimburse anything that exceeds the amount of your rent, including an hourly rate for labor. This isn't part of your job." He looked at her for a long time, then took her into his arms and kissed the top of her head.

"I don't even know how to tell you how much I appreciate everything you do for me."

She pulled back and patted his cheek. "Right back at you."

SHEM FINISHED THE RENOVATIONS QUICKLY. He planned to surprise Mar with October's rent when they had their regular lunch meeting at Sanctuary. Today's topic was her vacant old shop.

When they arrived, Menyara was standing in the doorway with Dev.

"I can't stay for lunch. The rain is coming. I wanted to invite you to a memorial for Cherise. It will be ten years next week." She gave them the details of the ceremony and hurried out into the light rain.

Shem and Mar brainstormed plans for the old shop over lunch, but Shem looked out of sorts, so Mar cut their meeting short "in deference to the approaching storm." Shem was relieved.

It was raining sideways when Shem pulled into the

driveway. He was heading for her place, not his. Mar grabbed a towel and opened the front door for him. He slid out of his wet jacket and left it on the porch before he entered. He didn't say anything as he toed off one shoe. He struggled with the other shoe before he bent to untie it. He sniffed as he stood up, and she saw that his eyes were wet. She took his face into her hands. "Looks like you're raining, too, sweetheart. How can I help?"

That kindness brought racking sobs. She pulled him into her arms and held him tight until he calmed. They were both wet when they broke apart. He still hadn't spoken. Mar rubbed his arms. "You're shivering." She handed him the towel. "There are more in the bathroom. Grab the blanket from my bed on your way back. I'll start the fireplace and make cocoa." He nodded, grateful for some space to regroup.

He winced when he saw himself in the bathroom mirror, rain soaked and red eyed. The dam that restrained his emotions for most of his life had broken and he was swept away in a flood of uncertainty. Get a grip. Get a grip. Get a grip. He toweled off and headed for Mar's bedroom. It was a different kind of quiet there. He picked up the blanket and breathed in Mar's lingering scent before making his way to the living room. He was on the couch leaning forward and staring into the fire when Mar handed him the mug. She sat beside him on the couch. He sipped the cocoa.

"Ten years, and I still miss Nick every day. I was so mad at him for leaving me behind, and I never got to tell him I was sorry."

"Sorry for...?"

"For how my asshole brother Noah treated him. Nick was kind and smart, and so much fun. Noah hated him. He demoralized Nick any time he had the chance. Noah hated me, too. I can't even say some of the things he did to me. Nick rescued me so many times. I never thanked him or told him I loved him."

He was crying again, softly this time. She put an arm around his shoulders, and he leaned into her gentle rocking. "I owe him, Mar. He was everything to me. He fed me, he taught me, he listened. Without him, I would have been in the streets." He took a breath.

"Cherise was mean to him. I don't want to celebrate her life. I want to celebrate his."

"You do that every day that you live the life he wanted for you. He'd be so proud of you."

He lifted a shoulder to wipe his eyes on his shirt sleeve, leaned his head back and closed his eyes. When he was dozing, Mar curled up on the sofa and fell asleep with her feet touching his leg. Hours later, she half woke to him putting the blanket over her. He kissed her cheek and whispered, "I love you, Mar." Then he curled up at the other end of the couch and slept.

DUTIFULLY, Shem attended the memorial. He took Mar's hand and closed his eyes when Menyara spoke about Nick. Afterward, the group went to Sanctuary for food, drinks, stories, and music. Most stayed into the night. Acheron played a set with The Howlers. His weeping guitar took the heavy metal band to a different dimension. When the set ended, the crowd was silent.

MAR STOOD ALONE on Sanctuary's loading dock when Acheron walked past.

"Playing your heart tonight, Ash?"

He scoffed. "What heart?"

"The one that's been in a vice for a decade." He stopped then and turned to her.

"That's about how it feels."

Helping him would be tricky without touching him or looking into his eyes. In her mind, from her core to his, she projected a pink light for her words to ride on.

"Your guilt is binding your grief, Ash. It makes for a great blues riff, but you have done enough time. It's okay to move through it now."

He was still for a long moment, then he gave her a nod and turned to leave.

"Thanks for the music, Ash."

He turned back, "How do you do that? Is it a therapy thing or a psychic thing?"

"Both, maybe. I seem to connect with people where their darkness meets light. The tears of the righteous are in the shadows."

"And the ones who don't shed tears, are they evil?"

"Nah. Mostly they're just shadow puppets."

SPENT, Mar lingered on the dock and thought about anniversaries, how they sneak in and open old wounds without mercy. She tossed intentions to the universe. Healing and comfort to the bereaved, peace for Nick, clarity for herself. She felt Shem approaching before she felt his arms wrap around her from behind. He pulled her close and whispered in her ear.

"Can I get those little magics now?"

She felt pink light coming from him. Her heart smiled.

DREAMING OF NEW ORLEANS

KRIS KELLN

1

S tepping out of the airport MacKenzie Galanis
looked around. She couldn't believe that she'd
finally made it to New Orleans. This had been a
dream of hers for as long as she could remember. It
had taken her working three jobs with no real social
life for the past few years, but she was sure it would all
be worth it.

Hiking her carry-on higher on her shoulder, she
reached for her suitcase and headed towards the line
of taxis. She nodded at the first driver who smiled at
her, as he walked to open the trunk of his car. After he
loaded her bag, he held the door open for her.

"Where to, *Chére*?" He asked with a thick Cajun
accent. As he started the car, he met her gaze in the
review mirror.

"Umm," she rummaged through her bag to find
the notebook she had written the information for the
trip. "It's in the Quarter," she muttered as she
searched.

Hearing that much, the driver nodded and pulled
away from the curb, driving out of the parking lot. Finally finding her notebook, "It's on Chartres Street,"
she told him. "It's Hotel Prov..."

"Hotel Provincial," the driver finished. "I know where it is. Enjoy the ride," he told her as he drove through the city towards the French Quarter. Putting her things back into her bag, she leaned back and watched the scenery as they drove towards the hotel.

2

Grabbing the bag, Remi thanked the man before turning to walk away. Being here early meant he had a great selection of vegetables before all the idiots in town picked it all over and left only rotten produce.

Glaring at the people in his way, he ended up walking into someone. "Oh, *mes dieux*. Watch where you're going," he snarled but stopped short as the woman looked up. She was the most beautiful woman he'd ever seen outside of the preternatural, but he knew she wasn't one of his kind. Being an Arcadian bear, he knew when another of his kind was near, and this woman was not. She had long black hair that curled around her face, with the most luminescent blue eyes he'd seen outside of the dream gods. He itched to feel those curls against his palm. Reaching for her hand, he smiled, "Here, let me help you up."

MacKenzie froze as the most gorgeous blonde man with piercing blue eyes stood before her, offering to help her up. He was the man she'd been dreaming of for months. Looking exactly as he had in her dreams. 'Hell,' she thought to herself, 'this, this here,' she'd dreamt of him helping her up last week. Taking his hand, she allowed him to help her and smiled at him.

"I'm sorry, I wasn't watching where I was going," she told him, gesturing to the map in her hand. "I was looking to see where I was going next."

"*Non, Chérie*," he smiled at her. "Forgive me, I was distracted." Still holding her hand Remi winked. "The sight of a beautiful woman always distracts me. My name is Remi Peltier." He raised her hand and kissed the back of her knuckles.

"MacKenzie Galanis." She blushed and stammered, "Ah, my friends call me Kenzie."

"Pleasure to meet you, Kenzie," Remi smiled. "I live around here, perhaps I can help," he took the map from her.

"The bellman at the hotel told me there was a great place to try N'Orleans gumbo. Sanctuary, I think he said," Kenzie explained. "He said it was close by, but I think I'm lost," she sighed as she looked around the street and back to him and chuckled. "I think I turned at the wrong voodoo shop."

Remi laughed, "That happens here a lot. I know exactly where Sanctuary is. I can show you. You won't need this." Folding the map, he held it out to her.

"That would be great," she shoved it in her bag. "Is the gumbo as good as they say?"

"I'd like to think so," he grinned. When she raised her eyebrow in question, he chuckled. "I'm the cook at Sanctuary. It's my family's bar," He explained. Picking up his bag of produce, Remi gestured for her to follow him from the Farmer's Market. "So, what brings you to N'Orleans?" he asked.

"It's something my parents had always wanted to do. They died when I was young. I decided to make this trip for them."

"I'm sorry to hear that. Where did you live after that?"

"I was adopted by a couple, but we never bonded. Sadly, they've passed as well."

"Oh, *Chérie*, I'm so sorry." Remi patted her arm in sympathy. "So," he smiled, "Where does Kenzie call home when she's not travelling? What do you do for fun? Are your friends going to miss you while you are here?"

"I'm from New York. There isn't a lot of fun happening," she sighed, "I was working three jobs to make this trip become a reality. There isn't much time for that with how busy I am. I don't have many friends. A lot of people don't always understand when I don't have time to hang out."

Kenzie wasn't sure why she was telling him things she'd never told anyone before, but she felt a connection to him, and she just felt he wouldn't judge her for being different. She did keep the fact that she could move things with her mind and often 'saw' things before they happened to her a secret. She'd learned a long time ago that people didn't understand things like that.

3

"I have to go around back," Remi nodded to the bags in his hand. "You go on in and get a table. I'll bring you out gumbo and cornbread right away."

"Will you join me?" she asked him shyly. "If you want to," she added quickly. Turning towards the door, she gasped. Turning back to Remi, then back to the door, she froze and stared.

Remi glanced to the door and laughed. "I should have warned you." He nodded towards his double. "That's my brother Dev, we are half of a set of quads."

"Quads, oh lord your poor mama," she laughed. Seeing the pain flash in his eyes, she sobered, "I'm sorry did I say something?"

Shaking his head, Remi gave her a sad smile, "*Non Chérie.* It's just that our parents died a few years back and it still hurts to think about them. I should have said something earlier." He gave her a smile and a soft laugh, "But you are right. We have a big family, 14 kids, all boys except ma soeur Aimee."

"I change my statement," she snorted, "Poor Aimee. All those brothers," she shook her head. "Yikes."

Laughing at that, Remi gestured to the door, "You go ahead, tell them I sent you. I will join you right away." He smiled again and headed around the building after watching her walk towards Dev and Max who were manning the door.

"Morning, *Chérie*," Dev greeted her as she got to the saloon-style doors of the bar.

"Hi," Kenzie said shyly, "Ummm, Remi told me to tell you he sent me, and he'd be joining me for lunch." She stammered a little. Being around this many beautiful men was doing nothing for her self-esteem. Not only was Remi's quad gorgeous, but so was the huge blond bearded one beside him.

Dev gave her a quizzical look and glanced at Max, who was standing beside him, "Who Chérie?" he asked her.

"Remi," she repeated, watching them look at each other.

Giving her a weird look, Dev gestured to himself. "Tall, blond, looks like me?" Kenzie nodded. "Okay if you say so," he snorted and gestured for her to follow him inside.

"Hey, Aims," Dev called out to the tall blonde waitress walking by. "Remi said to seat her, and he'd be joining her for lunch," he said with an amused smirk.

When the waitress turned around, Kenzie could tell that this was the sister Remi had mentioned. She smiled at Kenzie then turned to Dev, "Our Remi?" she asked in disbelief. Nodding Dev grinned. "Okay," Aimee said slowly turning back to Kenzie.

"Well, if Remi is joining you, I will set you up over..." Her voice dropping off Aimee stopped and cocked her head like she was listening to something. Kenzie felt a bad feeling go through her, but she couldn't hear anything that would have caught the woman's attention. Looking over at Dev, "Remi!" Aimee said in a panic.

4

Not sure what was going on, Kenzie watched as Dev touched the earpiece he was wearing. "Remi needs help in the alley," he snarled. "Come on Max," he called to the other guy at the door, and they raced through the bar. Not sure what she'd find, but worried about her new friend, Kenzie followed Aimee as she raced after them.

When she got to the alley, she found Dev, Remi, and Max fighting four rough-looking thugs, who started to leave when they saw there were reinforcements. One of them looked back with a snarl and shot Remi with something before running off. Remi dropped to the ground with a painful growl and started to flash back and forth between a man, and ... She had to be seeing things, but she could swear that it was a bear.

"Shit," Dev swore. "Damn jackals had a Taser." Racing to Remi, Dev knelt by his side but didn't touch him in case he was affected too. Glancing back at the others, he cursed when he saw that Kenzie had followed them out. "Aims," he pointed towards Kenzie. "She shouldn't be here. You know what to do."

"No," Remi called out when he was back to man

for a minute. Nodding to Kenzie, he struggled to keep form. "Don't wipe her mind." He then gave in and went back to flashing.

Looking over at Dev and Fang, Aimee walked towards Kenzie, placed her hand on her arm, and turned the woman to face her. "How about we forget about this and get you a table," she said smoothly as she tried to move Kenzie back towards the back door.

Kenzie gaped at her. "Get me a table...are you freaking kidding me? Remi is..." She gestured to where Remi was laying on the ground, "Well, I don't know what he's doing. But I'm staying here until I know he's okay." Kenzie moved away from Aimee, trying to get closer to Remi but couldn't as Dev and Max stood in her way.

Aimee walked over to where Fang was standing. "Well, that's weird," she muttered. "I've never had a human not follow my suggestions before," she said quietly. "What do we do about Remi now?" She gestured to her brother on the ground. "We can't have him shifting in the alley for long, people are going to start to notice."

Dev shook his head. "It looks like it's slowing down," he pointed out. "Hopefully, he'll be able to hold form soon." Glancing at Kenzie, he looked back to his family and shrugged.

Straightening he walked over to her. "So, how long have you known my brother? Remi doesn't care about," he paused. "Well, really Rem doesn't care about anyone. So why would he care if we wipe your memory of this? And you seem rather calm about it."

"She's not that calm," Fang snorted. "I can smell her fear from across the alley." Gesturing to Remi, "You two got this," he asked Dev and Quinn. They nodded. Fang glanced at Max. "You should get back to the door, and I've got to get back to the bar." Turning back to his mate, he kissed Aimee. "Let me know if you need any help," he said as they headed back into the bar, giving Kenzie another glare.

Aimee walked over to where Kenzie stood, shifting her weight from foot to foot. "It's okay Cherie," she smiled warily. "We are just worried about this whole," she paused, waving a hand to encompass the alley and Remi. She looked around, muttering in French.

"Mess," Kenzie suggested helpfully. "And to answer Dev's question. Remi and I met this morning right before coming here." At her answer, Aimee gave Dev a freaked glance. "But don't worry," she continued. "I've got my own secrets. I don't intend to tell anyone else's." She glanced back at where Remi looked to be passed out as a man, then flashed again. "Even as big as this one," she said. "I'd probably be locked up if I told anyone that their cook was a bear."

"Yeah, well," Aimee said softly, "I think it's better if you just stay here for now." She glanced towards her brother. "Until we can talk to Remi at least." Turning back to Kenzie, "I'm Aimee," she introduced herself. "You've met Dev. The other brother is Quinn."

"I guessed that," Kenzie gave her a nod. "Remi was telling me about you all on our walk over here from the Market." Her eye caught the loose jumble of colorful vegetables scattered from the bag. "I'm Mac-Kenzie Galanis, but I go by Kenzie," she paused noting the looks between Aimee and her brothers. "Why do I get the feeling it's unusual for Remi to share?"

Dev snorted, "That's an understatement. Let's see, how to put this. I'm the friendly one," he paused as both Aimee and Quinn laughed. Glaring at them he continued. "Cherif, you haven't met him yet, he's the oldest and acts it, Quinn over there is the quiet one, and, well, Rem is the grumpy one." Looking at her he shook his head, "Remi doesn't talk to people, not if he can help it. So, him sharing about the family, yeah, that seems weird to us." Aimee and Quinn nodded their agreement.

"She's different," Remi said on a gasp as he struggled to sit up.

5

R acing over to him, Kenzie dropped to her knees, "Oh-my-god. Are you okay?"

Squeezing her hand, he nodded, "I will be." Glancing at his siblings, he sighed. "I see you've met some of my family." His brilliant but exhausted gaze returned to her. "You seem very calm for having just seen me flash back and forth between a bear and a man," he cocked his head. "Should I ask why?"

Kenzie sighed and gave him a half-smile. "Well," she started, turning to look around the alley. "I'm good with strange." Holding out her hand she looked back at the step and as they all watched, a garbage can lid floated towards her where she held it in front of them for a few seconds, then sent it back to the can, placing it carefully back in place. "You turning into a bear, that's a new one, but yeah, I have plenty of my own secrets."

"Okay," Aimee got their attention as they all watched Kenzie. "How about we take this inside and have Carson take a look at Remi, make sure he's going to be okay." Seeing his glare, Aimee held up her hand. "For me, please," she smiled. "I'd feel better knowing he checked you over." Still grumbling Remi finally nodded.

Dev stepped forward to help them but when he reached out to help Kenzie to her feet, Remi growled at him. Rolling his eyes at his quad, Dev snorted. "Relax Grumpy bear," he held out his marked hand. "Mated, remember." He stepped forward again and helped Kenzie get up under Remi's glare and then reached to pull his brother up who swayed on his feet. "Okay, I was going to ask if you wanted to walk up to Carson's office, but I think we're taking the express elevator."

Before Dev could do anything, Remi turned to Aimee. "Bring her up. Please," he nodded towards Kenzie. Remi gave Kenzie a smile as Dev then flashed them from the alley.

While she was still looking around wondering where the hell they had gone, Kenzie heard Quinn and Aimee talking behind her.

"He's different with her," Quinn said quietly. "Wonder what's up with that?"

Aimee nodded, "*Oui*, he certainly is. And I don't know why, but I'm sure we will find out."

"Where did they go?" Kenzie asked as she fastened her attention on them.

"One of the perks to being a were," Aimee told her. "We can flash to places. As to where they went," she pointed down the alley. "They went to our doctor's office which is upstairs in our house over there," Aimee nodded to the building beside the bar. "I'll take you up there as Remi asked. However," she stopped and looked at Kenzie seriously. "Our family lives there, our kids are there. You bring trouble," Aimee leaned into Kenzie's face and locked their gazes. "You bring trouble and there will be nowhere you can hide that we won't find you."

Kenzie knew that Aimee hadn't warned her, she'd made the threat a promise. "I would never hurt anyone," Kenzie assured the woman. "I have lost too many myself to be the reason someone else loses their loved ones."

Aimee studied her with a steady gaze her for a minute and nodded, "Yeah I can see you mean that. Okay then, let's go see Remi," Aimee led the way over to the house and took Kenzie up to Carson's office on the second floor.

6

K enzie fluffed the pillow and put it behind Remi's head. "Are you sure you're okay?" she adjusted the blankets around him.

"I'll be fine," he assured her. Reaching up he took her hand. "Sit down, Kenzie.". He rolled his eyes as she sat down carefully beside him. "Believe me, I'm not made of glass," he teased. "This is not how I planned to spend my afternoon," he went on. "I had planned to have lunch with a pretty lady, get to know her more, and possibly ask her what she has planned for tomorrow."

"You don't mean that," she protested. "You were being nice when you agreed to have lunch with me. Guys like you don't want to spend time with girls like me."

He snorted. "Firstly, I'm not that nice. Ask anyone here," he told her. "Secondly, what are you talking about, girls like you?"

Waving a hand to gesture to all of her, Kenzie explained as if speaking to a child. "Girls like me, plain girls." Then she looked at him. "Gorgeous guys like you don't hang with people like me."

Putting his finger to her lips, Remi shook his head.

"Guys like me love to hang out with beautiful girls like you," he insisted, ignoring her protests. "I'd like to see you again tomorrow. You never did get to try my gumbo. Meet me here around noon tomorrow. We can have lunch, talk more about, well, today, and then I will take you sightseeing. Please?"

Still not believing him, Kenzie agreed to meet him at lunch. "But I'll leave you now to get some rest, you look tired."

"Maybe a little," he admitted. "I'm going to get Dev to walk you back to your hotel. It's getting late, and the Quarter is no place to walk around by yourself." He told her before a huge yawn took over.

"Dev, I need you to walk Kenzie back to her hotel." Remi sent the message through their telepathy. "What the hell? I'm busy *mon frère*," Dev grumbled, as usual for the big guy, then sighed. "Oh Christ. Yeah, I can do it. Have her meet me downstairs."

"Dev will meet you downstairs," Remi told her. He lifted her knuckles to his lips. "I will see you tomorrow."

As they walked in silence Kenzie could tell Dev wanted to say something to her. "What?" she finally asked as they stopped outside her hotel courtyard.

Dev glanced around and then back to her. Rocking back on his heels, he crossed his arms over his chest. "Look, I know Remi seems to trust you....and I want to trust his instincts, but..."

Shaking her head, Kenzie gave him a peeved look. "I had this conversation with Aimee, and I promised Remi too. I will not say anything to anyone. Cross my heart." She made the crisscross motion over her chest. "I would not harm any of you. You seem like nice peo-ple...er...well, you know what I mean. Your secret is safe." She told him. "I like Remi, I want to spend time getting to know him, and he offered to take me sight-seeing tomorrow."

Dev gasped, "He did what?" He started laughing when Kenzie repeated that Remi offered to show her around New Orleans after they had lunch the following day. "Oh man," he shook his head. "They are never going to believe this one." Still chuckling to himself, he waved goodbye. "I'll see you tomorrow."

7

The last couple of weeks had been amazing. Kenzie was sad that her trip was ending. Her flight home was booked for the next day and tonight was the last time she'd see Remi. She had no idea if he wanted to see her after she went home to New York or not, but a girl could dream.

Every day of her trip she'd met up with him to either go sightseeing or simply hang out together at Sanctuary watching their house band, The Howlers play. She enjoyed meeting his family, who all seemed to work in or around the bar.

Sightseeing had been fun with Remi, as he had made sure to show her all the best places. He'd even shared some of the spots that the locals reserved for themselves and didn't often share with the tourists. Her favorite being a sunny day they had had a picnic near the ocean.

It was on an outing to Café du Monde for beignets and chicory coffee that she had shared her secrets with him. If Remi could trust her with his family's secret, she could do the same. Telling him that along with telekinesis, she had pre-cognitive abilities both awake and dreaming, had been a relief for her. It was nice to be with someone who understood being different.

Tonight's going to be special she thought to herself as she finished her make-up in the mirror. He'd promised to make her a romantic meal, just the two of them. Looking down at her dress, she hoped he liked it. Grabbing her purse and phone she locked the door and headed downstairs where she found Remi waiting for her. 'God, that man is yummy looking,' she sighed.

"Hi," she greeted him with a kiss. She pulled back a bit. "I thought we were meeting at Sanctuary?"

Smiling, Remi returned her kiss and then handed her a single red rose. "I have another surprise," he told her. Taking her arm, he whisked her outside to where a horse-drawn carriage waiting for them. "Better than walking to the bar," he assured with a wink.

"Much better," she agreed as he helped her into the carriage.

The evening ride through the Quarter was fantastic but entering the dining room of the Peltier house was even better. Remi had laid out a beautiful table. After seating her, Remi went into the kitchen and brought back two plates with Grilled chicken, roasted vegetables, and rice.

"It looks delicious," Kenzie told him as she went to take her first bite. "Tastes that way too."

"Merci," he thanked her and started to eat his meal. "I've got something sweet for dessert too," he added.

After they were finished eating Remi brought out honey cakes and coffee. "Again, very delicious," Kenzie told him after taking her first bite of the cake. It was delicate layers of creamy filling and soft sponge cake with sweet taste of honey to tease her taste buds.

Enjoying the meal, the two of them talked about anything but her leaving the next day.

"Rem," Kenzie began. "I wanted to ask about the marks on some of your family's hands. What's that about? I noticed that they are similar but different. Well, except for Aimee's. Hers doesn't match the other women in the family."

"Those are," Remi paused. "Well, they are mating marks. When we find our mate, who is set by the Fates, the mark appears so we know."

Thinking about this, Kenzie looked at him, "Do they appear when you meet them, or is there something more to it?"

"We have to...um...sleep with them," he told her quietly, his gaze on the pristine tablecloth over the table. He looked up at her. "We don't have any say in who our mates are, the fates are sometimes cruel bitches, but we have to have sex with each other and then afterward the mark will appear on our palms."

"Does it happen instantly?" Kenzie rubbed her thumb across her palm. The thought of sleeping with someone once and having their whole lives decided for them was a little scary.

"No, we have three weeks to decide if we wish to be mated. Well, actually, it's mostly the females who make this decision."

"What happens if she decides no?" Curiosity got the better of her and she had to ask.

"Well," Remi heaved a big sigh, so full of emotion Kenzie didn't blink until he finished his explanation. "If the female says no, the male is left impotent until his mate dies. She is able to be with others, but we are only able to have children with our chosen and accepted mates."

Sitting there quietly after he explained this, Kenzie

frowned. "Is that why we haven't?" She waved her hand between them. "I mean...you never tried to..." She looked at the floor. "You wouldn't want to chance that with me."

"Gods no," Remi raced to assure her. Seeing her disappointment, he realized what he'd done. "I just didn't know if you wanted to be with me."

"That's crazy." She shook her head at the misunderstanding. "We've been fooling around my entire trip. I just didn't think you wanted to sleep with me. Thought maybe I was too human," she found a smile.

Gathering her into his arms, he kissed her. "Never too human," he brushed his nose against hers and flashed them up to his room and had her lying on his bed before she changed her mind.

Sheltered in his arms, Kenzie gave herself over to a soul-searing kiss that left her breathless and wetter than she'd ever been. Reaching down, she pulled at his shirt. "Off," she moaned against his mouth, wanting to feel his skin against hers. No sooner had she said the words than their clothes vanished, and Remi gave her a wicked grin and kissed her deeply again.

"The fun of being me," he teased her between kisses as his hands roamed over her body. He'd never wanted to be inside a woman as badly as he felt right now, about this woman. As weird as it was, he was possessive and never wanted to let her go.

Taking her into his arms, Remi put her on her side and laid down behind her. Keeping her wrapped tightly in his embrace, he used his leg to widen hers, and with one hand caressing her body, he entered her from behind, driving himself deep. His moan answered hers as he felt her body flutter around his. With each moan she let out, Remi quickened his strokes, sending her body spiraling ever higher. Feeling her close, he moved his hand faster against her, amplifying her pleasure until she burst apart in an earth-shattering orgasm, which had him following her over the edge soon after her.

Kenzie felt Remi's ragged heartbeat against her back as he held her tightly while they struggled to breathe regularly again. He had broken her for another guy, she knew that and hated that she had to leave him tomorrow. Pulling his arm tighter around her, Kenzie turned slightly to kiss him over her shoulder where he rested his head. No sooner had they started the kiss when she felt a burning on her palm. Pulling back with a hiss, she watched as he also held up his palm with a matching mark. "Holy shit, we're mates."

Seeing the look of shock in her eyes, Remi held her close. "Shh, Kenz," he said softly. "Sleep now, we can talk about it tomorrow." Giving her a tender kiss, he settled her in his arms and snuggled behind her.

_____

8

Waking up to the sound of her alarm, Kenzie stretched and sat up. Blinking she looked around her. "What the hell?" She was back in her bedroom.

She looked down at her bare hand, no mating mark.

She felt the world close in on her. It had all been a dream, a very vivid dream; but it was still only a dream. She wanted to cry but knew it wouldn't change anything. Remi wasn't real, he was just a figment of her imagination. A perfect dream lover. No one so perfect for her could exist in the real world.

Getting out of bed to start her day she glanced at the calendar. Seeing the date, she glanced down the hallway and saw her suitcase sitting by the door. Today she was leaving for her trip to New Orleans. That must have been why she dreamt of the adventure. If only, she thought as she headed to the bathroom to get ready for her day.

It was a nice dream to imagine meeting a handsome stranger, she smiled at that thought. Then remembered how many times her dreams had come true. This couldn't be true, could it? There wasn't a race of people that could turn into animals... She shook her head. That was simply crazy. Wasn't it?

HOT WINGS AND HOWLERS

KIMBERLY FORREST

1

Jackelyn "Jack" Phillips took a deep, cleansing breath to calm her nerves as she stared at the Sanctuary Bar on Ursulines. With her being newly arrived in New Orleans, the place had been recommended to her by her cousin Eric. Now there was a guy who had luck in spades. Jack's mother had always said he could fall into a shit pot and come out smelling like a rose. Somehow, despite what could best be described as a mediocre academic record, her cousin had landed one of the cushiest jobs in history. He made an obscene amount of money running errands for some eccentric rich guy who couldn't go out during the daytime. Jack could only be so lucky. Her bank statement practically laughed at her every month when she opened the thing.

Though, she supposed, she did have some luck. She'd been accepted to her first-choice school where she'd be studying her second love, anthropology, under Professor Soteria Parthenopaeus. Her first love, however, was what had led her here tonight to Sanctuary. Music, specifically playing guitar.

She'd been worried when she'd arrived in New Orleans that she wouldn't find a group of musicians

willing to take her on. Her first night in the city, she'd
taken a walk down iconic Bourbon Street, with its
palm trees and neon, the smell of fried food that had
set her belly rumbling with hunger, the people
shouting and laughing, and above all of that, the
sound of music. Right there on the street, a man was
slapping out a rhythm on an overturned bucket while
his buddy played the trumpet. It had put a smile on
Jack's face and a spring in her step as she began
walking to the beat and swaying to the music. Further
down, another group of brass players was lighting up
the night with their song. This was the home of Jazz,
and while the style was phenomenal, and something
Jack could appreciate as a listener, it was not her preferred style to play. Having voiced that worry to her
cousin once she'd gotten back to her place, he'd recommended she get in touch with The Howlers, a rock
band that frequently played at Sanctuary, and ac-
cording to Eric, played just the type of music she
loved.

Her stomach churning with nerves, she swiped her
sweaty palms down her denim-covered thighs and approached the door. Once she was playing, she knew,
those nerves would disappear, she'd be too into the
music to notice or even care if anyone was watching
her. Unfortunately, the time leading up to that point
was a whole different story.

"Hey, there," said the rather large and strikingly
handsome blond man sitting outside the door. "You're
new. We like new," he added with a wink and a grin.

Crossing his rather impressive arms over his chest,
he shot her a playful look of mock-sternness. "You're
not going to start any trouble, are you?"

Jack shook her head, only to spy the bow-and-
arrow tattoo he sported on his bicep. "That's the mark

of Artemis," she pointed out, as if he weren't already aware. "You're a fan of Greek mythology?"

His responding grin hinted at secrets as he replied, "You have no idea."

Before she could follow up on that statement, he glanced over her shoulder at the guitar case on her back and asked, "You playing with The Howlers tonight?"

The nerves that had diminished for a moment, thanks to her distraction with the guy's tattoo, shot right back up. "Er, to be decided," she replied, shooting a nervous glance at the door.

"Well, good luck. Be sure to grab yourself some hot wings."

Hot wings? On a nervous stomach? No way. Not unless she wanted the band's first impression of her to be her throwing up on their shoes. Well, she supposed they'd definitely remember her that way.

With a weak smile of thanks, Jack entered the bar and her stomach dropped as she saw how busy it was —especially for a Tuesday. Who had ever heard of a bar being busy on a Tuesday? She almost laughed at the irony. When she'd spoken on the phone to the guy who represented The Howlers and he'd set up the date, she'd been relieved, expecting low occupancy and therefore, a low-stress environment. So much for that hope. At least the music, currently playing over the bar's sound system, was right up her alley, which boded well for tonight's audition.

The place was huge, much bigger than how it appeared from the outside, and looked rustic in design. There were three levels that Jack could see, with sections for the bar, what looked like a restaurant, and a billiards section with the stage and a dance floor.

The sight of that stage had her swallowing hard. A

shot of liquid courage was definitely in order. Making her way to the bar, Jack spotted a coffin in the corner with a skeleton inside, and a small plaque that read, THE LAST GUY WHO ASKED AIMEE OUT. Jack chuckled and shook her head as she slid into an empty spot at the bar next to a young woman dressed like a Goth. Her long black hair had a vivid streak of red in the front that perfectly matched the red stripes on her tights. A black bustier with shiny metal clasps running down the front, black mini-skirt, and tall black combat boots completed the outfit.

Waiting for the busy bartender to notice her, Jack heard the woman next to her let out a long, almost heartbroken sounding sigh.

"Are you all right?" Jack asked.

Another deflated sigh as the woman looked up from a rather impressively sized bowl of ice cream, smothered in some sort of dark reddish-brown sauce Jack couldn't identify.

"There's a hot wing-eating contest tonight," the woman told her forlornly. "All you can eats, but the akri says 'No, Simi, no hot wings for you.'" She shook her head. "Tragic. Simply tragic."

Indignant on the woman's behalf, Jack drew herself up. "Well, that's not fair. If you want wings, you should be able to have them."

The woman's face noticeably brightened. "That's what I told the akri, but he says I needs to leaves the wings for the peoples."

Jack blinked at the odd, almost child-like way the woman spoke but quickly shook it off and offered, "Would you like me to speak to someone for you?"

Her question provoked a wide grin. "You would do that for the Simi?"

"Of course. Just point me in the right direction."

"You quality people," was said with a sharp nod of the woman's head. "What's your name?"

"I'm Jack."

"Hi, Jack!" Another of those wide grins that were positively infectious. "You and the Simi are going to be friends, I think."

Unable to do anything but return that smile, Jack nodded. "I'd like that." Having just moved to the area, she didn't really know anyone. A friend would be welcome.

"My akri plays guitar," Simi suddenly remarked, her chin jutting out to indicate the case on Jack's back. "He plays sometimes with The Howlers. Are you playing with The Howlers? They quality peoples too, just like you."

Opening her mouth to reply, she was forestalled by the appearance of the bartender. Before Jack could mentally switch gears to place an order, her new friend piped up, and said, "This is Jack, she's Simi's friend and deserves double-scoops pronto."

The bartender grinned at Simi and then Jack before he took off to fulfill the order. Bare minutes later, Jack had a large bowl of ice cream in front of her, sans whatever sauce was on Simi's.

Peering at Simi's bowl, she wondered what sort of ice cream topping the other woman was enjoying. It didn't look like your typical hot fudge, caramel, or strawberry syrup.

Simi must have noted her curiosity because she suddenly asked, "You want some?"

"What is it?"

"Good stuff," the woman said, turning slightly to dig into her small, coffin-shaped black bag with bat wings on the side. With a triumphant smile, she pulled out a bottle of what turned out to be barbecue sauce and proudly showed it to Jack. "See?" Simi said, tapping the label. "Special recipe. Hot, hot."

Barbecue sauce on ice cream? Well, Jack supposed there were worse combinations, but right now, Simi was waiting for an answer. "I better not tonight," Jack gently told the woman, hoping not to offend a potential new friend. "Nervous stomach."

Simi just shrugged good-naturedly and tucked the barbecue sauce away. "Not everyone can has a strong stomach likes the Simi."

Jack grinned in reply and scooped up a big spoonful of ice cream, lifting it slightly in a toast to Simi's stomach before putting the spoon in her mouth. Cold chocolate had just hit her tongue when she spotted a woman with a tattoo on her forearm, just like the guy at the door had sported. Once she swallowed, she casually remarked, "I guess a lot of people around here have a thing for Artemis."

It had been said more to herself than for Simi, but the woman scowled blackly, muttering, "Nasty old heifer goddess."

Taken aback by the vitriol behind that statement, Jack repeated, "Heifer goddess?"

"Artemis," Simi confirmed grumpily. "She a mean old heifer. The Simi hates her."

The words had been said in a manner that suggested Simi had actually met the heifer—er... Artemis —but as that was an impossibility, Jack could only assume that the stories Simi had heard about the Greek goddess of the hunt had vastly differed from those that Jack had grown up with.

Curious, she was about to ask, when they were approached by a tall, rangy-looking man with a ready smile. "Hey, Simi, how's it going?"

The question prompted one of those bright smiles

from Simi, her hatred of Artemis, for the moment, forgotten.

The man then looked to Jack, "Are you Jack Phillips?"

Her throat suddenly dried up and her nerves reappeared with a vengeance that made her hands shake. Fisting them at her side, she nodded, too afraid any words she attempted to utter would come out as so much gobbledygook.

The man introduced himself, though, for the life of her, Jack wouldn't have been able to repeat his name if asked.

"Come on over and meet the others before you play."

Okay, okay, she thought, her mind going into full panic mode. You've got this. You can do this. Be cool. So, of course, she ended up tripping over absolutely nothing as she went to follow the man.

"You got this, Jack," Simi suddenly proclaimed. "The Simi will cheer for you."

Throwing her new friend a grateful smile, Jack somehow managed to follow the man without falling on her face.

The Howlers currently had five members. There was Angel, the lead singer; Teddy, who played bass; Colt, who was their lead guitarist; Tripper, who also played guitar as well as keyboards; and Damien, their drummer.

They were an intimidating bunch, despite the fact that they each smiled at her and offered words of welcome.

"So, Eric," Colt said, tapping a callused finger on the table. "He's your brother?"

"My cousin," Jack managed to squeak out past her suddenly parched throat.

While Colt nodded in acknowledgment, Angel added, "You understand we're not looking for someone full-time?"

Jack nodded, adding with heartfelt sincerity, "I just want to play."

A few more head nods from the members of the band, their eyes glinting with understanding. For them, too, Jack guessed, the music was an addiction that needed to be fed. It screamed in the blood. A passion that demanded to be indulged.

"Then, let's hear you play," Colt said, flicking his fingers toward the stage.

The interview portion of the night was apparently over. Definitely short and to the point. Now it was up to her to prove that she deserved any more of The Howlers' time and attention.

As Jack made her way to the stage, she was trembling so badly she was surprised her bones didn't shake apart. A few deep breaths as she pulled her baby out of its case, she did a quick check to make sure it was properly tuned, then plugged the cord into the amp, the low buzz soothing her like a lullaby. This was it; this was her moment. She felt the familiar weight of the strap settle on her shoulder, the cool, smooth surface of the Gibson's body under her fingers, and as the song currently playing over the sound system abruptly cut off, a welcome calmness suffused her. She could do this. Closing her eyes, she struck the first chord of Seether's Breakdown.

Her fingers moved with confidence and her surroundings seemed to melt away. No bar, no people, no worries. This was what happened every time she played. She was lost in the music, and the feeling was sublime.

Another guitar joined her, a harmonious coupling

that sent chills down her spine. Vocals, drums, and keyboard as The Howlers joined her on the stage. It was perfection, and it brought tears to Jack's eyes.

As the last note faded and cheers erupted from the crowd, Jack couldn't hold back her grin. "That was amazing. Thank you," she told the band, sincerely.

"Oh, we're not done," Angel told her with a grin just as Colt began to play another song, and Damien, on the drums quickly joined in, setting up the beat. Godsmack, she recognized, her head nodding as she found the rhythm and joined in, letting Colt take the lead while she backed him up.

They played an entire set, unplanned, unscheduled, just the six of them, jamming for the pleasure of it and the enjoyment of an ecstatically cheering crowd. It was glorious. Arguably one of the best moments of Jack's life.

As she left the stage, still riding an adrenaline high, Simi was there to greet her, practically bouncing up and down in her excitement. "That was amazing, Jack."

Others came forward to add their own compliments, crowding around, patting her on the back, and Simi suddenly put herself in front of Jack, arms out to the sides to hold back the crowd. "Back up, peoples, let the Jack have some room to breathe."

Looking over her shoulder, Simi grinned. "Not to worry, Jack. The Simi will be your bodyguard."

"Thank you, Simi," Jack returned, nearly bubbling over with giddy delight. "I think we need another round of double scoops, maybe even with some special recipe, hot, hot."

"Now you're talking the Simi's language."

Laughing, they made their way back to the bar where an extremely tall and extraordinarily good-looking man in a long duster coat and sunglasses was standing, a fond smile on his face.

"Jack, this is my akri," Simi said by way of introductions. "Akri, this is Simi's new friend, Jack."

Like Simi, his hair was black with a red streak in the front, though his fell neatly to his jaw. Looking between the two, Jack asked, "Are you guys brother and sister?"

Her question sent Simi into a round of giggles that elicited a fond smile from the man.

"You did great tonight," the man said, turning his attention to Jack and adding, "I'm Ash Parthenopaeus."

"Really? My new professor at school is Professor Soteria Parthenopaeus. Is she you guys' mom?"

While Simi was practically rolling with laughter at Jack's question, dark eyebrows rose over the man's sunglasses in an expression of surprise. "She's my wife."

Jack's mouth fell open and her cheeks heated to near explosive levels of embarrassment. "Oh, my God! I just assumed she was old, you know, being a professor and all." Smacking her hands against her face, she shook her head and let out a pitiful groan. "Please don't tell her I called her old."

"Don't worry," Simi said, patting Jack on the shoulder. "Akra Tory is quality peoples like you and the Simi. Can we have double scoops now?"

"Yes," Jack immediately replied. "Maybe if I stick my face in the ice cream my cheeks will finally cool down and I can pretend I didn't just insult the woman who will have control over my future academic success."

Ash let out a little 'heh' sound of amusement. "It

was nice to meet you, Jack, and don't worry about Tory, she's got a great sense of humor."

"But you won't tell her, right?" Jack blurted hopefully.

With a wave that was in no way reassuring, he wandered off and left Jack to her misery, as she imagined meeting the professor and having the woman hear her name and realize that Jack was the student who had called her old. She'd probably say something like, "You didn't hope to pass, did you?"

With a pained groan, Jack dropped her head. Turning to Simi, she repeated, "He won't tell her, right?"

"No worries, Jack," Simi replied, rubbing her hands together as a bowl of ice cream was placed in front of her. "The Simi gots your back."

Jack blew out a relieved breath. "Thank you, Simi."

Simi grinned and pulled out the bottle of special recipe barbecue sauce, dumping a liberal amount on both of their bowls of ice cream. Honestly, Jack had to admit after taking a cautious taste, it wasn't anywhere near as bad as she thought it would be, and she quickly forgot her embarrassment.

All in all, it was a great night. The Howlers had agreed to let her jam with them, and play with them at Sanctuary occasionally, and she'd made an amazing new friend in Simi. Jack even managed to snag a platter of hot wings, much to Simi's delight.

"See?" Simi remarked with a bright grin, hot wing in hand, "I knew you was quality people."

THE FUGITIVE JACKAL

T. ELIZABETH GUTHRIE

Kenzie slowly crept down the alley she'd seen her bounty duck into earlier. She'd been chasing his worthless hide for the last two weeks and had finally caught up to him in New Orleans. *Tonight's the night I get my guy, and tomorrow, I can collect my money. Winner, winner, steak dinner!*

As she neared a darkened doorway, her senses started to tingle alerting her to danger. She'd never been sure where the power had come from, but she suspected it was one of her Celtic ancestors. She didn't care since it never failed to keep her safe. This time was no different. As the feelings bombarded her, she made sure to stay alert.

The young man came out of the dark with fists swinging. She could tell he was injured, which was why she expected him to fight instead of being able to disappear. *My first shot hit him for sure.* She was glad he couldn't go anywhere and was forced to face her.

Kenzie dove at his legs, taking them out from under him. He landed on the ground with a loud 'oof' as the air whooshed from his lungs. She jumped up and stood over him, chest heaving. "Now you little punk. You're coming with me."

Colt stood at the edge of the alley and watched the young jackal get his butt kicked by a sexy female. He couldn't tell if she was a shifter or not, but he'd bet his next paycheck she wasn't. Either way, he couldn't allow her to take the idiot and possibly expose their secret. "I don't think so, beautiful," he said.

Kenzie whirled around and saw a tall man standing in the shadows. "Back off, jack. This one is mine."

"Again, I don't think so," he said, and moved toward her.

Kenzie crouched into position to take him on when a sudden bright light lit up the darkness and she was blinded. Going on instinct, she grabbed the first thing she touched and hung on as she felt the ground drop from beneath her feet. She landed with a thud on a hard floor but was up quick in a defensive stance, in case she needed to fight.

"What's this?" asked Carson as he pointed toward the woman and the young man that was in Colt's arms.

"How in the world did you do that?" asked Colt. "That shouldn't be possible."

"Who are you people?" Kenzie asked, making sure to put the wall to her back.

Carson walked further into the exam room and gestured toward the bed. "Put Andric on the table so I can check him out." Then turned to Kenzie, "Who are you?"

Before she could answer the question, Andric managed to say, "That witch shot me." Then passed out.

"Well, at least we know what happened to him," Colt walked around the table to stand in front of her. "Now, back to finding out who you are." He couldn't help but notice the way her dark hair fell around her shoulders, the deep brown of her eyes, or that her lips were made for long, sweet kisses.

Kenzie's first thought was how tall and wide the man in front of her was. He looks like a tank. A very yummy tank. Falling back on her training, she realized he had to stand well over six feet tall. "Yummm," purred her instantly horny witch. Determined not to show any emotion she drew herself up to full height with hands on hips. "That's none of your business and I demand you turn over my bounty."

"Your bounty?" asked Carson as he bound the worst of his patient's wounds.

"Yes. I'm a bounty hunter and that little punk has slept with the wrong married woman," she snarled.

"Who hired you?" Colt asked as curiosity got the best of him.

"None of your business. Now, give me my bounty and I'll happily leave." Kenzie tried to be civil, remembering the old saying about flies and vinegar.

"We can't let you have him, I'm afraid," replied Carson as he straightened and stripped off his gloves. "As a matter of fact, we need you out of here. Now."

"Not without him," Kenzie said, jerking a finger in Andric's direction.

The two men sighed and looked at each other. Colt shook his head and closed in on her. "Be a good girl and come with me."

Kenzie sneered. "I've never been a 'good' anything, much less a woman who obeys." She feinted to the left, hoping to throw the big guy off. When she saw him move in the wrong direction, she dove between his legs to slide out the other side. Knowing she only had the one shot at getting Andric out of the clinic, she grabbed him and flipped him over her shoulder in a fireman's carry. Then took off.

"What the heck? How did she get by both of us?" snarled Carson, as he tore out the room behind Colt.

"She's a fast little thing, ain't she?" Colt commented then laughed.

They caught her before she made it to the stairs. Carson took Andric, while Colt wrapped his arms around Kenzie. She fought like a caged tiger, and he barely retained his hold on her. "Calm down. I'm not going to hurt you."

"I know you're not," she replied breathlessly, but she went completely still. There's more than one way to get free.

Colt didn't trust her sudden compliance, so he tightened his arms around her making sure she couldn't move. He carried her back into the exam room where Carson was putting Andric back on the table.

Andric let out a little bark. "Stop that. We're trying to protect your hide, so be quiet," Carson admonished.

At the odd sound, Kenzie glanced at the young man. Her bounty suddenly shifted forms and became a weird looking dog. That was the last straw for her overworked mind, and she fainted.

Colt looked down at the lovely bundle in his arms when he felt her go limp. "Well, damn. That didn't go as planned at all."

2

K enzie floated and kinda liked it until her memory returned. She stretched to make sure she was able to move and not being restrained. Then she opened her eyes. After doing a quick pat down across her body, she was pleased to find that the small but hidden arsenal was still intact. She swung her feet over the side of the bed. "Well, okay girl, get it in gear and grab your guy," she said softly to herself.

Her bounty was still knocked out, but she knew she could get him outside. She had no desire to come face to face with anybody else.

As she moved toward the other bed, the door opened, and the handsome doctor walked in. Knowing she was caught, she froze.

"Ah, I wondered if you were awake," he said. "You've been out for over an hour."

"No way!" she replied, astonished at the news.

"Yes, way. How are you feeling?"

Kenzie went to answer, but was interrupted by a beautiful, petite blonde. She was followed by a guy who could easily pass for a male stripper. Shaking her head, Kenzie wondered if they had the market cornered on sexiness. She closed her mouth and remained quiet.

"Why is she still here?" the blonde asked, pointing toward her.

"She fainted after watching Andric shift. What was I supposed to do with her?" He turned to Kenzie and introduced himself. "I'm Carson Whitethunder, the resident doctor and you are?"

She sat back on the bed and tried to smile. "Not important. For your information, I don't believe what I thought I saw, so you can let me go now." She took a deep breath to calm her jangly nerves. "I'll be taking my bounty with me, if you don't mind."

"Well, we do mind. Andric is an idiot, but he is one of us. As such we have a duty to protect him," said the blonde.

"Don't forget our secret," added the man behind her.

Kenzie glance between the three of them. "I don't know any secrets, except my own, and those I never tell. But I will tell you all this. That 'idiot' of yours is a wanted man. If I don't take him back to the person who hired me, another bounty hunter will."

"Who hired you?" asked the doctor.

"None ya," Kenzie snapped.

The man with the blonde laughed. "I think I like her." He put his hand on the blonde's shoulder and fixed his smile on Kenzie. "Just call me, Fang."

The blonde looked over her shoulder and glared at him. Kenzie briefly wondered what their relationship was before being brought back to the conversation.

"Ma'am. We're trying to be nice here. Please, work with us," Carson said.

Kenzie frowned at him. "Do. Not. Call. Me. Ma'am. Or I will be forced to hurt you."

That seemed to get the attention of the blonde better than anything else. "Fine. Let's start over. My name is Aimee Kattalakis. My family and I own and run Sanctuary."

Knowing when to act nice and when she needed to be a badass, she chose the former. "I'm Kenzie and I'm a bounty hunter. I'm here to collect a fugitive wanted by a pissed-off husband. Nice to meet you all." As a second thought she asked what Sanctuary was.

Aimee was about to answer when Colt walked in and interrupted her. "We'll answer your question when you answer ours. Who wants Andric so bad?"

"Damn it, bear. How can you move that quiet when you're so big?" asked Fang.

"Shut up, both of you. Now, can we please keep this civil?" Aimee asked, and turned back to their un-wanted guest.

"Who are you?" asked Kenzie as she looked past the others and directly at Colt. He towered over the others and the sight of him caused butterflies in her belly. Her witchy side sat up and took interest.

"That's Colt," Aimee answered for him and jerked her thumb over her shoulder in his general direction. "Will you tell me who's after the idiot? Please?"

Kenzie sighed and looked around at all of them, a de-bate going on in her head. "I can't," she admitted softly.

"Or won't?" asked Colt with a little growl.

Kenzie wasn't one to back down. "Listen here, big boy. I don't owe you any explanations." She closed her eyes and took a deep breath to calm herself. "I'm not trying to be overly rude, but I really must be getting back. Please let me have my fugitive."

Colt moved past the others. "You're not going any-where, little girl. You already know too much, and we can't risk it." He stood nose to nose, which was saying something since he stood six-foot-five to her five feet.

Not to be cowed by the big man, she stiffened and leaned in. "Get out of my space or you're going to sing soprano." He pissed her off with the macho act. When he didn't move, she brought her knee up so quick that none of them saw it coming. After the solid impact, Kenzie rolled over backwards and landed on the other side of the exam table. She watched him drop to one knee and cup himself. "I warned you."

Aimee stepped in to diffuse the situation. "Hey, let's go downstairs and have a drink. We can continue this little chat in a more civil manner. I think Colt might need a few minutes to regain his composure. You don't want to be around when he does."

Kenzie tore her gaze away from Colt to look across the room to Aimee. She decided that the other woman was probably right and nodded. The big man was only now releasing his injured parts. She moved around the table and followed Aimee out of the room, leaving the men behind.

"What would you like to drink? It's on the house."

Kenzie noticed the guard at the bottom of the steps but didn't say anything. "I don't drink alcohol, but I'll take a Dr. Pepper. If you don't mind."

Aimee glanced back at her with a friendly smile. "I rarely do myself. I have a thing about not being in total control at all times." She went to the bar and or-dered two sodas then carried them over to a table in the back and settled into a chair. "Now, let's talk, just you and me. No men to get in the way to say or do something stupid."

Kenzie lifted her glass in agreement.

3

Aimee looked over the rim of her glass. "Tell me the story of what happened with Andric."

"It would seem that the little idiot decided to mess with the wrong wife. He's known for being a womanizer and word has gotten around about his penchant for married women. I was hired to find him and bring him back to face the husband." Kenzie lifted her own drink and took a sip.

"Hey, Aims, can you come back here and settle something for us," a voice from the bar called out.

She sighed and rolled her eyes. "Children. What can ya do? Sorry about this but it'll only take a minute."

Kenzie watched her leave and sat playing with the condensation on the glass. She saw Aimee shaking her head for a second time. Then she walked off with the employees following her.

She decided to take that opportunity to slip out of the building. Nope, not gonna stick around to be interrogated any further. She rose from the table and wasted no time making a beeline for the door. She walked outside then paused to glance back over her shoulder.

Nobody followed her and she slowed down. The hotel wasn't far only a couple blocks over and she made it in no time. She went straight to her room.

As soon as the door was shut behind her, she collapsed onto the bed. Her mind spun in a thousand directions. How did my bounty change into a weird-looking dog? There's no way I saw what I thought I saw. Nobody in real life does that. And what about Colt? How can a man that looks that good make me want to jump his bones and drive me crazy at the same time? Her thoughts were in such turmoil that she neglected to hear the soft knock on the door until it opened. In walked the very man she'd been thinking about.

Kenzie was off the bed and reaching for the knife tucked into her boot when a large hand closed over hers. It was like being held in a vice. "Let go of my hand," she said through gritted teeth.

"Fine." Colt spun her around until she was wrapped in his arms. He held her effortlessly as she struggled. "You snuck out little bounty hunter and it's rude to leave without saying goodbye."

She froze hoping he would loosen his hold. "If you had given me the fugitive then I wouldn't have had to." He didn't let go. Instead, he tightened his grip as if anticipating that she'd try something. "Colt, right?" She decided on a different tactic.

"Yep," he affirmed. He liked the way she felt pressed against him. Mmm, sweet curves.

"Well, Colt. I'm going to be nice this time and ask. Will you please let me go?"

He hesitated. "Since you asked so nicely," Colt replied, and instantly let go. He hoped he wasn't making a big mistake.

"Thank you. Why are you here?" She stepped away from him and rubbed her arms.

He grinned. He hadn't wanted to let go. "You left before we had the chance to have our own little chat."

"I have nothing else to say to any of you." Kenzie looked at him trying her best to appear sweet. "Unless you want to hand over the little weasel."

Colt laughed. "While Andric is many things, a weasel is not one of them." He walked over to the bed and dropped down. "No, I don't want to hand him over. However, I would like some answers from you."

"Then, we have nothing to discuss, and you can leave." She went to open the door, but he moved so fast she didn't have a chance to turn around. He reached over her head putting one hand against the door to keep it closed, then leaned against her back. Excitement made her heart pound, and her voice took on a sultry tone. "What are you doing?" Uh oh. Why did my voice change like that? What the heck is wrong with me that this turns me on? Why am I not trying to get away?

"Making sure we're not interrupted. Like I said, I have some questions." He pressed a little tighter against her to hold her in place. Damn, she feels good.

"Get off me, you macho jerk." Kenzie's anger grew along with the excitement, and she was determined that the first one was going to win out.

He chuckled but didn't move. He leaned down and breathed against her ear. "Why? I rather like it here."

Kenzie blushed. She liked him there too, but this wasn't the time nor the place. Maybe I can use this to my advantage. Taking the chance that he wouldn't realize what she was doing, she pushed back against him. Her butt rubbed against his growing erection and she felt him stiffen against her. "There are other ways to get information from me." She heard the purr in her own voice.

Breathing in her scent he bent his head slightly and bit back the moan threatening to sneak out. "Yeah?"

"Yes. Would you like me to tell you? Or show you?" she asked, moving slightly.

Goddess, yes to both ideas. He closed his eyes, took a deep breath, and inhaled her scent again. Then took a step back. "Show me," he said calling her out.

She spun around and raised her knee. Kenzie was disappointed when he moved enough to protect himself. She darted across the small room, grabbed the knife out of her boot top and spun around to face him. "Now, I really think it's time for you to leave."

The dark expression on his face told her how pissed he was. "This is not over little girl," Colt said. He opened the door and walked out. Slamming it behind him.

The pictures rattled on the walls. Kenzie let out the breath she'd been holding. She dropped onto the bed, trying to get her nerves to settle down. "I'm in so much trouble with that one." She knew she had to grab her fugitive and get the heck out of town.

4

K enzie used the next few days to figure out how to get back into Sanctuary. She didn't want to be seen by anyone, just in case Aimee had told the others about her. One of the kitchen staff walked out the back door to throw trash into the dumpster and she made her move. She grabbed a piece of wood lying in the alley and wedged it into the doorframe. That way it couldn't completely close.

She waited for half an hour to make sure no one else came out then slipped inside. There was only one guy working in the kitchen and he had his back to her washing dishes. She walked through the door that led upstairs into the main house. No one was around as she crept up the steps.

The door to the exam room was open. She walked in to find Andric sitting up in bed. His fingers raced over the keypad of his phone.

He looked up to see her standing in the doorway. "How the hell did you get in here? I know there's a guard at the door."

"I'm just that good, dog boy. Now, come along nicely so I don't have to hurt your ass. Again," she replied. Kenzie had shot him with a 9mm.

"I'm not going anywhere with you. I've already told you that I didn't sleep with his wife," Andric denied hoping she'd accept his word this time. "I told you all this before you shot me."

"Surely you don't expect me to believe that? He has proof it was you." Kenzie started toward him.

He moved to get up, but pain had him laying back against the pillows. "Then it's been fabricated because I swear, I didn't sleep with her. That old man wants me for a very different reason. He knows what I am and will stop at nothing to get his hands on me, or another of my kind. No matter what I do, I can't let that happen. I won't let it happen."

The look he gave her made something she'd overheard Vanderbilt say suddenly make more sense. He'd been on the phone when she arrived for their meeting, and she'd waited outside the door so as not to interrupt him. "Now listen, I have a good lead on a shifter, and the perfect hunter to get him into custody. She's never lost a bounty and comes highly recommended," Vanderbilt had confided from his side of the conversation. She hadn't heard the reply from the person on the other end.

When he hung up, she paused then knocked. Their meeting had taken less than thirty minutes and she'd been on her way to find Andric. Not thinking anything of the phone conversation at the time she'd forgotten about it. Until now.

"I promise." He lifted his hand and made a cross over his heart. "I did not sleep with his wife. You have to believe me," he implored.

"Make me believe it," she replied. Shoot. Could he be telling the truth? Have I been played by Vanderbilt? Giving him a chance to explain she hoped it would alleviate her own doubt and clear her conscience. After all she had shot him.

Andric explained about coming across Vanderbilt's radar when he crashed a party the man was throwing. "He didn't like his young wife looking at me and called security to throw me out. Granted, I might have been a bit difficult, not wanting to leave. One asshat pulled a stun gun and shot me with it. I shifted back and forth between my human and animal sides. Vanderbilt saw it and decided he wanted the power to shift. Now he's trying to catch me to experiment on."

Kenzie remembered some of the tales her grandmother had told, about creatures that could shift. She hadn't wanted to believe them back then or now. I need to get to the bottom of this. Still, I don't have to make it easy for him. "Vanderbilt showed me proof you were sleeping with his wife. There were several photos of the two of you together. By the pool. Going into a hotel. So, unless you can prove that you didn't, I'm taking you back to Texas and turning you over to him." Even as she said it, she didn't like the idea at all. Holy crap I'm going soft. Not much of bounty hunter if I keep acting like this.

"I can't prove any of it," he said and fell silent. Then it hit him. "But this." He shifted. One second, he was a human, and the next, a jackal. He had to concentrate through the pain to shift back. "Does that do it?" he asked panting from the effort.

Kenzie didn't know what to think or do. She felt the world around her going black once again as her mind refused to believe what her eyes had just seen. She never felt the large arms wrap around her before she hit the floor.

"What the hell did you do, boy?" Colt cradled the beautiful little bounty hunter close to his chest.

"I had to convince her of my innocence, didn't I? She didn't believe anything I told her about Vanderbilt and why he wants me so bad. I had to show her," Andric explained.

Colt carried Kenzie over to the other bed and laid her on the covers. He grabbed one of the smelling salts from the top drawer and popped it under her nose. She came up swinging. "Hey now. Calm down. Nobody is going to hurt you."

"What happened?" Kenzie asked then looked over at Andric as she remembered. "You! You became a dog."

"I am not a dog. I'm a jackal. Get it straight, human," Andric said in an offended voice.

"Yeah sure. Okay. A jackal." She turned to Colt. "You're one too?"

"No. I'm a bear," Colt explained.

"Unh hunh and I'm a unicorn. Right," Kenzie rubbed the bridge of her nose. What is happening here? Am I dreaming? Have I gone insane?

Colt and Andric both laughed. "I seriously doubt you're a unicorn, since those don't exist."

Andric grinned. "But dragons do, and we have one sleeping upstairs."

Kenzie was too shocked to answer.

5

S he looked from one man to the other. "Darn it. You guys are pulling my leg. Dragons aren't real."

"Did you just try to cuss?" asked Colt with a chuckle.

"She can't," said Andric. "I don't think she knows how."

"I can too. I simply choose to use better grammar, thank you very much." She stood and looked at Andric. "Now, where were we? Oh yeah. You were getting out of that bed and coming back to Texas with me." Her mind still refused to believe what it had witnessed.

"No, I wasn't, and we weren't talking about that. We were talking about the dragon that lives in the attic."

"Damn it, Andric. Shut up, will ya?" asked Colt. He turned to glare at Andric.

Kenzie put her hands on her hips and tried to ignore that little inner voice that was asking her about her sanity. "Wait a minute. If I remember correctly, you said you were a bear, so why can't there be a dragon in the attic?"

"You're too tiny to look mean," Colt replied, wearing a huge grin.

"Shut up and quit trying to change the subject!" She turned back to Andric. "Get out of the bed and come with me or give me proof of Vanderbilt wanting to experiment on you." Her phone started ringing and she answered it without looking. "Hello?"

"Where the hell is that worthless little weasel you were supposed to bring back to me?"

"Hello, Mr. Vanderbilt. We were just talking about you."

"Who is we?" he asked.

"I'm hanging out with new friends and your name came up."

"I don't give two craps who you're talking to. What I do care about is the fact you aren't doing your job and bringing me that experiment. I want him back here immediately," Vanderbilt's voice carried from the speaker on the phone. Colt and Andric heard parts of the conversation and exchanged glances before turning back to her.

"You said 'experiment' not fugitive. I thought he was caught with your wife?" asked Kenzie as a bad feeling washed over her. The truth about Andric and the older man's wife was becoming clearer with every passing second.

"Listen you worthless little..." Vanderbilt stopped and took a deep breath. "Just bring him back to Texas and I'll give you a half million-dollar bonus."

"I don't think so. If you want him come, get him yourself. I'm officially off this hunt." Kenzie hung up as he started to scream at her. "Well, that didn't go well." She told them what he'd said and about the slip up. "Now that I have the full story, I guess I should apologize for shooting you."

"Although I'm not really sure that's an apology. Thank you," Andric said.

"Don't thank me. I'm trying to decide if I'm relieved that I don't have to figure out how to get you out of here or worried about what that old man is doing to people." Kenzie sighed. She knew what she had to do. "Look, I'm not going to say a word about anything I've seen or heard here. So, no worries. Besides, nobody would believe me in a million years anyway."

"We appreciate that," replied Colt.

Andric nodded in agreement.

"I have to go. I'm going to start my own investigation on Vanderbilt and find out what he's doing. If he's kidnapping people to experiment on, then I'm going to shut him down."

"Want some company?" asked Colt. "I have a little vacation time built up. I can take it to lend you a hand."

Kenzie stared at him. She knew if he came along, they'd end up lovers at some point. Would that be such a bad thing? She told her inner libido to shut up —for now. "Sure. I'd love the help."

"Give me a few minutes to gather my things and let Aimee know. Then I'll be back." Colt flashed out the room.

"Darn it. I wish he wouldn't do that." Then it dawned on her to ask, "Hey, how did he do that?" Kenzie looked at Andric with wide eyes.

"Well, if I answer your question, I'd have to kill you."

She looked at him with a deadpan stare. "Try it, dog boy."

He laughed and told her to take a seat. "I have one hell of a tale to tell you."

RAVAGED ANGEL

MARY E JUNG

1

CLAIMING SANCTUARY

The humid New Orleans air was a palpable omen as Melody paced the parking lot of Sanctuary. A famous biker bar known to most locals, it stood resolute under the moonlight, as if daring deadly beasts to crawl out of the darkness and step over its threshold. By the scent of danger in the air, Melody would venture that gauntlet was picked up more times than not. The neon lights were a beacon to her thundering heart as she watched the bouncer lean against the brick wall. She knew he watched her like the predator lurking beneath his skin as his nostrils flared, trying to catch a hint of her scent. Melody masked most of it, but there were parts of her DNA that would mark her as a demigod. Whether he picked up on it or not remained unknown.

She couldn't imagine why Menyara sent her to this place. She was going to be chewed up like rawhide and spit toward the Pontchartrain before she even entered the building. Melody couldn't stay outside forever, and eventually, that nonchalant bear was going to turn grizzly in more ways than one. Melody twisted her fingers agitatedly and inched toward the entrance, willing her gumption to rise from the shadows of her shivering soul.

She tried to dress the part to blend in but felt uncomfortable in the roguish costume. Normally, Melody wouldn't wear anything provocative, but this was a place filled with leather and attitude. The black jeans tucked into her boots constricted like a python but did wonders for her backside. The black corset top emphasized her petite waist and voluptuous cleavage.

Melody grabbed a strand of gold tickling her shoulder and twirled it feverishly to the rhythm of her heels clicking against the pavement. She halted before the monster guarding the door and found her tongue forgot how to form words. This was a terrible idea and every cell in her body screamed to run as fast as her legs could pump. She gulped and tried to drop her hair, but it got caught in a knot and ensnared her fingers pathetically. Melody cursed under her breath as she clumsily extricated herself and straightened under the keen eye of the guard bear.

The tree trunk arms of the bouncer didn't unwind as he assessed her for dinner. His gaze couldn't have been more blatantly obvious, and she tried not to whimper as the unnerving seconds ticked by. When the bear unfolded his arms, Melody jumped three feet backward and stumbled like an idiot who missed trapeze training. He didn't change his stoic expression as he opened the door wide with a gesture to enter. Gathering her heart off the pavement, she scurried into the bar like a rat. The bouncer spoke into the headset as her feet crossed the entrance, but she was too distraught to make out the words. All she had to do now was follow Menyara's instructions perfectly. Find Aimee and tell her the whole story of her escape from Apollo, then pray she wasn't eaten alive.

Long ago, the sirens were handmaidens to the goddess Persephone. One day, the sirens lost the young goddess to one of the original Olympian gods. Demeter, Persephone's mother, gave them the ability to fly and the power of song to lure the goddess back from Hades, the god of the Underworld. Persephone never returned to Demeter or her handmaidens, and the sirens were blamed for their ineptitude and carelessness. They were cursed to be exquisite in looks and compelled to sing the lamentations of Demeter's lost child forever. Those who heard the song perished by jumping into the sea and drowning, but if anyone escaped the spell, the sirens died instead.

Melody's mother was one of the original sirens who met her fate when the Odyssey traveled through the Aegean Sea. When Orpheus played his lute and evaded the death song, all the sirens jumped into the sea and drowned. Melody was a baby when her mother died and was left in the care of her older sister who lived on Mount Olympus. Chastity later helped Melody escape Apollo to live on the hidden island of Anthemoessa. Two days ago, Apollo burned it to ash.

Melody was a different creature than her siren relatives and carried god powers mixed with the siren traits. As a result, she was a wealth of contradictions that baffled the gods and ensnared her father's attention. Her song could bind and save, heal and curse, it was prophetic and enlightening, and it captivated the soul. Those godly gifts are what led her to Sanctuary.

Inside was cooler than the insufferable degree outside, but the onslaught of commotion made Melody inwardly scream. She didn't know where to turn or what to do. The door was behind, the rambunctious bar in front, and all around the preternatural world overwhelmed her vision.

Her chest constricted as she slid onto a barstool and took a moment to think. As if in answer to her roaring benediction for silence, the noise faded, the lights dimmed, and a soft crooning sound came from the stage. Melody raised her head like a puppet on a string and turned toward the sound of an angel singing. Transfixed by the accent that enriched the lyrics, Melody drifted into the music like a dreamer on a cloud.

She was tethered to the song as it wrapped around the room in wonderous vibrations. Every uncertain thought and feeling washed away with the melodious tide that came from the low purring of the singer's voice. Her eyes widened at his beauty and magnetism that pulled her like gravity. Under the stage lights, he looked heavenly, with his dark hair brushing the collar of his black shirt, and rippling muscles clutching the microphone like a holy relic.

Her powers unfurled as Melody listened to the luxurious intonation and drifted on the mellifluous tones toward something ineffable. Amber and gold strands undulated before her vision, while tendrils of warmth licked down her spine. Wings of glorious white light swooped around the room as the air thrummed magnetically with each beat of the drums. She was captivated and electrified as the notation unraveled in the air to reveal every composition of the piece. These gifts from Apollo she loved and cherished whenever they flourished.

The song ebbed and Melody was forced back into reality, but she hated to leave the pocket of comfort the music created. As the band switched songs, a male wolf appeared with a rag slung over his shoulder to take her order. She was flung back into the tumul-

tuous wreckage of her mind at her clairvoyant revelation.

When Melody was young, Apollo hunted her with
his prized pack. He bound her wings and laughed
from his chariot as the wolves ravaged her flesh. It was
agonizing and took weeks to heal. She vomited some
nights when the nightmares eroded her slumber. Her
luminous father was nothing more than a belly-slith-
ering serpent of evil that was spawned from the
abysmal hell of the Olympians.

"Do you want anything?" The male asked as he
wiped down a wet spot on the bar.

Melody snapped back from her reverie and
whipped her head back and forth. Bile gurgled in her
throat, but she swallowed it down and jumped off the
stool. She wanted to put as much space between her
and the wolf as possible. Melody looked around spot-
ting the pool tables and video game machines in the
back. It was the perfect distraction for her until the
bar closed and she could speak with Aimee. It would
be as far away from the wolf, the noise, and the overwhelming supernatural onslaught that pounded her
senses from the moment she set foot in Sanctuary.

She made her way to the back and selected a game
nestled into a dark corner. Melody pulled a small
purse out of her cleavage and jostled coins into the
machine. She never played one of these human con-
traptions before, but it looked interesting. Melody
looked back to the stage with longing and wondered if
there was a way to savor that sound forever.

2

SIREN SONG

S anctuary closed for the night, and it was time to
face the music. Straightening her top, Melody
crept toward the bar to continue her mission. She was
getting odd looks and a few whispers from the were-
hunters settling into the closing shift. No one should
be in the bar except for those residing in Sanctuary or
working. She gleaned throughout the night which
bear was Aimee, and it was to that blonde she fixed
her gaze. Menyara assured her this place would keep
her safe. There was no reason to doubt that sincerity,
but it was hard to have unshakable faith when the
gods did nothing but spit on her since birth.

The bearswan turned her head in Melody's direction and raised a quizzical brow at her nervous fidget-
ing. An audible gulp echoed through Melody before
she opened her mouth to speak.

"Aimee? I was sent here by a voodoo priestess
named Menyara. Is there somewhere we can talk?"
Once she started speaking, the rest rushed out.

Aimee's ponytail swung when she angled her head
and regarded Melody with interest. She held her
breath waiting for an answer and flicked at the end of
her hair silently counting the seconds. What seemed

like an eternity later, Aimee nodded and led Melody toward the back of the bar and into her office. She shut the door and strolled around to take a seat. Aimee indicated Melody should take the chair opposite. Melody sighed with relief and fell into the offered seat. Her knees shook uncontrollably from her nerves, but she forced herself to meet the bear's calculating eyes.

Melody dropped her shields and let her scent fill the room so her identity would be uncovered. Aimee's jaw dropped as the full impact of Melody's heritage and power registered. Melody licked her chapped lips and blurted out her story. "I need a place to hide. My home was destroyed a few days ago by my father, Apollo. I was saved by my sister and sent to Menyara. Chastity believed the priestess could help, but I was sent here after our meeting."

Aimee was quiet for a minute before responding. "Who was your mother?"

"The siren Ligeia. She died when I was a baby. My sisters are also dead or enslaved. My father wants my voice to lure men into an army and take over Mount Olympus. I don't want to bring trouble, but I have nowhere else to go."

Aimee pursed her lips as she regarded Melody, and there was a moment where she thought of escaping. Asking to be hidden from a god was a monumental request. At long last, Aimee's eyes cleared of debate, and she came around the desk. She folded her hands decisively and said, "This Limani was set up for anyone seeking refuge. We will not deny you our help. Stay as long as you need."

Melody smiled as relief coursed through her veins. "Thank you. I mean no harm. You won't even know I'm here."

Aimee chuckled lightly and helped pull Melody to her feet. "A demigod is going to be noticed, hon. What's your name?"

"Melody."

"Well, Melody," Aimee began. "You are welcome here. We have only one rule. Come in peace or leave in pieces. I guarantee we take that seriously. So long as you do us no harm, we will keep you safe."

Melody's stomach growled ferociously from her last meal eaten at breakfast. Her body was demanding sustenance now that immediate danger had passed. "Is it too late to ask for something to eat?"

"Certainly not," Aimee reassured Melody and looped her arm around her shoulders hospitably.

"Let me grab something from the kitchen while you make yourself at home. You can wait at one of the tables, then we can resume our talk after you've put something in your stomach."

Melody led Aimee guide her out of the office and into a chair near the stage. She drifted into quiet contemplation as she waited for her food. This had to be the worst day of her life, and that was saying something.

Melody stared at the stage and wanted to hear the beautiful music again. It calmed her savage soul and pulled her from the depths of Hell. Without realizing it, Melody stepped up to the stage and ran a tentative hand over the sound system. A tether to that miraculous liberation pulled her to the keyboard.

The lure to perform was so potent Melody couldn't stop her fingers from poising over the white and black keys in sumptuous anticipation. Tendrils of yellow and gold power rippled around the instruments and sound system. Wires connected into sockets, frequencies popped and radiated as everything aligned to her needs. There was no instrument she could not play, and the piano had always been her favorite. The mic dropped to her level as Melody turned on the keyboard and pressed her first note.

Middle C.

The purest of all notes, it was the diatonic tone to build all others. It sent a shock wave through her nervous system as her soul responded to the vibration. She hit it again, harder this time, and closed her eyes with the invigorating ripple that hijacked her senses. Her second finger skipped a third, then to the seventh note. Her left hand floated on an illustrious current toward the bottom registers. The C suspended as Melody walked a bass chord. It was slow and dipped deep into the harmony. Melody struck the seventh note again with her right hand. She switched scales and slurred into D minor.

The progression built until the song burst forth with brutal force. She tapped her foot, and the drums began to pulse, the guitars strummed. The instruments synchronized to her dynamic masterpiece, as long and wide tones pulled and undulated through the atmosphere. Melody became a musical necromancer as the husk of her heart began to beat. It escalated into soulful yearning as choirs of magic filled her head.

With a masterful intake of breath, she began to sing. It was unimaginably beautiful as notes glided on an illustrious tone. The excruciating deliverance swelled from her vocal cords to create a lyrical revelation. The music bowed to her like a queen. It bent and waved, harmonized, and drove with divinity with each flip of her tongue. It permeated her cells and poured into Sanctuary like the breath of the gods.

She slowed the piece phrase by phrase and dissolved the world back to silence. The overtones echoed in her mind and lingered in her beating heart. The music suspended inside Melody, and she felt liberated from the disaster of her life. Her lashes fluttered open, and she beheld the shocked stares of those left in the bar.

The cooks came out of the kitchen, those busing tables hovered mid-wipe with slackened jaws, even the bouncer pulled out his headset to marvel at her song. The power she infused into the room was something soul-wrenching and death-defying. She never really let herself go before, because of what Apollo would do with her powers.

"Do that again," a heavily male voice spoke to her right.

Melody dropped her gaze to see the leopard who sang in the band. His brown eyes were intense, and the flecks of gold within danced as if they were on fire. She'd never seen anyone look at her with such reverence. She couldn't breathe as he jumped on the stage and pulled the guitar over his shoulder. Melody felt her mouth open and close like a fish as he turned to her with his eyes shining bright and fingers poised to strum.

Normally when a siren sang, it put people under a spell, but this male was half animal and made from the gods. It occurred to Melody this may be a group of beings that could resist the call of the siren. He wasn't reacting to that part at all but mesmerized by the part connected to Apollo. He wanted her music, and that thought hurled her out of fear to land in a place of destiny.

As one the rest of the band joined them on stage and took up positions where their instruments rested. She moved aside for the keyboardist and grabbed the mic next to the leopard. Her body was on autopilot as it prepared for another song. She cleared her throat and began to sing "Zombie" by the Cranberries. The male grinned in approval at her choice and strummed his guitar with tantalizing fingers. He turned to the mic and joined Melody in a duet. She dissolved into the sensual catharsis of their vocalization as harmony stroked melody like a lover at dawn. She smiled as vivacious sensations permeated her system and they became perfectly in tune, as if they were meant to make music with their souls.

They finished the song and he held out his hand in greeting. She gulped and took it gently, trying to figure out what lay in his pulsating amber eyes. His grasp was firm when she tentatively laid her palm into his open hand, and warmth spread through her veins like a summer breeze.

"Angel," He introduced himself and she felt compelled by his hypnotic voice.

"Melody," she responded, and wondered if it was odd she held his hand a little longer than necessary.

He let go after a beat and put the guitar back on the stand. He straightened and turned back to her with awe written across his features. "That was amazing. I've never sung like that with anyone."

"Thank you," Melody replied with a blush. His words struck like a flint against the tinderbox of her heart.

"Well," Aimee interjected, "I think we know where you belong in our motley crew. How do you feel about joining the Howlers every now and then?"

Melody sputtered at the suggestion and didn't want to reject the offer but was afraid of the consequences. "That's very kind of you, but I'm not even sure how long I will stay."

Angel rubbed his chin contemplatively and backed up Aimee's proposal. "A voice like that isn't meant to be hidden, Melody. You have a gift. You don't have to sing during open hours. You could join us for private jam sessions. Think of it as singing for your supper." He winked at the end and gave her a devilish smile.

Melody was breathless against his charm, and the way he said her name sent shivers across her flesh. It made her stomach flip and her toes curl as his lips sensually wrapped around each word like warm chocolate. Melody lived in isolation most of her life and was hunted for her gifts. She only whispered her songs to the winds and was never able to stay in one place long enough to make friends. It was worth breaking out of her fears to experience something sublime with the Angel again.

"Okay," Melody conceded, and glanced to the microphone with prophetic expectation.

"Welcome to the Howlers."

She beamed as Angel clapped her on the shoulder and hopped off the stage. Aimee had placed her food on the table, but she paused before sitting and turned toward Angel. "Thank you."

He inclined his chin and turned to clean the stage with the other band members. Melody sat down and looked at the food ravenously. She pivoted toward Aimee, who was shaking her head at something one of the busboys said. Melody caught her eye and waved the bear over.

"Thank you for your kindness."

Aimee sat next to Melody. "You've been through a lot. I can see it in your eyes. It costs nothing to be kind to someone in need."

Melody took a bite and thought about remaining

at Sanctuary permanently. She needed to come up with a plan to fight Apollo. Her entire life she cowered before her father. Melody let him abuse her and destroy everyone she loved. She couldn't waste immortality in fear and tonight felt like a step in seizing her fate.

"Is it possible to keep my father out of Sanctuary?" she asked Aimee as she sliced into a perfect medium-rare steak.

Aimee grimaced at the question but answered honestly. "The way our wards are set up we have to let everything in, but we don't have to let them out. We can't keep a god from our doors, but we could put up a good fight. You don't have to worry. There's plenty of muscle here to keep you safe. You aren't without your powers either, you know. You could stand your ground."

Melody wished she believed that. "I'm too afraid."

Aimee tapped the table with her fingernails thoughtfully. "I can introduce you to Grace Alexander. She's a psychologist who specializes in supernatural trauma. We even know a few people that ran afoul of your father. She's helped them. It might give you the confidence you need."

Melody couldn't believe the extent Aimee was taking to ensure her protection. The compassion she was shown tonight obliterated her melancholy. She wanted to find the spark inside her soul and make it blaze.

"I would love that," Melody said. "Any help is greatly appreciated."

She finished eating and yawned from bone-deep exhaustion. Melody hadn't slept in two days and all the new events were sucking the life from her body. She rubbed her face, trying to focus on the conversation, but Aimee understood and gestured to the stairs. "We'll get you set up in a room. If you need anything, just let me know."

Melody smiled gratefully. "Thank you."

She stood with Aimee, but Angel hopped off the stage and intercepted their path. Melody's eyes widened as he spoke quietly to Aimee and wondered what else he might want. The bearswan nodded gratefully, patted his arm, and turned toward her office again. She paused to say good night to Melody and let her know everything was fine.

Melody turned back to Angel in confusion, but he jerked his chin toward the stairs and said, "I'll take you up. Aimee has to finish the paperwork for the bar."

Melody followed Angel up the second landing to a room at the end of the hall. Angel punched in the code on the lock and opened the door for her to see the accommodation. Melody paused in the doorway to looked up at Angel fascinated by the way his aura appeared feral, yet deeply layered like the earth. There was something about this leopard that called to Melody. Maybe it was the shadows that flickered in his eyes, but she sensed Angel had a story of his own.

"Good night," she said, and stepped over the threshold.

"Good night, songbird," he replied, as he leaned against the frame with one hand.

Her ears perked at the teasing note in his voice. "Technically I'm a siren and demigod, not a bird."

He chuckled at her obvious answer and stepped back so she could close the door. "Songbird suits you better."

She shut the door and looked about at her new home. There was a bed, a television, and a dresser. Meager trappings, but Melody had nothing of value to store and was accustomed to survival over luxury. She padded to the bathroom and a pleasurable sigh escaped her lips. A shower would be sumptuous.

She peeled off her clothes and turned on the water. The sound of the faucet reminded her of the waterfalls on Anthemoessa. Exotic flowers caressed the basin where she used to bathe, and beautiful ferns fanned over the rock bed. The trees were a canopy of green that shielded from the sun. This wasn't a tropical cove, but the water serenaded her into tranquility.

Stepping into the stream, Melody washed away her worries and grime. The warmth kneaded her muscles, and she surrendered to bliss. She scrubbed until she shone like the twinkling stars that speckled the night sky. When she was finished, Melody begrudgingly left the shower and conjured a new set of clothes. It was good to be a goddess sometimes. She poked at the controls for the television before deciding she preferred the quiet.

Slipping into the bed, Melody breathed in peacefully. As her body fell into slumber, she heard the plucking of a lute. It was far away, but Melody knew that sound distinctly. She shot up from the bed and looked around frantically for her father.

He was sending out a homing beacon with that horrid lute. The sweet intoxicating sound haunted her nightmares, rattled her senses, and it was death if she answered its call. Melody searched her powers for something to deafen the lute's lure, but terror overrode her senses.

A flash of light heralded a pack of wolves as her father opened a portal between realms. She screamed and charged for the door, but a wolf jumped in front of the exit. Melody backed away from the snarling beast, but another closed in from behind.

She felt the old horrors rear up at her helpless-
ness. Apollo would find her no matter where she went.
The only thing she could do now was fight. Gritting
her teeth, Melody dug into her power and blasted the
wolf in front first. It yelped as her bolt hit him and
singed his flank. She whirled around and attacked the
other.

It dodged her blast and bit her leg, sinking deep
enough to bring her down on one knee. With a roar, a
leopard burst through the room and attacked the
pack. Teeth and claws collided as the animals engaged
in deadly combat. Melody lunged for the bed with her
throbbing leg. The wolves swarmed the leopard, but
his enormous teeth sunk deep into their ranks, felling
them in a few minutes.

Melody held back her bile at the four mangled
bodies in a bloody heap. She panted with astonish-
ment as the leopard transformed into Angel, who
wiped his mouth from the gore. He reached for her
hand and hustled Melody out of the room. Aimee and
the werewolf from the bar charged down the hall as
they charged away from the scene. Melody hid behind
Angel at the sight of the wolf and gripped his shirt,
afraid another attack was on its way.

He turned toward her petrified expression and
clarified he was a friend. "That one won't harm you.
He's Aimee's husband. Come on, let's get you out of
here. They will take care of the rest."

Melody didn't argue as he teleported them from
the hall to a clinical room. Melody pressed a hand to
her leg and hissed. She hobbled over to a chair and
flopped down.

Angel knelt and lifted her chin gently, searching
her gaze as he spoke. "Are you alright? This is our resi-

dent clinic inside Sanctuary. Carson is our practitioner. He will stitch you up."

Melody knew it would heal in a matter of hours, but she appreciated the consideration. Fighting back gave her a sense of power she never experienced before. The adrenaline was high as she realized for the first time her father's creatures could be beaten.

"It hurts, but I'll heal. How did you know the wolves were in my room?" Melody asked, trying to keep her mind off the ooze.

Angel dropped her chin and took a chair beside her. "Your scream broke the sound barrier. We felt the wards ripple when they breached our defenses but weren't sure whom they were after. Thanks to your incredible lungs, we were able to get there in time."

Melody jumped as the door to the clinic opened and Carson entered. Angel stood and filled him in on Melody's condition. She didn't want to look at the damage, but it felt like the fires of Hell burned her flesh. Carson moved about gathering supplies, while Angel helped Melody onto an examination table. She was getting dizzy and gripped the edges to keep from passing out. Angel took her hand to steady her nerves.

Carson came with a syringe and bandages. "I'm going to give you something to keep you calm. Most of this stuff won't knock a supernatural entity out, but it will give you enough comfort you won't thrash while I stitch up the wound."

Melody gritted her teeth and hung onto Angel. "Just do what you need to," she whispered through chattering teeth.

Carson gave her an injection, then cut off her pant leg. He set about cleaning the bite then pulled out a needle and thread. Melody winced at the first prick to her flesh, but Angel drew her attention away from Carson.

"Those weren't werewolves that attacked you," he stated, as she dug her nails into his hand.

"No," Melody shook as sweat trickled down her brow and nausea rolled in the pit of her stomach. "Those were Apollo's favorite pets."

"Why's he got such a hard-on for you?"

"Because of my powers. My voice can bind most men to my will."

Angel swore as he understood the magnitude of her situation. Angel kept her talking until Carson was done. He washed the blood away and gave her another shot of anesthetic.

Melody couldn't imagine what her father would inflict if he enslaved her to his cause. She looked up into the dark eyes of the leopard who came to her rescue and understood why Menyara sent her to this place. It wasn't just a refuge it was a place for her to learn how to become strong.

Taking a deep breath, she addressed Angel. "Can you teach me to fight?"

Angel's brows shot straight up in surprise at her sudden demand. She held his gaze with a determined purse of her lips, but his lips twisted roguishly in response. "It would be my pleasure."

SANCTUARY

CARRIE HUMPHREY

1

Kedah opened one eye, knowing that if she opened both, she would officially be awake and wasn't ready to commit to that nonsense. The sun had already set—she could feel that. Though it was early in the evening, she had no desire to be functioning on her first day off in over a week.

However, the man that had been snuggled into her side, sleeping peacefully, was now up and rummaging around the closet making unnecessarily loud noises. "What are you looking for?"

The man in question peeked his head out beyond the door and grinned. His hair was wet from a shower she hadn't heard running, and from her current view, it appeared he wasn't clothed yet. That got her attention. She opened the other eye and sat higher in the bed.

"Good morning," Doran's voice rumbled across the distance between them, caressing her skin and bringing a blush to her ears. "Have you seen my jeans?"

"How did you function before me?" she snorted then shook her head. "Second shelf to your left. The good pair would be the darker ones. But, why?

Tonight we're supposed to have off. Stay in bed. Do nothing. Right?"

She heard an 'ah-ha' muffled in the closet and rolled her eyes with a smile. After a few moments, Doran came out looking like a dream in denim. Between the jeans he wore, the black shirt that stretched over his muscled frame, the leather jacket hanging off his arm, and the boots in his hand, he looked like a biker ready for trouble. She wanted to be the trouble he was looking for.

"To what do I owe the pleasure of this view this evening?"

"We're going out," he stated with a heart-stopping smile.

"Oh, really? Like a date?"

"I'm not sure the Sanctuary is date material, but I guess it could be. I want you to meet some friends of mine who recently sent out an invitation." He walked to the edge of the bed and sat down. "I can only assume they heard I had settled down, or hadn't heard that I was causing trouble, and worried." Shrugging, he continued as he put his boots on. "Honestly, they are probably more curious about you than seeing me. I seem to have a certain reputation that people are finding hard to see broken."

Leaning in, he brushed a gentle kiss on to her lips, pulling away with a resigned sigh. She understood the feeling, and if it were up to her, which apparently it wasn't, he'd stay right where he was. He seemed so excited to be going out, something she rarely saw from the man who showed almost no outward emotion. She wouldn't hesitate to follow him anywhere to keep that excitement intact. "The Sanctuary? Not sure I've heard of the place."

Doran shook his head. "You wouldn't have. It's a

bar and grill down in New Orleans run by the Peltier family. Last I knew, Aubert and Nicolette were running the joint, but I'd imagine one of their twelve cubs may be in charge by now. My bet's on Aimee."

Kedah blinked several times as she tried to unpack everything he had said so casually. "New Orleans? Cubs? Twelve kids?"

He smiled. "Sometimes I forget how new you are to this immortal, paranormal world." Standing, he held out a hand for her to take, and pulled her to the edge of the bed. Pushing the covers aside, she stood and then he wrapped his arms around her body. Inhaling his scent, she laid her forehead on his chest, hugging him back.

"The Peltier's are a family widely known though the were-community. Though it is a functioning bar and grill, it's also a sanctuary for weres, paranormals, and passerbyers that have nowhere else to go. I'd imagine Jensen based this place on theirs, albeit rather loosely. We could do with a good bar in this town."

He wasn't wrong. Briarberry, the tiniest town in rural North Carolina, barely had a stop light. A bar of any caliber would be a welcome upgrade.

"You've wandered from the subject at hand," she laughed, giving him a squeeze, then stepping back.

He winked at her. "Well, we could, and you'll see why I say that when we get there. Anyway, the Peltiers started the bar after losing family, children if I am remembering correctly. Now they feed the hungry, take in the lost, host the most amazing Metal bands, and are a force not to be disturbed. As far as prominent families are concerned, they're top of the food chain."

"You called their children cubs, because?" she asked, trailing off to give him time to answer.

"Because I can. Aubert, or Papa Bear as he likes to be called, stands well over seven feet tall. Everyone else in the family stands a good six feet or more and is as menacing as you could imagine. Good hearts though, but beasts in a fight, and must-haves on your side of right and wrong."

She thought Doran was a huge man standing on his own six-foot frame. It was hard to comprehend the idea that there were people bigger than him. What was she about to walk into with her little five-foot-nothing self, fangs, and two left feet? "Are we sure I won't get run over in there? I do have a pretty solid track record of being clumsy."

He laughed and hugged her tight before pulling away. "You'll be fine. Your two left feet seem to be getting better. Don't fret."

"I'm not fretting," she pointed out. "I'm stating a fact." Reluctantly, she stepped away and into the closet to find her own clothes. Opting for a similar style, she shimmied into a pair of jeans, grabbed a deep crimson tank top and a jean jacket. Her boots were the same style as Doran's, though hers came with spots to house her throwing knives. Grabbing her wrist cuffs off the shelf and sliding them to cover the scars she didn't like to share with the world, she walked out to Doran. His gaze seared into her. "What?"

"Never mind going out. We should stay in," he growled, his voice sending chills down her spine.

"Oh no," she tsked. "I did not get out of bed and dressed for you to change your mind. I'm going to brush my teeth, pee, and do my hair. Then we can go." Turning away from her soulmate before he became any more distracted than he already was, she put a little extra swing to her hips as she walked to the bathroom.

"I'll make coffee and blood for ya. This is not a place you'll want to lose control in," Doran grumbled from somewhere behind her.

Looking in the mirror, she smiled at herself as she brushed her hair. Being a vampire had its perks. One of which being perfect hair all the time. She'd question the why's but didn't want to jinx her good luck. Satisfied she was as decent as she could make herself, and finishing the rest of her business, she left the bathroom and headed to their small kitchen where a mug of blood and a mug of coffee awaited. She hated drinking from the bag and adored her mug collection, so she appreciated Doran's effort to keep the ick factor of blood drinking to a minimal by using her favorite things.

Drinking the blood first, she switched out the mugs and propped her hip against the counter. "Anything else I need to know before we go?"

Doran looked thoughtful for a moment then shook his head. "Not that I can think of. However, you know me. I've probably pissed someone off, so do not be surprised if words get tossed around. Words or people. Kinda depends on who's there."

With wide eyes knowing he wasn't wrong, she asked, "Should we be armed?"

"No. Weapons will be taken at the door. Believe me, you cannot get them past security. I've tried."

"Of course, you have," she chuckled. Looking over the rim of her mug, she watched Doran check his phone and then smile at whatever it was he was reading. It was such a nice change of pace to see him grinning at something other than her. She loved that he adored her but was a firm believer in couples having relationships and experiences outside of being together twenty-four/seven. This was the first time in months she'd seen his attention diverted.

"You're looking at me with a funny expression," he commented, as he looked up and slid his phone into his back pocket.

Shaking her head, she finished her coffee, set the mug in the sink, and took Doran's outstretched hand. The nice thing about having him in her life, aside from all the obvious reasons, was the travel. Being a fallen god certainly had its perks. In just a thought, they traveled between North Carolina and New Orleans, landing in a dark alley with hardly a sound.

Standing still for a moment, Kedah looked around to get her bearings. The building they were behind had walls that were a faded white brick, aged by weather and worn by use. Coming from inside, music thumped so loud she could feel the vibrations under her feet.

Her nose twitched as a barrage of smells assaulted her at once. Beyond the normal smells of stale beer and age, there was an intriguing mix of various were-animals that she could identify, and some she couldn't. Whatever was in the building they were about to go into resembled what she assumed a zoo would smell like to her heightened senses.

"Oh," she breathed out. "There are so many animals in there."

Doran barked out a laugh. "I'd be quiet about that particular opinion. There are a lot of weres in there, and although most of them act like animals, they aren't fans of being called such."

"Charming," she grumbled while trying to shake free the overwhelming feel of nerves that churned in her gut.

Making their way around the building, she looked

up, and up. The bar and grill was less a restaurant and more a house, if looks had the final say. Standing at least three stories, and stretching as long as several town homes, the building was enormous and not at all the bar her mind had created. There were old, run-down buildings across the barren street, and if you ignored the typical noises that a bar created, the place looked like an unassuming residence and nothing more. However, she was beginning to discover that things in the realm of the paranormal were always what wasn't expected. The learning curve she was adjusting to astounded her.

Sounds of motorcycles revving mixed with voices and music, gave the ambiance of a hole-in-the-wall establishment. Which, surprisingly, made her relax as they continued forward. There was a presence about this place that reassured her she was welcome.

As they rounded the building, the crowd she had been hearing took form. Most were dressed similarly to her and Doran, with leather being the go-to fashion statement.

Spying the line that trailed out of the front door, she sighed, assuming they would be waiting for a good while before going in. But instead of taking them to the back, Doran made for the bouncer blocking the front.

The man guarding the door was positively huge. Standing well over six feet, he had blond hair pulled back in a low, tight pony, with piercing blue eyes and a scowl that could level a prison.

Then something Doran had said clicked, and she jerked to a stop. She turned so her back was facing the bouncer. "He's a bear," she muttered through clenched teeth. "Why the hell didn't you tell me the family was a bunch of bears?"

Doran grinned. "I did."

"Calling them cubs is not the same as saying they are bears," she hissed.

Leaning down, he kissed her cheek. "Maybe, but your reaction was priceless for both me and him." Turning back to the bouncer, Doran nodded before speaking. "Dev."

"Doran?" Dev questioned, then turned his scowl into a smile. "Where the hell have you been, man? It's been what, fifty years?"

"You know damn well I can't sit still," Doran laughed as he pulled the other man into a brief hug that ended with a slap on the back.

Looking between the two men, she stood stunned. Doran had always been laid back with her, but never with others. Seeing him so casual with Dev was a refreshing departure from his usual stoic self, though it was odd as hell to witness.

Dev peered over Doran's shoulder and winked. "Who is this lovely lady? Surely, she's not here of her own free will. Blink twice if you're in danger," he said smoothly. She wished she could tell if he was joking or not, but erring on the side of not, she tried for a reassuring smile.

"This is my soulmate, Kedah," he explained without hesitation.

"No shit. Really?" Dev muttered as he looked between the two of them. "Kedah, you must be a goddess to have settled this man down."

"Not sure about that," she laughed. "It's nice to meet you, Dev."

"It's my absolute pleasure to meet the woman responsible for knocking Doran down a level. A task, I might add, once thought impossible. Come on in. VIP is in the back. Howlers take the stage in about an hour.

Food's fresh and the beer is flowing. If you're still here later we should catch up," Dev said.

"Sounds great. Thanks." Doran nodded at Dev, took her hand, and pulled her though the door. She ignored the sounds of groans and complaints of those waiting in line and laughed at the shouts Dev gave to the crowd to shut them up.

The moment they crossed the threshold of the bar, things went from loud to deafening. As a human, it would have bothered her to hear this much chaos as one sound. Now with her heightened sense of hearing, she could pick out individual noises that she could hear separately and clearly. It was organized chaos and to her pleasant surprise, it was not a bad thing.

Following Doran to the back of the bar, she watched the crowd move as they passed. She could pick out the werewolves and a few other animals by smells she recognized. There were a lot of beings she could not seem to identify. Being a vampire, she assumed she'd get a few glares or nasty looks, but no one paid them any mind. All the stereotypes she had thought were a thing didn't seem to be within the walls of The Sanctuary.

Sliding into a booth, Doran kissed her hand before letting it go and waving to a tall woman who turned, saw him, and smiled as brightly as Dev had. She also looked a lot like Dev, with the same blond hair, blue eyes, and build. A pang of jealously swarmed in Kedah's stomach as the woman came their way.

"Doran!" Leaning down, she gave him a brief hug then smiled at Kedah and offered her a handshake. Taking it, Kedah felt instantly better, and relaxed into the booth. "It's been a while. Where have you been hiding?"

"Over at The Den with Jensen." Doran nodded towards Kedah with a gleam in his eye and a smile she was getting used to seeing. "Aimee, this is Kedah, my soulmate." The last bit of jealousy deflated immediately.

"Soulmate?" Aimee questioned, then smiled as she looked between them. "Good for you. What brings you in tonight?"

"Just dinner and drinks. We've had a few rough weeks."

Aimee raised a brow and snorted as she shook her head. "You're a liar, but I'll take the compliment as it was intended. Usual for you? And," she looked at Kedah. "Blood or something else?"

"At the risk of being the odd one out, I'll take anything you have that's fruity and filled with tequila."

Aimee grinned. "Bears and weres you may see here. Yes, they appear big, scary, and mean. When it comes to drinks, you'd be surprised to learn that we go through more mixed drinks than beer."

"Truly?" Kedah asked with a laugh.

"Absolutely. Are you hungry? The burgers today are amazing, but don't tell the chef I'm hyping him up. I'll never hear the end of it."

Doran turned to look at Kedah, who shrugged her shoulders. "Sounds good to me."

"Burgers it is. Thanks, Aimee," Doran said.

It didn't take long before drinks and food appeared. Aimee was right, the burger was the best thing she had ever had. Though when she thought about who ran this place, she tried not to think about how fresh the meat was. Which was silly since she occasionally drank blood from a vein. Honestly, she wasn't holding up to the standard of vampire that she thought she'd be.

As they sat and listened to the set that was playing

before the main band took the stage, several people recognized Doran and came to catch up. He introduced her to everyone and pointed out names and faces of others as they passed.

"You came here a lot, didn't you?" she asked.

"A fair amount. It's one of the only places I found that I could be me and not a damn soul cared one way or another," he said with a sad pause. "For lack of a better word, it was refreshing."

"I can totally understand that." Taking a sip of her drink, which was delicious, she sat with a grin as Doran lead the conversation. From what Kedah could gather, there had been more than one occasion he had been to The Sanctuary after hours for various reasons, most of which involved breaking up fights and disagreements.

As a second round of drinks came, and empty dishes taken away, more familiar faces appeared. One patron went so far as to go the opposite direction, causing Doran to smile wickedly at the action.

When the Howlers took stage, she had to admit they were fantastic, despite heavy metal not having been on her musical radar. The music was loud and vibrated through her body. All traces of stress she hadn't realized she had been holding on to, disappeared.

Noticing her state of euphoria, Doran wrapped an arm across her shoulders and leaned in, kissing her on the cheek. "You look like you're in your element."

"I hadn't known this was my element." She eyed him curiously. "But something tells me you might have guessed."

He chuckled. "The thought had crossed my mind."

"How so?"

"Music, if done right, has the ability to block out

reality and bring a sense of passiveness to those with active minds. I noticed when you work, you always play something from the computer, and even if you can't see it, those around see the change. The lessening of tension as you move with the beat. I assumed that being in a bar with one of the best bands ever would double the effect."

His attentiveness to the things she enjoyed made her heart swell. "You assumed right," she said with a grin. Leaning in, she kissed his cheek and went back to watching and listening to the band.

Crowds of people moved in waves as the music rose and fell. Drinks passed hands among the loyal patrons. People of all kinds mingled as if there weren't a care in the world. It was an incredible sight to see, and an even better one to feel. There was no tension, no fear, no worry. Just music, happiness, and the comfort of good company.

That was right until a commotion caught her and Doran's attention. Without warning, a blur of a person came running across the room. Someone shouted, and before Kedah could blink, the commotion turned into the beginnings of a fight. The blur turned into a man who stopped in front of the band, balled up his fist, and knocked another man to the floor.

"What the heck is Dev doing?" Kedah asked, confused.

Doran shook his head, slid out of the booth, and stood. "That wasn't Dev."

Squinting towards the disturbance she could see that she was wrong, though whoever it was had the same giant build. His hair was a different color, for one. He was also not a bear, though she couldn't pinpoint what he was. Something seemed off about the man. It was as if he wasn't in control of himself.

The crowds of people parted, giving room to the two men who were circling each other. No one stepped in to stop the fight. No one spoke. Yet the band continued to play, their faces clearly annoyed.

"Is someone going to break that up?" she asked, keeping her eyes on the men.

Doran took her shoulders and turned her slightly towards the stairs that hugged the wall. A woman, tall and lean, dressed in leather pants and a simple black shirt descended the stairs like fury gliding on air. "Nicolette's got it."

"Oh no doubt about that," Kedah muttered as she studied the woman. She wasn't the only one. Half the bar turned to see Nicolette coming their way. Then parted to give her a clear path. Doran chuckled, grabbed Kedah's hand, and led her towards the fight.

The man that started the disagreement took the distraction as his cue to drop another punch, sending the patron staggering. The other man scowled as he tried to catch his footing. Kedah looked between the two, then to Nicolette. She knew that whatever was taking place was about to be short-lived.

A growl from the man who was regaining his footing echoed around them as they got closer. He launched and brought the fight to the ground in a mess of tangled limbs. The men rolled, stopping only when one straddled the hips of the other, his hand around the man's neck. As he applied pressure, a strangled breath rushed out.

Kedah stopped, which pulled Doran to a halt. He looked at her concerned, but before he could say anything, Nicolette approached.

"Doran," the woman exclaimed. "I heard you showed up."

"Nicolette," he said with a nod. "A fight in your bar? That's new." He raised a brow in question.

She shook her head and sighed. "Grab him for me, will you?"

"Yes, ma'am."

Kedah watched as Doran spun and flashed himself to behind the man that started the fight. He grabbed him by the neck and yanked him away from the one on the ground. Keeping the momentum going, Doran moved through the crowd. People scrambled to give him room, allowing him the space to move freely.

"Oh damn," Kedah muttered. She'd seen him in a fight before, but this seemed more a natural move on his part. It was impressive to watch.

"You must be Kedah, the one responsible for taming the beast," Nicolette said with a sweet smile. She held out her hand which Kedah took and gave the woman a firm shake.

"I don't know about taming the beast, but I'll claim him, that's for sure."

"Believe me, you have claimed and tamed a good one. Come on, let's see who started another fight in my bar for the third day in a row. I swear, it's like a full moon around here, without the damn full moon," Nicolette groaned as she took off towards Doran.

Nicolette led them up the stairs, down a hall and into the last room on the left. No one spoke aside from the man in Doran's grasp. He muttered profanities as they moved while struggling to be released, neither of which helped his case.

Inside the room, the door shut, and all noise from the bar ceased. Doran tossed the man into a chair and gave him a pointed look that dared him to move. Smartly, he stilled where he landed.

"You want to tell me what that was about?" Placing

her hands on her hips, Nicolette looked down at the man with a piercing gaze. One that would have had Kedah talking before the woman could take her next breath.

Kedah didn't get the impression that this was a woman who backed down from any situation. She saw the frustration in her eyes as she waited for the man to speak. It was odd that he seemed out of control until they reached the room and now sat like a statue. That didn't bode well for anyone. Nicolette growled low in her throat as she turned to walk to the far wall, pulling her phone out as she went. Kedah knew she wasn't the only one concerned.

"We have a situation here and I am out of reasons as to why," Nicolette snapped. She was quiet for a moment, then nodded before hanging up without another word. Kedah had no idea what was happening. Judging by the tension in the room, it wasn't good, and it wasn't normal.

"How long have the fights been going on?" Doran's concern was palpable and another sign that things were far worse.

"This isn't normal?" she asked.

"No," both Nicolette and Doran said.

"Did you call Acheron?" The seriousness in Doran's tone told Kedah that calling this man was a last resort.

Nicolette nodded. "You two go back downstairs and enjoy the rest of your evening." She moved to the door, opening it for them. "We were curious about where you had run off to, and it's nice to see you weren't getting into trouble. Thanks for the help with this idiot." Nicolette leaned in and gave Doran a brief hug, then nodded at Kedah with a smile.

Kedah thought about what she could do to help,

feeling drawn to do something. "Sometimes I can get a deeper read on people. Past verbal cues. Do you want me to try and see if I can't get information from him?" she offered. She could feel the man's anger, though behind it was something more, something complicated. He felt like a puppet, being controlled by an invisible force that she was sure he wasn't aware of.

"That's okay. You guys go back down and enjoy the rest of the night," Nicolette answered.

"If you change your mind, I am sure Doran could get me here anytime you need."

The woman beside her turned sharply, giving her a wary look. "You don't know this family or this place. Why would you offer kindness so readily?"

Opening her mouth, she was about to speak when Doran cut her off. "Kedah has a sixth sense about people. It's a gift, a precious one. She has shown kindness to those that deserved nothing but the worst the Gods could offer. It might do some good to have an outsider poke around in the minds of the ones starting the fights to see if there is something there you are not catching. With me here, of course."

"What a rarity," the older woman said with a smile. "We may take you up on that offer one day. Now go back down and enjoy your night." She gave them a wink and shooed them back towards the stairs.

Doran bowed at the hip before taking Kedah's hand and moving them from the room. As they walked away, she heard Nicolette's voice ring out like she was summoning the demons of Hell as the door shut with a slam.

At the top of the stairs, Doran paused. She glanced up to see him staring at her with a wicked grin. Before she could question the look, he tucked his thumbs into the waist of her pants, pulling her forward so her body pressed into his. He stepped forward, which forced her to step back, and when she bumped against the wall, he leaned down and whispered, sending chills down her spine. "You are a wonder."

She blushed, and before she could respond, his lips came down on hers, searing a kiss right down to her soul. His hands moved to cup her waist as his body pressed into hers, giving her only enough room to move her arms up and around his neck. She pulled him tighter against her body, moaning as he swept his tongue along her lips.

"Oh, God. This isn't even your house," a voice shouted from the bottom of the steps. "Get a room or go home." Kedah froze, having forgotten where they were. She glanced to the side to see Dev clearing two steps at a time before stopping beside them. "I take it back, get a room later. I've never seen Doran so docile. I need to know how this happened."

Doran muttered something in a language she didn't understand, before giving her a quick kiss. Reluctantly he stepped back. "Later, love. We'll finish this later."

"Duh," she laughed, then took the extended elbow Dev offered her. The bear led them down the stairs to the booth they had been sitting in. As they slid into their seats, Aimee came over with another round of drinks, the band seemed to kick up the volume, and Doran smirked at the look Dev was giving them both.

"Let me tell you about the time this little vampire with two left feet fell down the stairs and landed in my lap," Doran began.

"I didn't fall down the stairs," she muttered, then rolled her eyes when Doran took her hand and kissed her knuckles.

"Yes, you most certainly did," he chuckled as he continued the story, omitting nothing to her dismay.

A sanctuary, by definition, is a place to seek refuge and safety, and this place was no exception to the rule. From what she could see, those welcomed within the walls of The Sanctuary may have come in as strangers, but that didn't mean they left as strangers.

ONE FATED NIGHT

L.J. SEALEY

"**G**irl, you need to live a little." Denise shoved her elbow into Clara's arm. "You're so uptight sometimes."

Clara rolled her eyes and figured that tonight, fighting with her friend was futile. She'd worked with Denise at Concrete, a club on the other side of town, for almost a year, successfully keeping her identity secret from her friend. Humans didn't respond well to anything out of the ordinary. But Denise had started to ask questions, which was the only reason Clara was even considering having a few drinks at Sanctuary.

Clara was a Wolfswan. Being a Katagaria, her base side was animal. It meant she was stronger, most comfortable, in her wolf form, and was the reason she chose to sleep during the day. It meant always having to turn Denise down for lunch dates and shopping trips. It was horrible having to lie to her friend, but she had no other choice. Tonight was her night off and she'd promised it to Denise. A couple of drinks wouldn't hurt. She'd give her friend an hour at Sanctuary, then head back home.

Clara had missed letting her hair down, and Sanctuary was great. So was the band, The Howlers. Her feet were throbbing. They'd been on the dance floor in front of the stage since the moment they'd arrived, and she'd had way more to drink than planned. The crowd hollered out with wolf whistles and applause at the end of the band's first set. Clara watched her friend who was completely oblivious to the fact the place was full of otherworldly creatures. There were plenty of humans inside, but Clara suspected they were as unaware as Denise about who, or what, they were rubbing shoulders with.

"Woohoo. Aren't they great?" Denise called over the loud music that had replaced the band.

"Yeah. They really are. I'm glad you made me come here tonight."

Denise gave her a smug smile. "See, I know exactly what you need."

"Well, I'm glad you do, because right now, I need to go home. I'm beat."

"Whuut?" Her friend faced her head on, placing her hands on Clara's arms. "Don't you fail me now. It's barely 1 a.m. The night is still young." That last part was said with her hands in the air and a twirl. Then Denise's large chocolate eyes landed on Clara's, caging her in so there was no escape. Her brown bobbed hair swung across her face as she danced along with everyone else. Those puppy eyes weren't going to work this time.

"Denise." Her friend was now ambling backwards into the crowd. "Denise! I'm going to get a cab."

"Really? Don't go," said with a pout that wasn't going to change Clara's mind.

"I have to. But you stay. Enjoy yourself." Clara started to back away from the puppy eyes Denise liked to use to get her own way with everything. "I'll call you tomorrow."

"Clara." Her protest died when a dark-haired guy started to dance with her. "Okay," she said, her attention already elsewhere. "Text me when you get home. Promise!"

"You got it." Smiling to herself, Clara made her way out of the club, walking past the line which now stretched down the street. Taking her cell from her purse, she cursed trying to focus. Damn, her head was all wine-fuzzy. Clara was so busy trying to punch the right pin code in the keypad to call for a cab that she didn't notice someone had approached her from behind until it was too late. A hand went over her mouth, and before she could do anything about it, she was being dragged down an alleyway.

2

"Did you think this black hair would fool me?" Scar's voice froze Clara's blood. She screamed with everything in her lungs.

"What the fuck?" She heard one of the Were-Hunters say moments later while she was fighting to get free. Then she saw a struggle between two members of the Hanson pack and a stranger. The male with the raven hair gave a good fight until Jonah's punch to his stomach knocked the wind out of him.

Where had the male come from?

It was a question Clara feared she wouldn't get an answer to when she saw the stranger slumped in Scar's hold struggling for breath.

Clara's stomach sank as she saw the knife in Scar's hand slam into the stranger's side. The male who had tried to save her cried out as the Were-Hunter she hated with every part of her being twisted the blade, the stranger's body going limp. Scar discarded him like a piece of trash before he made his way over to her.

"Cut the mutt's throat," he snapped. "That'll teach the rabid dog to mind his own business."

Scar grabbed Clara by the arm, and she knew her

freedom had come to an end. She'd evaded the Hanson pack for longer than expected after she'd escaped her time period. Now Clara would have no choice but to return to 1982 to mate with Scar. The thought of being owned by him for the rest of her life made her want to throw up.

Her heart thumped in her chest as she watched Dale pull the stranger's head up by his hair, preparing to end her savior's life with a slice of his blade.

Clara couldn't let him die. He didn't know what he'd gotten in the middle of. She had to do something.

"Wait. Stop." she cried. "You can't kill him."

Scar laughed, his arm going around her throat. "No? Who are you to tell us what we can or can't do?" Clara squirmed when he kissed her temple. "Do it, Dale."

"No." She pulled at Scar's arm trying to break his hold, but it was no use. "He's my mate!" It was the only thing she could think of. None of the members of the Hanson pack, or any other male for that matter, would be interested in used goods.

Scar pushed her away as if he'd just found out she had some deadly disease. "Bitch. You promised yourself to me."

"I did no such thing," she snapped back. "You thought you could just take what you wanted."

Scar huffed out a laugh as he backed away. "You would have been the mate of a panther, a privilege many would appreciate. Now you belong to this waster." He spat at the male.

Rushing over to the stranger, she stood between him and Scar. "I'll be free of you." Her lip curled in anger. "That's all I care about."

Scar gave her a snarl, staring at her with contempt

before addressing his pack. "Come. Leave the dog. They're welcome to each other."

With that, the pack disappeared, returning to a time Clara had long left behind. She stood frozen, unable to believe she was free.

A groan came from behind her.

Clara turned and fell to her knees beside the wounded male. "Are you okay?" Stupid question considering there was a pool of blood on the ground where he lay. "Oh, God. What can I do?" Placing her hand over his side she pressed on the wound, but then he started to change form, the pain knocking his control and forcing his body to return to his animal form. But he was trying to stay human, and it wasn't working. Causing him to shift from one form to the other.

Shit. She couldn't compress the wound like this. He tried to speak but nothing came out. Then his wolf appeared again, the blood from his wound even more dramatic against his stunning white fur.

Sa—Sanctuary. The word was spoken from his mind right before he changed back.

"The club?"

He nodded now he was human again and tried to get up.

Clara went to help but he transformed again. There was no way she was lifting a wolf. "Shit. Can you stay human?"

Back to human again. "T...trying my...damn best."

"Well try harder. We have to get away from here." Throwing his arm around her neck she pulled as he moved onto his feet. "Can you flash there?" When they were standing, his weight almost took her back down again.

"Can't...do both."

"How about we do it together? Quickly while you're human. Now!"

It worked. The landing didn't go so well though. The stranger lost his control again, landing half on top of her and trapping her leg underneath his giant wolf body. She tried to free herself, but it was no use, and he was now out of it. Must have used the last of his energy to get there. Now how the hell was she going to get him inside?

The answer came as a door flew open and a tall figure stood there as though he was questioning what he was seeing.

The male came rushing over "What's going on?"

"He got stabbed. Asked me to bring him here. Can you..." She pulled again, but by now her whole leg was numb.

Clara gaped as the male picked the wolf up, carrying him towards the club's door like the thing weighed nothing more than a puppy. She quickly massaged the life back into her leg, reached for her purse, and got up.

"We have to get him inside. Then you can explain what the hell happened."

Clara followed.

"Go through to the bar and get my brother Fang. Tell him to come to the doc's room."

When the male disappeared, Clara had the strongest urge to run, but her mind replayed the agony in the stranger's face. All the blood. He'd put his own life on the line for her.

Cursing, Clara pulled the door shut as she went inside.

3

———

A knock at the door startled Clara. Fang, the male who owned Sanctuary, stuck his head through. "How's he doing?" He stepped inside.

Clara felt a little awkward being at the stranger's bedside after so long, but for some reason she couldn't leave. "He's settled."

Fang's hazel eyes went to the wolf lying on the bed. "I thought he'd left town already."

"You know him?"

"Not much. He sat at the bar a few times and we talked. I knew he was a decent male."

Clara knew that now too. "Yes. I was lucky he was there."

"Can I get you anything? You've been there for hours. You gotta be hungry or something."

Food was the last thing on her mind after everything that had happened. All she could think about was how close she'd come to a lifetime of hell. "I'm good. Thank you."

"Well, let me know if you change your mind. Call for me when he wakes." The big male left, closing the door behind him and leaving her alone with the stranger again.

Clara couldn't take her eyes off the gorgeous white wolf as she returned to stroking the soft fur on his forefoot. His breathing was relaxed, stomach moving up and down slowly as he slept off his injury. Dev had taken him upstairs into a sterile room, where a doctor had stitched the wound immediately. Now they were in a small bedroom down the hall, and Clara wondered what she was still doing there.

You owe him. If he hadn't come along and tried to rescue you, you'd be in 1982, trapped in a pack you hate, being used by half of the males in it.

A shiver travelled over her skin. She was safe now. All because of this stranger's selfless act.

Movement startled her.

The wolf nudged at the blanket that was draped by his head. *Could you cover me with this please?* His voice asked in her head, all gruff and husky.

She reached for it. "You cold?"

No. I just don't want my junk on display.

As Clara's breath caught, he shifted into his human form, and she found herself staring. It was inappropriate, but this was the first time she'd gotten a real look at him, and boy, he was good to look at. His short black hair was ruffled from the pillow. He had a handsome face, one with sharp cheekbones and full lips. His eyes were the most piercing blue she'd ever seen. She had to look away, turning her head to look at the dressing that covered his wound. She was glad she'd only laid the blanket up to his stomach. Her gaze moved over him. He was all muscle, his rippled abdomen and solid pectoral muscles enhanced by the shadows cast from the lamplight.

Clara's cheeks heated as she became aware that he was watching her. The fact he hadn't uttered a word, as if he were happy for her eyes to roam his body, made her heart race. When her gaze met his heavy stare for a moment, she froze.

What the hell was wrong with her?

Shaking herself she tried to ignore the sudden tension in the room. "How are you feeling?" Her words nearly didn't come out, and suddenly she felt the need to fiddle with the tie in the bottom of her blouse.

"I'm not sure I should answer that truthfully." His voice was low and breathy.

Christ, she felt the heat in his words in places she shouldn't. What was happening? Clara was too afraid to ask what he meant by that.

He gave a little cough and moved to sit up. "Good. Yeah, I'm good." Dark brows drew low, and he looked away from her. "Thanks for bringing me here."

"It was the least I could do after what you did."

"It was foolish jumping into a group of Arcadians like that. But I couldn't let them hurt you. That's all."

"No. That's not all." Tentatively, Clara reached out and placed her hand over his. "You have no idea what you did. I owe you my life."

He looked down at their hands. "They were going to kill you?"

Huffing out a laugh, Clara folded her arms tightly across her middle. Thoughts of what would have happened rushed back. She got up from the chair where she'd spent the last few hours and started to pace the small room. "That would have been easier."

"Why did they attack you?"

She hesitated, unsure if she could even talk about it, but he deserved to know what he'd saved her from. "I came here from another time almost a year ago. I time-jumped from 1982 to the past, the future, trying to leave a trail in as many time periods as possible so it would take them longer to find me."

"Who?"

"I escaped from my pack." Swallowing hard, Clara faltered for a moment before continuing. "I'd been promised to a male I hated and could do nothing about it. I escaped when one of the females came into season and the males were too busy fighting over her." Clara turned away as she swallowed down her tears. Fighting to keep her voice steady she said, "If they'd have taken me back with them, I would've spent my life being preyed upon whenever any of them wanted. Like a piece of meat. Scar wanted me as his mate but had promised the others I'd be fair game."

Cupping her hands over her face, she heard a rustling. The heat of the stranger's body warmed her back. Her heart began to race when her hair was moved to one side. A warm hand rested on her shoulder. His thumb rubbed back and forth. "Then I'm glad I chose not to walk away when they attacked you."

Without even thinking, Clara turned her head and nudged her chin against his hand. He raised his finger and stroked it over her lips. She trembled. In that moment, her body craved his touch. This male whom she'd only just met.

Was she crazy?

How on Earth could she have such a powerful reaction to him?

"What's your name?" His voice was husky and thick, as affected as she was.

"Clara," she breathed.

"Clara." His fingertips feathered across her jaw, tickling down the side of her neck. "Thank you, Clara."

Suddenly it was hard to hold her head up. "For what?"

"For staying by my side while I healed." His breath

dusted over her skin. "I felt your hands on me. Comforting me. Your touch helped me heal."

His lips grazed over her ear as he moved in closer, pressing his body against hers. "My name is Axe."

Soft lips kissed the sensitive spot in the curve of her neck, his breath shaky by her ear.

"Axe?" She had to let him know. "I don't ever do this." The truth was fear had made Clara avoid intimacy with males. After what she'd witnessed from her pack, the thought of a male touching her horrified her. Another reason why she was so confused by her reaction.

"Do what?"

"Let a complete stranger put his hands on me."

"And his lips."

Those lips kissed her again, this time on her jaw. Clara closed her eyes and turned her face towards him, her heart hammered in her chest. His mouth covered hers in a slow tentative embrace that took her breath. All thoughts rushed from her mind as she accepted his kiss. He turned her until she faced him, their lips never parted. Their kiss deepened. Her arms went around his neck. Something about Axe compelled her, drew her in like they were old lovers reuniting. A kiss that felt familiar but couldn't possibly be.

Strong arms pulled her in closer. Through the haze of passion, Clara felt his erection pressing into her lower stomach, reminding her that he was naked under the sheet wrapped around his waist. A thrill of nerves and excitement rushed through her. What was happening? All this time Clara had turned away from male attention. Untouched, she'd vowed to stay that way. Now she was putty in a stranger's arms.

Losing herself to him.

But she couldn't stop.

Didn't want to stop.

His mouth left hers and she dragged in a breath. A whimper left her throat as he kissed her cheek, her jaw, then moved to her ear. Light, feathery kisses. Intoxicating.

"Clara." Her name leaving his lips so roughly fueled her desire. "Christ, I've never felt this before." Lips on her neck, kissing over her racing pulse. "Do you feel it?"

"Yes," she managed to say, as his fingers brushed up her side. When he cupped her breast, she sucked in a breath.

In a swift move that appeared far braver than she felt, Clara lifted her blouse and pulled it over her head. No going back now. Not that she wanted to. She'd spent her whole maturity afraid of sex, believing it was always violent, only for the male's own pleasure, never knowing a male's touch could make her feel this way.

She wanted it, wanted everything Axe could give her.

Clara looked with wide eyes as Axe's fingertips caressed the tops of her breasts. Before she could blink, he'd undone the front clasp on her bra and pushed the material out of the way of his kiss. When he licked over her nipple her head fell back, hands running through his tousled hair as his tongue flicked her peaked flesh over and over.

"Oh, Axe." The moment she breathed his name he claimed her mouth again. This time his kiss was harder, more fervent. Then he lifted her, and her legs went around his waist. She got rid of the bra as he carried her over to the bed. He laid her down, crawling on top of her, bracing himself on his arms either side of her head. He was panting as hard as she was, losing himself the same way. Blue eyes pinned her, their sparkling depths drawing her in, hypnotizing her.

Axe closed them and took a deep breath as he fought for control. After a second, they opened again. "Where have you come from? Why do I burn for you so much?"

She had no answer because she felt the same way about him.

He lowered himself towards her, taking her mouth gently this time. His body pressed her into the mattress, every inch of him now touching her. Clara parted her legs as he settled between them, and she realized he no longer had the sheet around him. Trembling, Clara kicked off her pumps and helped get rid of her jeans. Only a thin piece of blue, silky material covered her most intimate place.

Never in her wildest dreams did she think she could feel this way. She was on fire inside, a throbbing heat between her thighs yearning for something she couldn't name.

Him.

Axe watched his hand stroking over her stomach, down over her panties, and in that moment her nerves were replaced by a need so strong she felt she'd burst.

Moving down her body, he hooked his fingers in the hem of her panties and removed them. Now Clara was fully naked under his ministrations and instead of feeling self-conscious, she felt more alive, freer than she'd ever felt before. The way he looked at her, the admiration there in his eyes, gave her the confidence to see this through.

Axe kissed his way up the inside of her thigh. "Beautiful," he whispered against her skin, then his mouth covered her intimate flesh and she cried out.

As he brought her to a shattering climax with his tongue, Clara lost the ability to breathe. Her whole body buzzed. Her vision hazy with a pleasure she'd never have dreamed possible. Then, smiling, Axe swiftly moved up her body. She tasted herself on his lips when he captured her mouth in a fierce kiss. And she gasped as his hardness nudged at her core.

Breaking their kiss, Axe cupped her cheek, pausing as he gave her a questioning glance. Embarrassment threatened to take hold, but Clara wasn't going to lose this moment.

"I want this," she said, reassuring him.

Axe nodded and pushed in ever so slightly, pausing to give her a chance to get used to him. "This will hurt at the start." He kissed the tip of her nose. "I'll make it feel good. I promise."

The stretch made Clara hold her breath as her body tried to accommodate him. But as she looked into his eyes, the gentleness he offered her in that moment gave her confidence. She held his hips and thrust hers up, taking him inside her. The shock of the burning pain made her cry out.

"Fuck," he growled in her ear, his head dropping to her shoulder. "I was trying to go slow." He started to move, and the burn subsided, replaced by a sensation that had Clara sucking in a breath.

She began to move with him. The pleasure building was overwhelming, stealing her breath. He was right. It felt so good. Their bodies now slick with sweat, their mouths fused, tongues dueled greedily.

Panting.

Moaning.

Both in sync with each other as they got lost in the moment.

Axe leaned on his elbow, changing his position

slightly and moving faster, thrusting harder. Clara moaned, gripped his arm and the bed covers. Overcome with desire as the tension built within her, and she chased the growing sensation she wanted so badly. She arched her back, head tipping back.

Axe cupped her breast, squeezing hard. "Fuck."

"Oh, Axe, I—"

"Fuck, yeah. So good." His words were ragged.

That's when she flew over, her body contracting around him.

One hard thrust, then another, and Axe joined her, burying his head in her neck as he groaned through his release.

It was the most intense moment of Clara's life. She'd done it. All these years she'd feared losing her virginity, and now she was lying under the solid body of a male she barely knew but felt so comfortable with, as they lay breathlessly in each other's arms.

As she came down from the glorious rush, her hand running lazily through the Were-Hunter's ruffled hair, she was hit by a wave of emotion.

Axe lifted his head, and it was the kiss that did it, the soft press of his lips. The gentle intimacy of this moment with her beautiful stranger brought the tears. Clara could do nothing to stop them running down her temples. As if sensing it, Axe broke the kiss and looked at her, wiping away the wet streaks with his thumbs. A frown appeared between his brows. "Are you okay? Shit. Was I too rough?"

She smiled at him and shook her head. "No. Not at all. It was perfect. I—"

Just then an almighty pain ripped through her palm. Clara cried out, and as Axe quickly rolled off her, she brought her palm up, gripping her wrist with her other hand.

"Clara? What's happening?"

"I—I don't know," she managed to say through clenched teeth. "My hand. It burns."

She clutched it to her chest, afraid to look. Then a warm hand covered her wrist. "Clara, let me see."

As the burn began to subside, she watched as Axe opened her fingers. His eyes widened. "Shit," was all he said, but the color had drained from his face.

"What is it?" When she pulled her hand from his hold and looked at it, her heart froze. The mating mark. Panic took hold. She looked at Axe and saw what she felt mirrored in his expression. "It doesn't mean we—"

"Don't." He got off the bed, running his hand through his hair as he began pacing the room. "Fuck."

Sitting up, she moved to the edge of the bed, wanting to go to him, but not daring to. Tears filled her vision, distorting the strong, naked figure in front of her. "Axe, please—"

Then he hissed as he grabbed his own hand.

Clara swiped at her eyes. When her vision cleared, her breath caught at the realization of what was also happening to him. The intensity in his eyes as he stared down at his hand. "You have the mark, too."

Axe must have seen the hope in her eyes. He shook his head and backed farther away. "I'm leaving town. That's what I was doing when I saw you."

"So, stay."

"Trust me, Clara. I'm the last male you want to be stuck with for the rest of your life."

"I don't believe that to be true."

He whirled around. "You don't know me."

Clara stood, grabbed the blanket, and wrapped it around herself. "I know... how you make me feel when I'm with you. I know it sounds crazy because we really haven't known each other long. But I'm not afraid of this, Axe."

He huffed out a laugh, looking down at the floor.

Clara went to him. Tentatively, she placed her hand on his cheek and guided his head up, seeking out the warmth of his eyes. "Stay with me. Here in New Orleans. Would you really lose that much if you did?"

"No. But you would. I'm a loner. I have no pack, no place to call my own."

"Then make this your home." She took his hand in hers. "Stay." Warmed by those stunning blue eyes as they stared back at her, Clara gave him a soft smile.

"What if I can't love you? What happens then? We'll be bound to each other no matter what."

"What if you can?" She tried to keep her voice steady, but it was hard to fight the shock of what had happened. She was standing in front of her true mate. Whom she may or may not be about to spend the rest of her life with. "I know this isn't what either of us expected, but it's happened, and there's nothing we can do to change it. I don't know why I feel so comfortable with you, but I can't deny that I do. What if we can be happy together? Isn't it worth a shot?"

It took so long for Axe to respond that Clara felt the rejection before he gave it. Then he did something unexpected. He bent down and kissed her. When he took her breath away, she knew that they were doing the right thing. Kissing him back, Clara wrapped her arms around his neck, and he held her close. For a moment, it felt like she'd always known his kiss. His arms.

It was a shock to feel so deeply connected to a stranger.

He broke away, then burrowed his face in the

crook of her neck. "I'll stay." His warm promise sent a shiver through her. Clara pulled back to look at him, her tears obscured his face for a moment. Then his thumbs smoothed them away.

"I can't promise this will work, but it seems the Fates have decided we should be together. All I can give you is what I am. If that's not good enough—"

Clara placed the tips of her fingers against his lips. "The fact you haven't run far away from me says a lot about how good you are, Axe."

He took her hand from his lips and looked at the mark that had scarred her palm. Then, placing his own over hers, their fingers locked together, and she saw his chest expand.

"My mate," he said, and the warmth she saw behind those ocean-blue eyes made her heart sing.

Smiling at her insanely handsome male, Clara thanked the gods for blessing her with such a perfect match. "My mate," she said back. He kissed her before lifting her up into his arms and carrying her over to the bed.

"So, we should seal the deal and get acquainted with each other some more, right?"

Clara laughed as he lowered her down and crawled on top of her. "Absolutely."

VALENTINE'S DAY AT SANCTUARY

SAM BRETON

A sh walked up to Sanctuary with a long and fast stride, his ankle-length leather coat blowing in the breeze. His long black hair blew forward as a gust of wind hit his back. He swept his hand through it and pushed one of the bright red streaks out from under his sunglasses and away from his eyes.

Sanctuary was one of his favorite places to visit whenever he was in town. It was a very well-known bar and grille, located on Ursulines Avenue in New Orleans, and was owned and run by a family of Were-Hunters.

Of course, most humans had no idea about that part, though. It's a place where all are welcome as long as they follow the rules: "Come in peace or leave in pieces." Cooler still, it was home to New Orleans' own band, The Howlers.

Ash had even had the pleasure of filling in on an occasion or two when they needed a guitarist. The place felt like home away from home to him. The Were-Hunters all knew him well and always welcomed him with open arms.

The Were-Hunter bear Dev was waiting by the door as usual and stood up straighter as Ash reached the entrance. He held his muscular arms tightly crossed against his chest, with the Dark-Hunter bow and arrow tattoo he got as a joke clearly visible. That stance would look very intimidating to anyone who didn't know him well. But Ash did and didn't flinch at all as Dev raised his eyebrow and took a step towards him.

"Why do you look like you're on a mission to kill a Daimon, Ash? You know something I don't?"

Ash arched a brow and smirked at the bear.

"Told Tory I would meet her here half an hour ago. Dark-Hunter shit took longer than expected and I broke my phone in a fight. Little worried I'll be in the doghouse, it being Valentine's Day and all."

Dev sucked in his breath while shaking his head, dropped his arms in sympathy and sighed. "Uh, yeah, that's not gonna give you any marital points. I think I may have to come in with you, just to see what happens. Have a feeling seeing you get scolded by your wife could be damn funny. Cracks me up that someone as intimidating as you is afraid of your wife. Then again, mine scares the shit outta me when I've messed up." He rubbed his chin and sighed again. "Funny how that works." he mumbled.

Ash raised both eyebrows. "I'm not finding it funny now. You want to start the music, so I can get in there?"

Dev snorted, stifling a laugh, and then spoke into his headpiece.

"Hey, Fang, could you start *Sweet Home Alabama*? Thanks."

Ash gave Dev a nod of thanks as he heard the music start playing, knowing that it would alert all the Daimons to his presence, so they could leave. After the first verse finished, he headed into the building.

He scanned the area in the dimly lit bar until his

gaze fell onto his adorable wife. Her soft brown hair fell to one side, and she rested her chin in her hand. She was sitting at the bar, talking and laughing hysterically with Aimee. Aimee was one of the proprietors of Sanctuary and beloved sister to all the male bears, each of whom were very protective of their beautiful, blonde-haired, blue-eyed sister.

Tory's laughter tapered off as she caught sight of him. She looked up with her brown eyes glistening, as he made his way across the room and stopped by her side. "Hey baby, I was beginning to think Aimee was going to be my Valentine this year. I'm glad you finally made an appearance." Ash felt his face go pale as his heart started racing. Aimee smiled at Ash, handed him his usual beer, and then turned towards another customer.

Ash kept his voice low. "I'm so sorry, Soteria. Things took way longer than I expected them to, and my phone broke. I wasn't in a place where I could flash without being seen. I got here as soon as I could." Tory smiled up at him. She always loved it when he used the Atlantean endearment of her name. His accent as he said it still gave her shivers.

"It's okay, Ash. I knew things must have just gotten crazy. I'm used to it and understand. I was just teasing you." She stood up and hugged him. Ash breathed an audible sigh of relief.

"Don't worry me like that, Sota. I never want to let you down."

"You could never let me down, Ash. You should know that by now." Tory got up on her tiptoes and placed a gentle kiss on his cheek. He smiled at her.

"I should, and deep down I do, but I still struggle at times. You're the best thing that's ever happened to me, and I don't want to screw that up, even now," he murmured, as he tucked a stray piece of hair behind her ear.

Tory slapped him on the chest. "Well, knock it off, because that's not ever going to happen." she said seriously. "Let's go celebrate our love, shall we?"

Taking his arm, she led him over toward the tables by the stage. The Howlers were on a break. It was quiet, other than the sound of the jukebox playing and the soft chatter of other patrons. Ash pulled a chair out for her and then joined her on the other side of the table. He took her hands into his and placed a kiss on her knuckles. "I love you so much Sota."

Tory smiled at her husband. "I love you too, baby. Do you know why I chose this particular table to sit at?"

Ash sat up and looked around. "No, I don't have any clue. Why?" He looked at her with an adorable, baffled expression that made her smile again.

"Because this is exactly where I was sitting the first time you ever sang to me. I still get goosebumps whenever I think about it. It makes me fall in love with you all over again just sitting here."

Ash smiled and then chuckled.

Tory looked at him a little taken aback. "What's so funny? I'm trying to be all romantic and sentimental, and you start laughing?" She smacked him on the arm. He sobered but continued to smile at her.

"I remember that night very well. Made me think of that "Tickle His Pickle" book you bought," he said in a low tone. "You learned a lot from it. Not that you ever needed any help in that department." He winked at her mischievously.

Tory cracked up. "I think I still have it. We should read some tonight and try it out." She gave him a devilish grin that made him chuckle.

"I'm going to hold you to that as soon as we get home."

As he'd finished that sentence, a fight broke out between two human males at a table near them. "That's my wife. You fucking asshole," yelled out an angry man, as he grabbed another guy who was sitting next to a beautiful, blonde-haired woman.

He yanked the guy out of his seat by his shirt collar. Instead of trying to talk his way out of it, the other man tackled him, and they ended up slamming into surly Remi, who had his back to them.

Remi lost his balance and stumbled forward until he landed on his knees. That only succeeded in slowing his fall a little bit, though, and his face ended up buried in Sasha's crotch, as the wolf tried to walk past him.

Ash almost choked on his beer, and Tory was in tears from laughing at the sight of it.

Sasha looked down in shock. "Uh, Remi, we really don't know each other well enough for that. And especially not in public." Remi stood up and shoved Sasha hard. "Fuck off, wolf!"

He then turned his attention to the human males who were still beating the shit out of each other, while the woman cried and begged them to stop. He stormed over to them.

Remi was terrifying on a good day. On a bad one, he could scare the piss out of Lucifer himself, which was one of the reasons he normally stayed in the kitchen, away from everybody. He gritted his teeth and exclaimed. "Come in peace or leave in pieces." Grabbing both guys by the shoulders, he dragged them out the door. The woman followed behind, crying hysterically.

Sasha looked over at Ash and Tory with a peeved

and unamused look on his handsome face. He ran his hand angrily through his short blond hair. "That wasn't funny. Why does the weird shit always happen to me?" he asked. "I was just minding my own business as usual, and bam. I really wish I could just go one day without shit like this happening." Then he stormed off towards the bar before either of them could answer.

Ash turned to Tory with both eyebrows raised. "Well, that was interesting."

Tory wiped the tears from her eyes but continued to giggle a little. "That's the funniest thing I've witnessed in a long time. My stomach hurts. Poor Sasha, though. I do feel bad for laughing, but the way that all went down was hilarious. I don't think anyone would believe it if we told them."

She wiped her face again and managed to calm herself down. "That's one of the things that I love the most about this place. There's always entertainment of some sort. You think Remi ate them? He hasn't come back yet."

Ash glanced over to the door, sighed audibly, and turned back to his wife. "Well, it is Remi we're talking about. Wouldn't put it past him. If he's not back in five minutes, I'll have to go and check. Was really hoping I wouldn't have to wrangle anyone tonight, though."

Tory looked at him with amusement in her eyes and a knowing smile on her face. She reached across the table and intertwined her fingers with his. "You know better than that. You never get an entire night off. But that's okay because you keep the world a safer place."

"He sure does." Aimee said as she walked up to their table to take their order. "We all certainly appreciate everything you've done for us and Sanctuary over the years, Ash. The gods know, we wouldn't have gotten by without you a few times."

Ash nodded at Aimee but stared down at the table. He wasn't good at accepting a compliment.

"No problem. You guys have done a lot for us also. That's what friends are for."

After Aimee took their order, Ash looked back over at the door. He groaned as he pushed his chair out from the table and stood, then he turned back and looked down at his wife.

"Looks like I'm going to have to check on Remi after all. I really hope he's not eating humans for a bear snack. I'll be right back."

Tory looked at him sympathetically. "Sorry. Be careful and hurry back before the food gets here. Now that you enjoy eating, I'd hate for you to have it cold."

Ash nodded and headed out the door. Dev and Remi were arguing just outside of it, but the humans were nowhere to be seen.

"Why were you even outside of the kitchen, Remi? You know shit like this turns you even more un-pleasant than normal, which is a major understate-ment. It's a good thing I was here to keep you from doing something really stupid." Dev stood with his arms crossed, facing his brother but keeping his dis-tance. Remi growled at him.

"It's none of your fucking business, Dev. I can be wherever the hell I want to be, and I don't need your or anyone else's permission. You're lucky I held back from hurting you for getting in my way and sticking your nose in where it didn't belong. I had everything under control. Go fuck yourself!"

With that, he blew past Ash without even so much

as glancing at him, threw open the doors so hard they almost came off the hinges, and disappeared inside.

Dev turned to Ash with a look of exasperation. "That guy seriously needs to take some anger management classes before an innocent gets killed."

Ash shook his head sympathetically. "Don't think that would help in his case. It'd probably piss him off more. I'm glad you were here to deal with him before I had to. I was worried, him being the surly bear that he is, that he'd killed them and had humans for dinner. That would have seriously ruined my night. Now you have a taste for what I get to deal with, though. Remi is nothing compared to some of my Dark-Hunters."

"Well then, I'm really glad it's you that has to deal with them and not me. Don't think I could put up with that on a nightly basis. I already feel like I need a drink, or five."

Ash shook his head in amusement and then made his way back to his wife. He and Tory talked between themselves for a while and reminisced about the past. They were in the middle of a good conversation and enjoying the quiet time together when a couple of young women stopped right in front of their table. One of them let out a very loud shriek, then covered her mouth with one hand and fanned herself with the other.

Ash groaned and whispered under his breath, "Now what?"

"Oh my God. It is them, Angela. I told you they were real." Claire said enthusiastically. Her long, wavy blonde hair and huge red hoop earrings bounced in her excitement, as she was finally able to calm down enough to speak.

"Breathe, Claire." The other woman said as she

gently shook her friend and helped to fan her. "They're probably just role players."

Ash and Tory looked at the women in confusion.

"Role players?" Ash asked, looking at Angela, who had her brown hair in a bun with a couple of pieces loose on either side. She was also wearing big hoop earrings, only hers were blue.

"Yeah, you are, aren't you?"

"No, I have absolutely no idea what you're talking about. Role players for what?"

Claire slapped Angela on the arm. "They're not role players, Ange. They're. The. Real. Deal. I'm telling you. We didn't think this place was real, but it is. This has got to really be Ash and Tory."

Ash exchanged a confused look with his wife, and then turned back to the women who were both staring at him wide-eyed.

"I am Ash, and this is my wife, Tory. Do we know you?"

Claire screamed again but covered her mouth, so it wasn't as loud.

"Holy shit." Angela hissed with excitement. "We're both huge fans of yours. We absolutely love the Dark-Hunter series. To a point of obsession. Your book is my absolute favorite one. Except for the parts where you're being treated so horribly. I can't imagine living through that. I'm so sorry." She reached out as if to put her hand on his arm, then pulled it back when his expression shuttered.

A wave of absolute panic and horror washed over Ash. "The Dark-Hunter series?" he asked in a raspy voice. His heart almost pounded out of his chest.

"Yeah, it's a series of books written by Sherrilyn Kenyon. Well, Sherrilyn McQueen now, but the books are published under Sherrilyn Kenyon. That's a whole other story though." She exchanged a nervous glance with Claire, and anxiously rubbed her fingers together.

"Poor thing went through absolute hell. We're glad she's out on the other side of that horror." Angela smiled at Ash shyly when he didn't say anything. "Sorry. I just realized how much I rambled. I tend to do that when I'm excited."

Ash couldn't hear at all because of the sound of his heart beating in his ears. All he could do was stare at her in shock. Tory spoke up for him.

"Wait, so you're saying there's a series of books based on our lives? That's not possible. We've never even heard of this author Sherrilyn McQueen. How could she possibly know about us?"

Claire stared at her in confusion. "I'm not sure how. But there's an entire series on you guys. There's also Were-Hunter and Dream-Hunter books, and a young adult series all about Nick, amongst others." Claire leaned back, suddenly the authority, and waved her hand in the air. "I've always said Sherri was way too much of a genius writer than should be humanly possible. Maybe she's an incredibly powerful psychic and doesn't even know it?"

Ash came out of the shock enough to speak, even though he was still in an absolute panic. "I don't know if that's possible, but there's something wrong with this picture, and we need to get to the bottom of it. You don't happen to have one of these books on you, do you?"

"Yeah, I think I have yours with me, actually. Hang on a second." Claire grabbed her oversized purse from her shoulder, unzipped it and then rummaged around for a minute. "Yup, here it is." she said as she pulled a huge, thick, paperback book out and handed it to him.

His heart sank as he saw the title that said *Acheron* with a picture of his symbol above it. Tory got up and walked over behind him. She leaned over his shoulder and gasped. He opened the book, and his heart sank more as he read the first few lines. Flipping through pages, his panic continued to grow until he was soaked in sweat. This was indeed a book about him, and all he could do was stare at the pages as a million thoughts raced through his mind. "I'm outed," he mumbled under his breath.

"Breathe, sweetie." Tory rubbed his back and looked back up at the two women. "We're going to need to know everything about this author, including how many fans she has. Does she have a website we can look at?"

Angela nodded. "Yes, and a Facebook page, as well as other social media platforms. She has thousands of fans worldwide. We call her the Author Goddess because she's so amazing, and we're her Paladins. We're like a family. You shouldn't worry, Ash. We all love you."

Ash stared at Angela with an intimidating look on his face. She took a few steps back.

"Yeah, that doesn't make me feel any better about this. I don't think you realize how catastrophic it is. The human world isn't ready to know everything about our world. I'm not ready for the people in my world to know everything about me, either. I also really don't think the fact that this is all real has fully hit you guys yet, and when it does fully sink in, it may not be good for your mental health. What's the website?"

"Mysherrilyn.com," Angela said quietly. She pulled it up on her cell phone then handed it to him. Once he had taken it, she nervously stepped back again.

Ash couldn't believe the size and quality of the site

as he scrolled through page after page of book lists and character names that listed full profiles for everyone. He knew almost all of them personally or knew of them. The detail was amazing and terrifying. She had other series listed as well, such as The League, and he wondered if that was a reality somewhere also. Maybe these humans had somehow crossed over into a dimension that wasn't their own.

As that thought crossed his mind, he relaxed a little. That could explain all of this. He scratched his chin and sighed when he realized that the possibility of that was unlikely, as he remembered she'd pulled the website up on her phone. There couldn't possibly be a way for her to connect to the internet in another dimension. His heart started racing again.

Aimee came to the table to deliver their food. "You guys OK? You look like you've seen a ghost."

Tory filled her in and showed her the website. After reading about the book called Bad Moon Rising, which was all about her and her husband Fang, she turned as pale as a ghost herself. "Savitar is going to need to know about this. The Were-Hunters are exposed to humans. How did this get past him?" Aimee's gaze moved from the humans to the book in her hand. She glanced at Tory and her gaze landed on Ash.

"I thought he was an extremely powerful and omniscient being that would foresee something like this happening and protect us from it. That's why he's our mediator." Ash sighed.

"I have no idea what's going on Aimee or how this author knows everything about us. How could we know nothing of her? You're right that Savitar needs to know about it, but I really don't want to tell him. It'll be about as fun as getting gutted. He's going to flip, and not just a little bit."

"Your phone's ringing, Ash." Claire said as she pointed to his backpack that was sitting next to the table. He looked at her without registering what she said and continued to talk.

"I don't want to bring Sav into this yet. I want to try and get to the bottom of it myself. I'm thinking we need to go and see Sherrilyn to get answers directly from her. I'm very curious to hear what she has to say."

"I definitely agree with that. Could I come with you?" Aimee asked. Ash nodded.

"That's fine, but I'd like to be alone with her when we talk about my story. I don't want you hearing details about my life. I hope you can understand that."

Aimee nodded.

"This has me freaked out." Ash said, turning to his wife.

"I know it does, Ash. I wish I could tell you that it's all going to be okay, but I can't. I'm worried too. Your phone's ringing." Tory pointed to his backpack.

"It has been for a while now." Claire added.

Ash turned and looked over at his backpack. He didn't even remember having it. Strange.

"My phone broke in a fight, Sota. That's why I was worried that you were going to be upset with me when I was so late getting here tonight. It can't be ringing."

Claire looked at him like he had six heads. "Well, it is. Aren't you a god? Can't you fix a broken phone with the snap of your fingers or something?" Ash had a weird feeling.

"Uh, yeah... I should be able to. Why didn't I?" He looked at everyone and they were all staring at him.

"Ash, are you going to answer that?"

Ash gasped and sat straight up in bed. Tory, who'd

entered the room to wake him, gasped and jumped backwards.

"You okay? I didn't mean to startle you, I got up to go to the bathroom, and your phone's been ringing off the hook. I was trying desperately to wake you because I think the Dark-Hunters need your help." She patted his shoulder. "You're soaked in sweat, and I was getting really worried."

He looked at Tory and took a deep breath. "They always need my help. What time is it?" He rubbed his eyes groggily and yawned.

"It's 1:30 in the morning." She replied quietly.

Ash sighed wearily, "I was having a wonderful dream that turned into the worst nightmare I've ever had." Tory sat down on the edge of the bed and rubbed his back gently.

"Breathe. It wasn't real. What was it about, do you remember?"

"Yeah, I remember every detail. It started off with us having a nice romantic night at Sanctuary on Valentine's Day. These two women came up to our table freaking out like giddy fan girls because we were real. It turned out there was an author named Sherrilyn that was authoring books about us and our world, and we were all exposed to the humans." He took her hand in his before catching her concerned gaze. "She had every detail of my life written in a book, Sota. I was more terrified than when you found Ryssa's journals. But it wasn't just my story, it was everyone's. There were fans all over the world that called themselves Sherrilyn's Paladins, and they referred to her as the Author Goddess. It felt so damn real." He rubbed his eyes like he had a massive migraine.

"Wow. That's crazy and I can understand why

you'd be so freaked out. I'm really sorry, sweetie." Tory hugged him.

"It's okay, I'm fine, now that I know it was just a dream."

Suddenly she slapped him on the arm.

"What was that for?" He asked, while rubbing it, pretending that it hurt.

"That was for taking that sip of my Sprite. I told you, you can't handle it. You're such a lightweight!" She joked trying to make light of the situation and get his mind off everything.

Ash laughed. "I guess you're right. Remind me not to drink ever again.

Tory smiled at him and kissed him sweetly on the lips.

"Don't worry, I'll keep it away from you at all costs. We don't need another mini-Atlantis. Or worse... Books about all our deepest darkest secrets. But what if it was real? You did really make a miniature Atlantis the last time." She mused.

Ash grabbed her and pulled her onto his lap while tickling her. "Hey. That's not funny." he teased back.

After he stopped tickling her, Tory smiled at him and rested her head on his shoulder.

"In all seriousness, though, I'm glad you woke up and realized it was a nightmare. It sounds like it was terrifying, and I didn't mean to downplay it. I hope you find out that the Dark-Hunters are okay."

Ash gently moved her over and got up fast. "I got so caught up with you, and my nightmare, that I forgot all about them. I guess they gave up trying to get ahold of me, since the phone stopped ringing. He picked his phone up and looked through the missed calls. Then turned back to Tory.

"I'll be back as soon as I can." He leaned down and kissed her. "I love you, Sota."

"I love you too, Papa Smurf."

Ash got back home after going to help his Dark-Hunters, took a quick shower, and quietly crawled into bed. His beautiful wife slept soundly. He smiled as he watched her sleep, and then laid his head down onto his own pillow. He started to close his eyes but couldn't sleep because of the thoughts racing through his head. Tory had been joking about it being real like when he'd created a miniature Atlantis, but what if he had created a reality where Sherrilyn was writing everything down, and everyone knew about them.

Someone could be reading about us at this very minute, he thought to himself.

"Now that's a scary thought." he whispered out loud. "A real Never-Ending Story of sorts. Yay. Now I'm never going to sleep."

He sighed and got up to go check on his kids. After making sure his boys were sleeping peacefully, he decided to log onto the Dark-Hunter website to see if there was anything interesting going on. When the page loaded, his heart sank into his stomach as his eyes fell on the same home page he'd seen in his nightmare.

"What the hell?" he gasped. "This can't be real. He clicked on the menu button that brought up more buttons he'd seen in his nightmare. Pulling up the Dark-Hunter series books he scrolled through the list until finding the one that carried his name.

He browsed the site for a long time and eventually ended up on Sherrilyn's official Facebook page. His racing heart slowed down with every kind comment he read on one of the posts that was a quote from a new book being released soon. The fans really did love the Dark-Hunters, and him. It made him realize that if people he didn't even know could love him despite all his secrets, maybe it was time for him to reveal who he really was to the Dark-Hunters. A huge weight would be lifted off his shoulders after thousands of years, but how would he go about doing it?

Ash opened his eyes. The sun was shining on his face through the windows behind his computer. The birds chirped loudly through the open window. Yawning, he stretched out his arms, sat up slowly, then rubbed his face where the keyboard had left marks on his cheek from sleeping on top of it. He couldn't believe he'd fallen asleep at his desk.

Tory was singing in the kitchen, and he could smell bacon cooking. He smiled as he heard one of his sons laugh. His phone started buzzing on the desk next to him. He reached over and grabbed it. It was a text from his daughter Katra asking if she could come and visit.

Ash started to answer her and then remembered finding the mysherrilyn.com website the night before. Needing to know if it was real or just another dream, he tried typing it into his browser and got the, "This site can't be reached." message. He then logged onto the Dark-Hunter website, and all was back to normal. He tried Facebook next to be sure, and there was nothing there. His stomach turned with a feeling of disappointment, which surprised him.

"Great, now I do wish it were real." he sighed. "I really do need to stay away from the Sprite." Then he turned his attention back to his daughter's message.

NEW BEGINNINGS

JENNIFER FORIST

I stood in line outside the famous Sanctuary Bar, flicking my ID against my fingers. I'd been anxiously waiting to get in for twenty minutes, and I was finally at the door. I glanced up at the three-story building that housed one of the most well-known bars in New Orleans. To humans it was just a cool bar, a place to hang out and play pool while the best metal bands around played great music. To shifters like me, and those of any species, it was a rare haven.

"Hello?"

I looked back at the bouncer working the door. "Sorry," I said, handing him my ID. The guy was huge, the black shirt he wore with the bar's logo hugged his biceps and showed off a muscular chest. His long blond hair and blue eyes did nothing to make him look less lethal.

"Satara, that's different. You been here before, Satara?"

I smiled up at him. "No, first time. I'm here to see Black Faith."

"Cool, they're good. I'm gonna give you a quick rundown. The rules are basic. No fighting, biting, or magic. Break the rules, we break body parts and you're banned for life. Got it?" He asked, tapping my ID against his fingers.

"Got it," I pointed at the sign above the door, "Come in peace, or leave in pieces, right?"

"Exactly—have fun."

I took back my ID and walked through the door. The lights were already dim, but at least the band hadn't started playing yet. I glanced around the busy bar. Towards the back, groups of people played pool or video games. Beyond the dance floor sat the stage. The band had already set up their equipment, but other than that, the stage was empty. I scanned the room as I moved through the crowd but didn't see him.

I squeezed my way up to the bar and ordered a rum and cola once the pretty blonde bartender noticed me. I wiped my hands on my jeans and adjusted my purple top. Pulling my long, curly black hair over my shoulder, I searched the crowd again, then shook my head. I wondered for the hundredth time what the hell I was doing. Last week I'd been passing through Shreveport and stopped at a bar where Black Faith was playing. They were amazing, but my real interest was in the lead singer. I hadn't been able to take my eyes off him. I'd spent the entire night in awe, this fire growing in me with every minute that passed. I felt a connection to him, and I didn't even know his name. When he'd announced their next show would be at Sanctuary, I knew I had to come.

"Here's your drink. Do you want to start a tab?"

I took the glass and nodded at the bartender. "Yes, thank you. Hey, when's the band supposed to start?"

"Should be anytime now."

"Thanks." I leaned against the bar and took a sip of my drink. Perfect. I looked around again, taking a moment to appreciate how cool it was to be here. Sanctuary was a rare gem. There weren't many places in the world where shifters, or other types of creatures, could gather in safety. The Peltier family, who owned and ran the place, was just as well-known as their bar. They were a family of Were-Hunters, bears, and as fierce as they come. They enforced the rules with a viciousness that left no room for argument. I'd always wanted to check the bar out, but rarely came to New Orleans.

And I'd followed a guy here that I didn't even know. I snorted at that and took another drink from my glass. I probably was crazy. Someone bumped into me, sloshing my drink over the edge of the cup. I caught the scent of wolf, turned to say something, and immediately forgot how to speak.

"Oh, sorry," he said, tilting his head to study me with chocolate brown eyes. He had his dark hair gelled back tonight, and he'd trimmed his scruffy beard, but there was no mistaking those eyes, or the sleeves of tattoos that covered his well-muscled arms. I licked my lips, staring up at him, wishing I could remember how to talk. "It's you," he breathed, a smile playing at his full lips.

I shook my head, clearing away the stupid that had struck me. "I'm sorry, what?"

He leaned into me, setting every nerve I had on fire. "I saw you, last weekend. I tried to find you after the show, but you were gone."

"Oh," I said, sounding as surprised as I felt. "You did?" There had been times during the night that I thought he was looking at me, but I bet half the girls in the bar had felt that way too.

"Oh, I definitely did. Did you come here to see

me?" He ran the backs of his fingers down my arm, leaving goosebumps on my skin.

"Would it be creepy if I said yes?"

He laughed, "I don't know, maybe a little." He shrugged, still smiling at me.

I laughed, relaxing a little, and took a drink. The rum warmed my chest, and I let out a small breath. "Well, that's good then, because I did come to see you."

"That is good. I was bummed that I missed you last time. Listen, I gotta get up there, but I'll see you at intermission, don't leave."

"I won't."

He smiled and moved for the stage but turned back. "What's your name?"

"Satara."

He brushed the backs of his fingers down my cheek. My breath hitched and white-hot electricity zinged through my body at his warm touch. The scorching look he gave me told me he felt what I did. "Satara," he said, "Beautiful. I'm Cassian, but you can call me Cash. I'll see you in a bit, Satara."

2

I watched Cash walk onto the stage and pick up his guitar. He put a black strap over his head and started messing with the knobs at the top. I grinned, turning back to the bar to order another drink. Next to me, a petite woman with caramel brown hair sat down on one of the black stools. She smelled like a wolf, and fear. I glanced around, not seeing anything out of the ordinary. The bartender brought my new drink, and I turned back towards the stage. Cash pointed to his drummer, then stepped up to the microphone.

"How's everyone doin' tonight?" The crowd cheered, people letting out loud whoops. "Alright. Well, we are Black Faith, who's ready to party?" After another round of cheers from the crowd, Cash played a few quick notes on his guitar. "This first song we're gonna play is called Divine Dreams. Tonight, I'd like to dedicate it to my beautiful new friend, Satara." He looked in my direction and smiled at me. I grinned back, my insides turning to mush.

I turned to the woman next to me as the song started. "That's me," I said, still grinning, "I'm Satara."

"Congratulations," She murmured, her fear still strong in the air. I noticed the other shifters had moved away from her, leaving us mostly surrounded by humans.

"I know, right," I said, hoping for a smile, no luck. "You know, I came here tonight to see him. I thought I was crazy. Turns out it was the best choice I've made in a while. What about you, did you come to see them play?"

She glanced at the stage and shook her head. "No, not really."

"Ah, hiding out then, huh?" She stiffened next to me, but I shrugged. "No worries, lots of people come here for that too, it's the best place in town to hide."

She glanced over at me, her ice blue eyes not meeting mine. "It's true then, what they say about this place?"

"Oh, yeah. This is a safe place for our kind. No one will hurt you here." She visibly relaxed and my curiosity spiked. "What's your name?"

She looked me over for a moment and must have decided I seemed safe enough. "I'm Grace."

"Nice to meet you, Grace. I'm Satara, can I buy you a drink? You look like you've had a rough day."

She chuckled and rolled her eyes. "More like a few days. Yes, I'd love a drink. A rum and cola, please."

"I think I like you, Grace." I ordered her drink and turned in my seat so I could watch the main attraction, Cash. Lord, the man looked like sex on a stage. His biceps flexed as he plucked his guitar. His face filled with passion while he jumped around belting out the lyrics to a raw, melodic song. The music ended and the crowd roared for more.

"They're good," Grace said, leaning towards me so I could hear her.

"Right? They're amazing. That singer, woo! He's something, isn't he?"

"He is cute."

"Cute?" I scoffed. "That man is smokin' hot." I fanned myself and Grace chuckled. "What about you, do you have a boyfriend?"

She shook her head, then took a long sip of her drink. "My uncle, he's our pack's alpha, he and my dad are trying to marry me off to his second-in-command. He's a horrible person."

I grimaced. "Yuck, they still do that?" Werewolf packs worked differently from were-hunters. I'd heard stuff but didn't know all the details. I wasn't part of the were-hunter world, we ran in different circles, and werewolves stuck close to their own kind. Personally, I'd been on my own since I was young, I preferred it that way. Watching Cash on stage, I thought that might change soon though. Werewolves don't mate the same way as were-hunters, but we do bond, and that can happen over weeks, or in minutes, which is what seemed to have happened with Cash and me.

"I don't think many packs force arranged marriages anymore," Grace said, bringing my attention back to her. "Apparently my uncle does."

"That's disgusting. What pack are you from?"

She hesitated. "Lakewood."

"From Mississippi? Ew, sorry to hear that."

"You know them?"

"I've heard of them. They're known for being scummy. No offense."

"Oh, trust me, none taken. They are scummy, misogynistic pigs."

"Is that who you're hiding from?"

She nodded and tossed back the rest of her drink. I signaled to the bartender for another. "Yup. I finally had enough and left. I'm sure they're looking for me. That's why I came down here. I heard rumors about this place. I didn't know if it was real or not. I'm hoping to have a few days to figure out what to do next."

I nodded, "That's some messed-up stuff. You need a shot, Grace." The music stopped and Cash announced they were taking a twenty-minute intermission, so I ordered three shots. My heartbeat picked up and my stomach fluttered as I watched him make his way towards me. His eyes stayed on me, even when several other females approached him.

He gave me a sexy grin when he reached me. "Hey."

"You were amazing out there, Cash. The crowd loves you. Oh, I ordered you a shot." I handed him his glass and slid one to Grace. "This is my new friend Grace, Grace this is Cash."

He held out his hand and Grace shook it. "Nice to meet you, Grace." He lifted his glass, and we all downed our shots. I sat mine down and grabbed my other drink, chasing away the burn of liquor. Cash stepped closer to me, putting his hand on the small of my back. Goosebumps broke out over my skin, and I leaned into him. "Will you get some food with me when I'm done?" He asked, his breath brushing across my neck.

"I would love that, yes."

"Awesome. We can eat here. They have great steak. Or we can go somewhere else, your choice?"

Before I could answer, the scent of Grace's fear drifted over to us, and I turned to look at her. She stood now. Her gaze fixed on the front door. "What's wrong?" I asked, touching her elbow. She jumped but didn't take her eyes off the door. I followed her gaze to a cluster of people up front. Two men dressed in jeans and sleeveless t-shirts stood out like a sore thumb. The shorter one had a hat and a beer belly. The other was taller and more muscular. "Grace?" I leaned closer to her, "Who is that?"

When she looked over, the fear in her eyes honestly shook me. It wasn't just the look of a woman running away from an unwanted situation, she was genuinely terrified. I realized this was a woman running for her life, one who had been hurt beyond anything acceptable. And that pissed me off. I moved closer to Grace as the men moved through the crowd towards us. Cash stepped in front of Grace and me, just as the men reached us.

3

—————

"Can I help you, gentlemen?" Cash asked the two guys, crossing his big arms against his chest. I caught a glimpse of the fierce wolf in him, and my own wolf growled in appreciation. She thought we'd picked well.

The taller guy spoke to Cash first. "We're here for the girl. She belongs to me," he looked around Cash to stare down Grace, "and it's time to come home."

"She doesn't want to go with you." I spoke.

The guy in the hat sneered at me, "She doesn't have a choice."

"That's where you'd be wrong," Cash told him, "This is Sanctuary, and it's protected by Omegrion sanctuary laws. No one is removed against their will, and she doesn't want to go so..."

The tall one glared at Cash, "Look, pretty boy, I don't know shit about Omegrion, and I don't care. Were-hunters don't have nothin' to do with me. She does—now move."

Cash shook his head, "It doesn't matter who you are, or what world you're a part of, when you're here, you follow Sanctuary laws."

"That's right," the bartender said, "see that scary-looking guy over there," she pointed to a man with brown hair and dark eyes. He looked like a half feral biker. "That's my mate, Fang. I'm Aimee, and this is our bar. When you're here, you follow our rules, or he'll make you."

The tall guy turned his attention to Aimee. "I don't give a shit who you are, her father promised her to me, and I'm taking her home."

Aimee shook her head when he reached for Grace. "I wouldn't do that if I were you. Fang and my brothers will have you out on your ass faster than you can blink."

Cash took a step forward, and I noticed several very scary-looking men moving through the crowd towards us. The noise level in the bar dropped, and the two men looked around. The tall one fixed Grace with a lethal stare as Aimee came around from behind the bar. "You can't hide in here forever, bitch. We'll be waiting." They turned to leave, brushing past two big guys who looked exactly like the bouncer I'd seen at the door. One of the big guys followed them out.

"I can't believe Dev let those two in," Aimee said. "Are you alright?" She asked Grace.

Grace nodded, looking at the small crowd that had gathered around us. "I'm so sorry. I didn't think they'd follow me this far."

Aimee gave her a thin smile. "It's no problem. That was pretty tame compared to some nights around here."

"That's true," Fang said, kissing her before he blended back into the crowd. Aimee gave Grace's shoulder a pat, then went back behind the bar. Everyone else returned to what they were doing, the noise level around us going back to normal.

Cash stood next to me, and I handed him his

drink, holding mine up. "Here's to a very interesting night." He smiled and clinked his glass into mine. Grace looked like she was about to cry, so I put my arm around her shoulder. "Hey, it'll be alright."

"No," she sniffed, "I don't think it will. He's right, I can't hide in here forever, and they'll be outside waiting when I leave. It was stupid to think I could get away from them."

I remembered what it felt like to be that hopeless. So many years ago, I'd been like her, struggling to separate myself from my past, wanting nothing more than to be free. "No," I said. "No, I don't accept that, and you shouldn't either. We'll figure it out." I looked back at Cash, disappointment blooming, but I knew I was doing the right thing. "I think I'll have to pass on dinner tonight. I'm sorry, I can't let her go out there alone."

The side of Cash's lip pulled up in a sexy-as-sin grin. He trailed his finger down my arm, taking my hand in his, and leaned close to me. "I know you feel what I feel," he nuzzled his nose against my neck, sending bolts of electricity coursing through my body. "If you think I'm letting my future mate deal with two losers without me—well, we need to get to know each other better."

Heat pooled in my core, and I resisted the urge to squeeze my thighs together. I reached out and ran my hand up his arm, enjoying the curve of muscle under my fingers. I stood on my tiptoes to whisper in his ear. "I can't wait."

He pulled back and looked down at me, mischief sparkling in his eyes. "I need to get back on stage, but do not leave without me," he glanced at Grace, then back at me, "either of you. You can both stay with me tonight. I got a huge room at The Roosevelt. We'll figure out what to do in the morning."

Grace looked at him in surprise. "You guys don't have to do this."

"Sure we do," Cash said with a wink, before he headed back to the stage.

"I have a plan," I said, peeling my eyes off Cash's butt and turning to Grace. "Have you ever heard of Stormridge?"

"No."

I hopped up on the bar stool and ordered another round of drinks from Aimee. Cash's band started back up, the smooth timber of his voice floating over me.

"Stormridge is a werewolf pack in Indiana. Hector is their alpha, he's a great man. The pack takes people in, offers them protection. It's a whole little town run by the pack. It's nice. If you want, I can call him."

"Are they your pack?"

I shook my head, taking a slow drink from my glass. "I don't have a pack. But Hector's dad took me in when I needed help, and they could help you too."

Grace twisted her glass around on the bar, thinking about my offer. "Do you think they'd take me in?"

"I can't make any promises, but I'll ask Hector to meet with you. It's up to him if he lets you stay." She thought it over some more, then finally nodded. I checked my phone, almost one in the morning. "I think I better wait until sunrise to call."

"Satara, can I ask you something?"

I pursed my lips. "Sure, of course."

"Why are you doing this?"

"Doing what? Helping you?" She nodded, and I shrugged. "You seem nice, I like nice people. And I've been in your shoes, sort of. My parents died when I was young, and my pack, it wasn't as bad as yours, but I just couldn't stay. I was eleven when I ran away. Thirteen when Hector's dad, Antonio, found me. That was the worst two years of my life. Antonio helped me just because he could. It won't cost me a thing to help you, so why wouldn't I?"

"Well, it's costing you a date at least."

I chuckled. "I'm not worried. I don't think he's going anywhere."

"I've never met anyone like you. Everyone in my pack is always angling for something, planning their next scheme. They'd never just help someone out of kindness."

"Well, it's a big world out there, Grace. And I think something better is just waiting for you to come along."

4

C ash packed away his gear as the bar emptied. He'd just finished introducing Grace and me to his band mates when Aimee and Fang came over. Fang tipped his head at Cash. "You guys were kick-ass. You free to play tomorrow night, too?"

Cash glanced at his bandmates, who all nodded. "Yeah, man, that'd be great. Thanks."

Fang turned to Grace. "You good?"

"I think so, yes, thank you for your help earlier."

"I can't stand assholes that don't take care of their women."

"Will you be ok to leave?" Aimee asked. "My brother says they're still out there waiting. I'd be happy to send over a distraction."

"Will you?" I asked, "That would be so helpful. Cash is letting us stay with him tonight, we just need to get out of here."

Aimee grinned at me, and I thought I saw a hint of bear in that smile. "It would be my pleasure. Come out in five."

She sauntered away, and Fang grinned. "I better go make sure she doesn't hurt them, too bad. See you tomorrow night."

Five minutes later, Cash, his bandmates, Grace, and I slipped out the front door of Sanctuary. Across the street Fang, Aimee, and the blond bouncer blocked our view from the guys after Grace. One of them pointed and yelled something, but Aimee swatted his arm down. The six of us jogged around the corner and out of sight. We all piled into a gray van with Black Faith painted on the side and drove to the hotel.

The lobby was silent at three-thirty in the morning. We quietly said "bye" to his friends, then followed Cash to his room. He hadn't been kidding about it being big. It was one of those suites with a kitchen and a separate bedroom. "Very nice, Mr. Rockstar," I said, looking around.

"Thanks," he said, looking almost embarrassed. He rubbed the back of his neck. "I, ah, I'm claustrophobic, so I need the space."

"Oh. Are you okay with us here?"

He ran his fingers through the ends of my hair with a smile. "Of course. You guys can take the room, I'll sleep on the couch."

I didn't bother arguing. I knew it wouldn't matter. So I said goodnight and followed Grace into the large, cushy bedroom. I lay in bed, tossing and turning with the knowledge that Cash was in the other room, and that we had bonded. I didn't even know his last name yet, but my body knew he was mine. I was giddy with the excitement of it. He was crazy hot, nice, and seemed willing to go along with whatever nonsense I got myself into. I couldn't wait to get to know him.

I woke up a while later, feeling like someone was watching me. Sure enough, when my eyes fluttered open, Cash sat in a chair next to the bed, watching me.

I sat up, tilting my head at him. "What's wrong?" I whispered.

"Nothing. I didn't mean to wake you."

"Were you watching me sleep?"

"Would it be creepy if I said yes?" He asked, using my words from earlier.

"Maybe a little," I said, carefully getting up from bed, going over to him and leaning down, "but I like it." I whispered in his ear. He held my gaze for a moment, little sparks of awareness shooting through me before he leaned forward and brushed his lips across mine. My need was instant. Even my wolf perked up, excited by our male. I couldn't wait for our wolves to run together. I took his hand in mine and tugged him from the chair.

He followed me out of the room towards the couch bed but stopped just before we reached it. He pulled me against his hard body, wrapping his fingers in my hair and kissing me again. His lips were warm and soft against mine, and my entire body hummed under his touch. I ran my hands up his arms, over his shoulders, and down his smooth back. Needing to see him, I pushed his shirt up, breaking our kiss long enough to pull it over his head. I ran my gaze over his magnificent body, biting my lip in appreciation. He growled low in his throat, picking me up and taking me to the bed in one smooth motion.

He laid me down, the weight of his body resting on top of mine. "I was planning on at least feeding you before we did this, but our dinner got canceled."

I wrapped my legs around his waist, raising my hips to grind against him. "You can feed me in the morning. I don't want to wait."

He kissed my neck, licking his way up to nip my ear. "Satara, my beautiful mate. I've waited a long time to find you. Will you come with me when the band leaves town?" He pulled back to look down at me, his brown eyes hopeful.

I gave him a soft smile and nodded. "Of course I will."

He leaned down to kiss me before pulling off my shirt, then my pants. His kisses became more urgent, his tongue sweeping across mine. I raked my nails down his back before unbuttoning his pants so I could touch him. He slipped his hand between us, sliding his finger along my core. I positioned his length against myself, lifting my hips to meet him. "I need you, now."

Cash didn't hesitate, he pushed inside me with a low growl, and I cried out at the perfection of it. His lips crashed back into mine as he moved faster, building up a blazing pressure inside me. He kneaded my breast, plucking at my nipple. I tightened my legs around him, meeting each of his thrust. He buried his face against my neck, slamming into me until I finally exploded with release. I cried out his name, digging my nails into his shoulders. His teeth grazed my neck, and as his release exploded inside me, he bit down, claiming me as his mate.

5

"I smell bacon." Grace muttered, padding into the small kitchen area, and flopping into a chair. Cash grinned at me, kissed my forehead, and dropped six pieces on the plate I had. I handed it to Grace.

"Morning, Sunshine." She groaned at me, and I handed her a cup of coffee too. Her next groan sounded happier. "Not a morning person, are we?"

"Not even a little."

"Well, I have good news at least. I talked to Hector this morning. He's willing to meet with you. I got on-line and ordered you a bus ticket to Indianapolis, you just need to get to Stormridge from there. The bus leaves at nine-twenty though, so we need to go soon."

"Thank you," Grace said, sipping her coffee.

We finished breakfast while Cash let his friends know he needed to take the van for the morning. Then the three of us hit the road. I gave Grace her ticket information and showed her the itinerary for bus transfers. I also gave her what little money I had on me for food.

"I don't know what to say. 'Thank you' doesn't seem like it's enough. You have no idea what you're giving me."

"I hope it's a fresh start. You still gotta win over Hector, but I think you'll do great. Watch out for Dakota though, he's Hector's second-in-command, scary dude."

"Thank you, Satara, really. I hope someday I can repay you."

"No worries, I'm glad we could help." We pulled into the bus station and Cash parked near the entrance. "Do you want us to walk you in?"

Grace looked around the parking lot, then peered at the glass windows of the building. "I think I'll be fine." She leaned across the seat and hugged me. "Thanks again, I'll never forget this."

I hugged her back. "Call me when you get there, let me know what Hector says, okay?"

"I will," she promised.

I watched her climb out of the van and go inside. Cash reached over and took my hand. "She'll be fine."

"I hope so. Thanks for being so cool about all this." I glanced over at him with a small grin. "I think you and I are going to get along very well.

He lifted my hand to his lips, kissing my knuckles. "I think so too."

Later that night I sat at a table near Sanctuary's stage, while Cash once again rocked the place. Aimee brought over a *Sex on the Beach* and sat in the chair next to me. "How'd it go with your friend?"

"Good, I got her on a bus heading north. I think she'll be okay. Thanks for your help last night."

"Anytime. It's terrible the way werewolves treat their women," she shrugged at me, "Nothing personal, I don't really understand your world much, and those guys were awful."

I watched Cash strum his guitar. He caught my gaze on him and winked at me. "We do live in very different worlds," I told Aimee, "But not all of our men are like that."

She saw where my eyes were and smiled. "No, I suppose not. He seems nice enough. You guys are always welcome here."

"Thank you." I said, before she got up and left. I sipped my drink, keeping my eyes on my new mate. We were going to Alabama next, and I couldn't wait to see what adventures awaited Cash and me there.

FROM HER DARKEST DREAMS

JENNIFER BECKER

1

———

The air around her suddenly changed. Delphi knew without looking that she was no longer alone. The streetlamp above her seemed to dim out, casting an eerie glow.

A shadow formed to her left. Then multiplied to five. Daimons. They watched her with hunger in their eyes.

Delphi widened her legs, preparing to defend herself. Her mother had taught her how to kill a Daimon. A wood stake through the chest, but she was weaponless. Which meant she would have to improvise. Suddenly, she was lifted off the ground and pulled into a small courtyard.

"Hello, little one." A deep melodical voice whispered against her ear.

"Let me go." Her struggles were useless. He held her in a tight grip. Strong enough to crush her bones.

"We will, eventually." He took a deep breath against the side of her neck. "You smell mouthwatering."

Then the Daimon was torn from her. She heard a grunt and the sound of flesh hitting flesh. Delphi turned to watch in fascination as a man fought off her

would-be attackers. He attacked with deadly preci-
sion. He was lethal and fierce.

She was so intent on watching, she didn't realize
someone sneaked up behind her until they had one
arm wrapped around her chest, pulling her tightly
against them and pinning her arms to her sides. Their
other arm pulled her head to the side, exposing her
neck. "I'm not going out without a piece of you," he
hissed before he struck. Delphi screamed as fangs
sank into the juncture of her neck and shoulder.

Delphi's arms flew out to both sides and the
Daimon fell back from her with a scream. A wealth of
knowledge suddenly filled her head. Power unlike
she'd ever felt before coursed through her veins.

As suddenly as it began, it stopped. Delphi collapsed as she came back to herself. Her legs refused to
support her yet she didn't hit the ground. Someone
was holding her. Her eyes fluttered open to see her
rescuer staring down at her. His eyes were soft and
caring. Nothing like the ferocious predator that tore
through the Daimons like rag dolls.

Delphi reached up and touched his face. The man
looked shocked at her touch, then leaned into it. A soft
rumble came from his chest, like a purr.

More images flashed through her mind, slower
this time. Of him and her over the centuries.

"Mate," she mumbled, before her eyes closed and
blackness consumed her.

2

Power radiated from the woman as if the Daimon bite unleashed something inside of her. She'd set off a power surge that any mythical creature within fifty miles would feel. She'd fried the Daimon that attacked her to ash. It wouldn't be long before creatures ventured out to locate her. Drawn to her powers.

Sanctuary, a bar and an actual sanctuary to the supernatural, was just down the road.

Thrax cradled the woman in his arms as if she were the most precious thing in the world. To him, she was. Mate. It was the one thing all species waited their entire lives for. As happy as he was to find his, it couldn't have happened at a worse possible time.

His brother, Diego, was currently hiding out at Sanctuary from a lion shapeshifter named Cassidy. Diego owed the lion a large sum of money. Thrax could pay it off, but he was tired of bailing his brother out. He'd come to Sanctuary to convince Diego to confront Cassidy, but his brother was being stubborn. He knew he was safe so long as he was within the red brick walls.

Sanctuary was the only place that didn't give a shit about animals with a grudge. Their law was absolute.

Any who sought refuge there were safe so long as they didn't attack another. Few were stupid enough to poke the bears.

Thrax needed to get his mate out of here before someone came up on them. Or worse, all of them. He was strong. A black panther. Lethal, deadly, but even he couldn't hold off an army by himself.

Thrax flashed them to his house above his business. It was warded and would keep her safe. Nothing could enter without an invitation.

Thrax settled in bed behind her, snuggling up to her peaceful sleeping form pressing his front to her back. The world shifted as he held her close, feeling a rightness settle in his chest.

3

Delphi came awake to a hair tickling her nose. She batted at it sleepily, not ready to wake up. She tried to burrow deeper into the blankets, willing her body to fall back asleep. A soft rumble vibrated against her chest as that annoying hair tickled her nose again.

She reached up to remove the hair and noted that it was connected to something that wasn't her. Delphi cautiously opened her eyes to black fur attached to a large cat. A panther, to be more exact.

Memories of last night came back to her. The Daimons. Her powers. Her mate. She'd known it the moment she touched him. Scenes played in her head of their future together like a movie. She'd seen the possibility of him rejecting her, but the future was always changing.

She smiled, looking him over. He was like a giant stuffed animal curled up next to her, his back to her front. She doubted he would appreciate being called a stuffed animal, though. Men didn't like to be considered cute and cuddly.

Did he know they were mates? Did he see the images like she had?

Delphi stroked her fingers through his fur. It felt soft, like velvet. Delphi couldn't resist, she rubbed his fuzzy ears, wondering if he was like a house cat and liked being scratched. She gasped when he suddenly turned over to face her in human form.

It was incredible how quickly he could transform. It was in a blink of an eye. His yellow eyes regarded her sleepily but also hungry. His arm wrapped around her back, pulling her flush to his chest. "I have something else you can pet." He smiled.

Delphi gasped when she felt his hard cock thrust against her core. "Oh yeah?" It wasn't wise to tease a wild animal, but he brought it out in her. "Something like this?"

She reached between them to grasp his bare cock. He was hot and hard and ready for her. Delphi could barely wrap her hand around him.

He groaned, arching into her hand. "Damn, woman. You enslave me." He leaned forward and captured her lips.

Delphi started at the abruptness of his kiss, then sank into it. His hands skimmed over her like she was made of the finest china and he was afraid to break her. He made her feel special, loved, cherished.

Delphi pulled back, realizing something. "What's your name?" She'd found her mate and didn't even know what his name was. A fact she found embarrassing given their position.

"Thrax Gataki."

She smirked at his last name.

"Is there something amusing about my name?" His eyes turned molten as his voice deepened.

"Not at all. Though I do have to say you are a cute kitten." She reached up and scratched his chin. The start of a beard scraped along her fingertips.

"Cute." He scowled, rolling from his side to loom over her. He nipped at her fingertips with his blunt teeth. "I am a ferocious jungle cat. A black panther. Top of the food chain."

"Does that make me your prey?" She quirked an eyebrow and gave a mischievous smile.

"Mmm," he licked his lips, "and I'm ravenous." His eyes started to glow again. His animal close to the surface.

"Are you going to tell me your name?" he asked, nibbling the side of her neck.

How was she supposed to think when he did that? "Delphi Sideris." She waited for him to recognize her last name. Her mom had been famous amongst the supernatural. A highly sought-after oracle. All the females of their line were oracles. Some more powerful than others.

Many demons tried to enslave them to use their powers. It was why her mother had taught her self-defense. They'd be drawn to her power and seek to use it.

Thrax pulled back with a look of puzzlement. She saw the moment he connected the pieces. "Sideris, the oracles."

"I am. I fully came into my powers last night." Now every demon and creature that could sense magic would be after her, drawn to her power. Seeking it for themselves. Would Thrax use her powers for himself? Or sell her to the highest bidder?

"You're safe, Delphi. I would never hurt you," he assured her in a calm, soothing tone, as if he sensed her growing concern.

"I know." She trusted he would never physically hurt her. Emotionally, mentally... that was a different story.

He eyed her skeptically. "You don't look convinced."

There was the old saying that actions spoke louder than words. "My people have been sought over the centuries. Everyone sought to use our powers for their own gain. I don't want to be used."

His gaze softened. "I have no use for an oracle, Delphi. I'm in control of my own destiny, not someone else's interpretation. No offense."

He was too good to be true. "You don't want to use my powers?"

"No, νεράιδα."

"But you have free and total access to a wealth of knowledge. I can tell you the outcome of every battle you'd enter. I can tell you all that and more, and you don't want it?" She shouldn't be trying to convince him to use her powers, she just wanted to understand why. It was her experience that creatures were self-centered.

"I am a wealthy business owner, Delphi. I have been for several hundred years. I started my own company from nothing. I believe in making my own way, not taking advice from an oracle."

"Would you let your friends use my powers?" He may not want them, but that didn't mean he wouldn't let others use her.

"One, I don't have friends, and two, no one will ever use your powers against your will while I'm alive." There was no deception in his tone.

Delphi relaxed in the bed. He didn't want her powers and would even protect her from others wanting to use them. "Thank you."

"You have nothing to thank me for, νεράιδα."

She didn't know why he insisted on calling her fairy. There was nothing similar between her and a fairy. It didn't matter, especially when his face buried in her neck. He bit down on the cord between her neck and shoulder. Her back arched off the mattress. Her hands wrapped around his broad back to pull him close.

He left a hot trail of kisses up to her chin. Delphi's fingers reached up and threaded through his long hair. It cascaded around her, a black silk waterfall.

Thrax rubbed himself into her touch as if to cover himself with her scent. "I want to feel your skin against mine." Before she finished speaking, her clothes disappeared.

Her eyes drank him in, not knowing where to start. His body was a work of art. Chiseled muscle over flawless bronzed skin. His were-genes healed him quickly from almost any injury.

Delphi's hands caressed his pectorals down to his perfectly cut abs. Her fingers glided over the ridges and divots before trailing further down.

Thrax snatched her wandering hands in one of his and held them in place. It wasn't forceful. She could pull free if she wanted. "You keep that up and it will be over before we've begun." His breath was harsh, his chest rising and falling in rapid succession like he had been running a marathon. He was on a knife's edge, and she wanted to push him over.

"That would be a shame." She wrapped her legs around his narrow waist and pulled him close, rubbing her dripping core against his cock.

Thrax reached his free hand between them. His fingers skimmed over her belly then to the juncture where she wanted him most. He separated her tender folds and slid a finger inside her.

They both groaned at the same time. Delphi's legs fell open of their own accord. He could ask her for anything right now and she would give it to him. Her head thrashed on the pillow from side to side as his fingers glided in and out of her at a slow and easy pace.

He kissed his way down the center of her body until he reached where his fingers were. Delphi screamed in ecstasy when his tongue swiped over her slit. He did it again, eliciting the same response. Her fingers scrambled for purchase, needing an anchor to weather the storm swirling in her core.

4

T hrax learned quickly what his mate liked. What made her wetter. What made her clamp down his fingers like a vise.

By the sounds of her moans, she was hurtling toward a climax. It was a good thing he lived in the penthouse above his office and his company closed on the weekends.

His little fairy was vocal.

Scratch that, he wished there were people closer by to hear his mate crying his name as he drew climax after climax from her. The animal in him craved it.

"Thrax, please." Her fingers clung to the back of his head, holding him in place. Telling him what she wanted.

Thrax redoubled his efforts. His lips clamped down on her nub as her body spasmed around him. He waited for the last of the tremors to fade before he slid to the side of the bed and watched her. A light sheen of sweat covered her porcelain skin. Her chest rose and fell as she tried to catch her breath. She watched him with hunger in her gaze.

"Your turn." She smiled as she sat up and draped a leg over his waist. His hands fastened around her waist and held her up so she couldn't lower herself down.

"No."

Delphi froze. Her eyebrows furrowed in confusion.

"Delphi, we can't." The words were hard to get out. He wanted to. More than anything.

"But you're my mate." Her voice was small and broken. The look of hurt in her eyes pierced his heart, but he had to remain strong.

"I won't endanger you or tie your life to mine. At least not now," he amended. Eventually he would. When this disaster with his brother and Cassidy was over.

"What do you mean?"

"My brother Diego is in hiding because a were-lion, Cassidy, is after him. If Cassidy learns I have a mate, he could use you to make me force my brother out. I won't endanger either of you." His vision turned red at the thought of what would happen if Cassidy ever got his hands on her.

Delphi's features smoothed out. He expected anger or hurt, but instead she remained calm. "Danger will always surround us, but we are stronger together. Bonded."

"Have your powers shown you this?" Had she seen something? He told her he didn't need her powers, and he didn't, but if she knew something that could help keep her and his brother safe...

"I don't need powers to know mates are strongest together."

Suddenly the air felt charged and the hairs on the back of his neck stood on end. He'd been in enough fights to know what was coming. "We're in danger."

No sooner had he spoken than four men popped into his room. With only a thought, he dressed Delphi and came off the bed in a crouch, ready to battle. By the scent of them, he could tell they were lions.

"Leave or die." It was the only warning he was going to give them. He didn't know how they got through his wards, but it was a problem for later.

"Our fight isn't with you, panther. We only want the oracle."

Over his dead body. Thrax transformed into a panther and launched himself at them. They were weakest in their human form, and he used that against them.

Before he reached them, he heard a feminine gasp behind him. He whirled around to see someone grab Delphi and disappear. He roared in disbelief.

"Tell your brother his debt is paid," one of them said, and then all disappeared, leaving him alone.

Diego had done this. Traded Thrax's mate for his freedom. Why else would they say his brother's debt was paid? How else could they have gotten through his wards? Only he and his brother could. Unless his brother told them how.

A rage unlike any he'd felt before consumed him. His brother was dead to him, and he would do the honors himself, sending him to meet their ancestors.

Thrax flashed to Sanctuary, straight to his brother's room. It was a risk going behind the bears' backs like this. He was breaking every single one of their rules. Attacking on their territory was a one-way ticket to death but he didn't care.

He'd get his pound of flesh before they got him.

Diego stood with his back to him, not even sensing he was no longer alone. It would be so easy to kill him. Panthers were known for their stealth, but he wanted his brother to know he was here for his head. To see his end coming.

"How could you?" His voice was low, menacing. His animal was in control. It wanted revenge for their mate being taken.

Diego whipped around so fast he almost fell on his ass. His eyes were wide with fear until he saw it was Thrax. They were similar in looks and height. Both had long black hair, though Diego's was a few inches longer. Thrax was taller, by an inch. The one big difference was Diego had blue eyes. "Shit, man. You scared ten years off my life."

"How could you?" he repeated, his humanity slipping by the second.

Diego realized his brother wasn't playing around. The scent of fear wafted through the room exciting his animal. "Thrax." Diego held his hands up to ward his brother back. Not that it would help him. Thrax was older and stronger. "Come on, it's me. I didn't do anything."

"The oracle," Thrax growled as he stalked closer.

Diego looked perplexed. "That's what you're upset about? What do you care about some random chick? You've never cared about women for more than an hour or two." It was true, he always put business before pleasure. That was before finding his mate. That's when everything changed.

"She's my mate," he snarled, then launched at him.

Arms wrapped around his middle and pinned him to the ground before Thrax could reach Diego. The scent of bear was strong. It was futile but Thrax thrashed under the bear, careful not to use teeth and claws. The bear would kill him in an instant if he tried it.

"Knock it off," a deep voice snarled.

It was Dev.

"He traded my mate to save his hide. He's dead to

me." He roared until his voice was hoarse. His body sagged under the bear's.

"You have a mate?" The bear sounded surprised but maintained his grip. "You don't smell it."

"I didn't know, bro. You know I would never do that to you," Diego denied, safely on the other side of the room.

Thrax didn't believe him. His panther demanded satisfaction. With renewed energy, Thrax surged to his knees before the bear got him back down.

"Remi, Quinn," Dev called out.

Two of his brothers, part of the quadruplets, came tearing into the room. Thrax was squished to the ground with the combined weight. He'd never get to his brother now.

"I said I was sorry," Diego whined like a cub of only a few decades instead of one over a hundred years old.

"You better explain quick, boy," Dev demanded of Diego. "No animal trades a mate to save a life... ever."

"You told me last night to find a solution, Thrax, and I did. When you left, there was an energy surge unlike anything I'd felt before. People in the bar were even talking about it. There were whispers of an oracle. I left Sanctuary and followed the energy to your building. Oracles are worth a lot of money. More than I owe Cassidy. I figured if I gave her to Cassidy, he'd forgive my debt."

"I'm going to kill him," growled Dev.

"Wait," Thrax called out, the roar in his blood starting to simmer. "No one is killing him."

"Now he sees reason," Diego muttered.

"Shut up. You're still on my shit list." Diego wisely held his tongue. "Let me up." His voice was calmer now. His animal back under control... barely.

One by one, the bears stood up. Rising smoothly to his feet, Thrax glowered at Diego. The bears stood ready to restrain him again.

"You," he pointed at his brother, "are coming with me and we're going to get my mate back."

Diego looked ashen but nodded. Good, he hoped his brother finally saw the gravity of the situation.

5

Delphi sat primly in the ornate chair across from the man she'd learned was named Cassidy. Thrax had mentioned him before. Cassidy looked like a king, sitting behind his monstrosity of a desk with rare and expensive trinkets scattered on top of it.

He didn't appear to need more wealth or power. He had it in spades. Whatever the reason, she wasn't going to be here long. Not only would her mate come for her—he may not claim her, but she was still his mate—she had a bargaining chip.

"Sir." One of the men who'd taken her walked into the room. "Thrax and Diego Gataki are here to see you."

"Send them in," Cassidy said, never looking up from his work, his tone bored.

Delphi's heart pounded as Thrax stalked into the room, his gaze focused on Cassidy.

"Cassidy." He dipped his head in greeting at the were-lion.

Cassidy looked up from his paperwork.

"Thrax, I thought my men told you our business was concluded when your brother told us about the oracle. Your brother's debt is paid in full."

Thrax's eyes narrowed to slits. "I came to renegotiate, because you can't have the oracle."

It was grating that they were talking about her when she was sitting right between them.

"Why is that?" Cassidy leaned back casually in his chair. His hands laced across his chest.

"She's my mate."

It warmed her that he called her his mate, but she remembered his words from earlier. They were mates in name only. She didn't bear the mating mark.

Cassidy jumped to his feet. His fists planted on his desk. "I beg your pardon?"

"She's my mate," Thrax repeated, louder. "Release her. I brought my brother as payment."

"Really?" Diego whirled on Thrax, a look of betrayal on his face. "I'm the last family you have."

Delphi gasped. He couldn't mean that. Diego was his brother. How could he hand his brother over for her? This was exactly the situation he'd been trying to avoid. Why he hadn't wanted to mate. He was backed into a corner. She couldn't let him do this.

"No, you will not," she said, rising from her seat.

"She does speak," Cassidy muttered.

Delphi turned on him and pointed a finger in his face. "Yes, I do, and I have a name. Delphi. Remember it." She turned to face Thrax. "You will not turn your brother over to him."

Thrax remained still as a statue, his gaze on Cassidy. The only indication he gave that he heard her was the tightening in his jaw.

"We seem to find ourselves in a quandary. Whatever are you going to do?" Cassidy chuckled like he didn't have a care in the world.

"Offer something you can't buy," Delphi said,

crossing her arms over her chest and taking a defensive stance.

Cassidy looked at her with an eager expression. As if this were what he'd been hoping for. "What would that be, Oracle?" Power crackled around her. The lights in the room flickered and the hairs on her arms stood on end. He was giving her a display of his power, but she wasn't frightened. He wouldn't hurt her. Cassidy needed her. A dead oracle was useless.

Delphi marched around the desk. Several people came charging up behind her, but she ignored them, her focus on Cassidy. Cassidy's expression was guarded but he didn't move when she stood in front of him.

Cassidy could easily overpower her if she tried to hurt him, but she didn't want to hurt him, just show him something.

She grabbed his hand and let her powers flow through her. Images bombarded her mind, but she focused on the course he was currently set on and pushed the image into his head. His body went rigid as they watched it together. When it had played out, she showed him another path, one that led to everyone getting what they wanted if he made a crucial decision in the next few moments.

When the images stopped, Delphi stepped back. "The choice is yours."

Cassidy blinked several times before he turned to address Thrax, admiration in his eyes. "You have some mate."

Thrax's gaze fell to her, the first time he'd looked at her since he entered the room, his chest expanded with pride. "I do."

"Our business is concluded, take your brother and go. The oracle too."

It had worked. Delphi couldn't believe it.

"We'll be in touch." Cassidy gave Delphi a meaningful look, then waved them out. A bodyguard ushered them out of the room.

She would be seeing a lot more of him in the future. "Until then."

"So that's it?" Diego asked once they were outside.

Thrax went to lunge for him, murderous intent in his eyes, but Delphi stood in front of him. "Go," Thrax snarled.

Diego didn't need to be told twice. One second, he was there and the next gone, leaving them standing alone on the street.

"I should go too." She didn't want to, but Thrax didn't want to claim her. She didn't want to be mates in name only. Delphi wanted his mark. She wanted that bond.

Before she could take a step away, Thrax grabbed her arm. She opened her mouth to protest when the world shifted. One moment they were on the street, and the next they were back in his apartment, in his bedroom.

Delphi moved to walk out, but he blocked her path. She moved the other way and he followed. "Let me go."

Thrax took her chin in his hand and forced her to meet his gaze. "Never."

Delphi's knees threatened to buckle at the possessiveness of his tone. It was what she wanted, but the fact of the matter hadn't changed. "You said you wouldn't claim me. I won't be with you and not be mated."

6

Thrax dipped his head down so their noses touched. Her sweet scent wrapped around him like a blanket. He'd be able to find her anywhere in the world by her scent alone. It was unique to only her.

"I plan to claim every inch of you." Then his lips descended to capture hers.

He drank in her gasp and used her surprise to drive his tongue in. The burning need to claim his mate consumed him to a fever pitch. He knew he should be taking this slower. You only mated once. He wanted this to be memorable, but he was impatient. He'd almost lost her. The thing he'd feared would happen, had happened. Only Delphi's quick thinking saved them from war. With no other obstacle in his way, he wanted to claim his mate.

Thrax willed their clothes away and flashed them onto the bed. "Tell me you want this," he demanded, trailing hot kisses down her jaw to her neck.

"I..." She squealed when he bit down on the cord of her neck.

"Tell me you'll be mine." He kissed the other side of her neck.

"Thrax," He heard the hesitation in her voice and his blood turned to ice. Had his stubbornness pushed her away?

He pushed up on his hands to look down at her. "What is it?"

"I'm confused. Not long ago you said you wouldn't claim me and now you are. What changed?"

Thrax sighed heavily. "I was scared to bind us together. To give my enemies something to use against me. I thought I was protecting both of us by keeping us unattached. When Cassidy took you, I realized I was being an idiot."

A smile bloomed across her face. "Not you."

He bared his teeth at her in a playful manner. "Watch it, νεράιδα. Suddenly, it didn't matter if I tried to keep us from bonding because you were already right here." He touched his chest, right over his heart. "Where you belong. My fears of someone hurting you may never go away, but I know now how strong you are. How strong we can be together." His tone was gruff, chock-full of emotion.

Tears pooled in Delphi's eyes. He was wondering what he said wrong when she pulled him down and crushed her lips against his. "I love you."

Her words were a balm to his heart and soul. "I love you."

"I'm ready. Mate with me."

"The mark won't appear until we make love this first time. After that, we will be mates."

"Then what are you waiting for? Make love to me."

He purred as his knee brushed her legs open, then thrust into her warm and welcoming heat.

FALCON'S FLIGHT

CATHY GRAHAM

Skye found herself in the middle of a wide plaza. She looked like a young teenage tourist, clad in shorts and shirt like many of those around her, but Skye knew she had nothing in common with them. They were all focused on enjoyment and thrills. Skye simply wanted to survive.

New Orleans was strange to her. She had underestimated how busy the town would be. The crowds were overwhelming to someone who led a solitary life as far away from humanity as she could get. She hurried to escape the press of bodies, diving into the nearest street in a rush to get out of the square. For over twenty-five years, Skye had been running and hiding.

Skye contemplated shifting and flying away, but there were too many people near. Seeking a quiet spot out of sight, she turned another corner.

The breath was abruptly forced from her lungs as she collided with what felt like an immovable object. She thought the man leaning against the wall around the corner hadn't even noticed the impact, but as Skye looked up, and up, and up again, she saw that he had turned his head to look down at her. He was an arresting sight—way too tall, too dark, too male. He was clad in black leather. His long hair was black with blood red tips, and it flowed down over wide shoulders and a broad chest.

Startled, Skye began to back away. He dropped his tattered backpack at his feet and grasped her shoulders before she even saw him move.

"Sorry, I shouldn't have stopped so close to the corner." Even his voice was disturbing to Skye, deep and low, with a hint of a lilting accent.

"That's okay," Skye stuttered, "I'll just..." Unable to continue, she began to edge around him, never losing sight of her reflection in the black sunglasses that covered his eyes.

He released her as quickly as he had grabbed her and waved her past him. "Sorry again."

Skye ducked her head and moved away, but before she had gone more than a few steps he spoke. "Go to Sanctuary, Skye. It's a bar at 688 Ursulines Avenue. You'll find what you need there."

Skye gasped and whirled back, but the man was gone.

She knew that men were trouble, but otherworldly men who disappeared in the blink of an eye were even more so. Avoiding trouble was the mainstay of her existence, so Skye knew she wouldn't be going anywhere near a bar called Sanctuary.

THAT NIGHT SKYE found herself staring across the road at the building that housed Sanctuary. She eyed the Were standing guard at the door. From his size, she thought he might be a bear.

No way was she going to go in.

Skye was surprised to find herself anywhere near

the place, but something about the tall stranger had compelled her to come. Who was he? How had he known her name? What help could a bar full of bears offer her?

Still, sanctuary sounded good after years of lying low. Maybe she should check it out.

Skye went to step out of the shadows but paused and looked down at herself. Shorts and a loose shirt might have let her blend in with the tourists earlier in the day's heat, but they didn't seem appropriate for a bar. She decided to keep the sneakers in case she needed to run, but she concentrated briefly and used her magic to change her clothes.

Happy her choice of jeans and a lace-edged top was suitable for such a warm evening, Skye checked her pocket to make sure she still had her wallet. She crossed the road at last and manoeuvred past the row of bikes lined up along the kerb. The bar was obviously crowded. It didn't sound at all like the peaceful haven its name promised.

"I thought you weren't going to come over, for a minute there." The Bearswain opened the door wide in welcome. "Hey, you're a little one, aren't you? Are you sure you're old enough to drink?" His tone made it clear he was joking, but Skye self-consciously drew herself to her full height of a hair under five feet. She glared up at him.

Sheer bravado made her respond. "Why are all the men in New Orleans so tall?" she complained. "Is it something in the water?"

He laughed and gestured at her to enter. "I like you, little bird. Tell my brother at the bar that I said your first drink is on me—and to make it with water so maybe you'll grow a bit."

"Your brother." Her jaw dropped. 'You mean there's another one of you?"

"More than one, but you can always tell me from the others by my tattoo." He indicated the strange double-bow tattoo peeking out from under the hem of his T-shirt sleeve. "Just ask anyone to fetch Dev if you get into trouble, and I'll come running."

"Maybe if I see you coming, I'll be the one running... away." Skye grinned impishly back up at him, somehow unable to remain afraid of the giant bear who welcomed her so warmly. She took a breath and stepped through the door he still held open.

Inside, Skye paused to look around with interest. The bar was dimly lit and as crowded as she had imagined. It was furnished with a ragtag collection of tables and chairs surrounding a small dance floor in front of an unoccupied stage. A few people were dancing to the music blaring from an old juke box next to the stage.

More people were playing pool at the back of the bar on tables that filled the area under a shadowy balcony. The bar was larger than it had seemed from the outside, yet to Skye it still seemed overcrowded.

Skye took a step back in surprise at the sight of a coffin in the corner behind the doors. Peering at it, she saw it was labelled, "The last man who tried to date Aimee." Shaking her head in amusement, Skye let her gaze travel past the coffin to a long, scarred bar that ran the length of the room.

Making her way through the crowd, Skye was startled to see another Were behind the bar, who so closely resembled Dev that she checked his arm for the distinctive tattoo. He smiled when he realised what she was looking for. "Dev doesn't move that fast. Didn't he tell you I was his brother?"

"He did mention you were his brother, but he didn't tell me you were his twin."

"Quad," responded a voice behind her. Turning, she saw another Dev carrying a drinks tray. "But I'm Quinn, the best-looking one."

"Four of you." Skye shook her head in disbelief.

A pretty blonde moved along the bar to join them. "Ignore them," she said. "I'm Aimee Peltier, and if my brothers give you a hard time, you all just let me know."

Skye pointedly looked at the coffin before turning back to Aimee. "So you're Aimee. With four brothers like these I'm surprised you get to date."

Aimee laughed. "If only. I have eleven brothers— we bears tend to have big families. It used to be a problem, but my mate is tough enough to handle them all."

Almost too quickly to see, Aimee grabbed the white towel draped over her brother's shoulder and swatted him with it as he leaned against the counter. "Cherif, have you got the lady a drink yet?"

"Not yet, but I would have if you all would stop interrupting." Grabbing the towel back from Aimee before she could hit him again, Cherif turned back to Skye. "What would you like, sugar?"

"Aah, I'll have a beer. Whatever is on tap, thanks." She handed over payment.

Quinn nudged her and pointed across the crowd behind him, to a corner of the room near the stage. "Why don't you grab a seat at that empty table over there and I'll bring the beer over to you."

"Thanks, I'll do that." Skye was still smiling as she made her way over to the empty table.

. . .

CANE FOLLOWED his father into Sanctuary.

They made their way to the bar where Cane saluted Cherif. "Hey, quad, how's things?"

"Hey, Cane, didn't know you were back in town. Hello, Carson, what can I get you?"

"Two beers—thanks, Cherif," Carson replied.

"I guess you're here to meet the little Were who came in a while ago. Pretty thing. I haven't seen her around here before." Cherif indicated across the room.

Turning they looked where he pointed, and both started in surprise.

They saw a tiny but beautiful young woman, with feathery bronze wisps of hair tipped with gold fluttering around her shoulders. Her eyes were wide as she looked around the room. She was perched on the edge of her chair as if she were ready to fly away at any moment.

"An eyas," breathed Carson. "She looks like one of the Falconi, but I thought they were all dead."

Cane was still staring at Skye when his father nudged him. "Close your mouth, son. We should go over and introduce ourselves."

Taking the beers Cherif handed them, they crossed the room. As they stopped next to her table, Cane waited until she looked up at them before asking, "Mind if we join you?"

Skye's eyes widened until their bronze-gold colour was almost completely swallowed by the black of her pupils. She saw two tall Native Americans, with wild black hair tipped with bronze, sharp features, and fierce hazel eyes. The taller one had his hair in a long braid. He wore casual pants and a loose shirt. The other wore his hair short and had a white T-shirt over tight dark jeans. "Tierces," she whispered. "I haven't met any hawks in so long I thought I was the only one left."

Cane smiled at her. "There are still Gerakian breeds around."

Carson smiled and nudged him aside. He smiled at Skye. "I'm Carson Whitethunder and this is my son Cane."

Skye looked from one to the other. "That doesn't seem right." She frowned with suspicion. "Cane seems older than you—how can you be his father?"

Cane grinned. "Time shifting can be confusing. I was born in 1723 while Dad was born in 1956—so I've caught up with him here, but he hasn't met my mother yet." He continued to look at Skye in admiration, drawn to her warmth and beauty.

"Remember, I don't want to know anything more about my future in your past." He shook his head at Cane. "Be careful what you say." Carson smiled. "I already know that I meet my mate and have at least one child. I don't want to upset the Fates by knowing more."

"Are you Falcons?" Skye sounded hesitant.

"Sorry, no. The only Falcon aeries left are in Europe and Egypt. We are Aquila. May we sit down?" Carson spoke softly and carefully, as if addressing a wild animal.

Blushing wildly, Skye nodded. "Of course. Sorry, I don't think I've ever met any Eagles before."

"Welcome to Sanctuary," Cane took the seat opposite her. "Sooner or later you will run into all kinds here."

Skye looked warily from one to the other. "You both live here?"

"Well, I do. Cane is visiting me. I work for the bears."

"Dad runs the clinic over at the Peltier's home." He grinned at his father. "That's how we met. I was hurt and my friends brought me in to Sanctuary. They didn't know that my father was the doctor here, or that I was supposed to avoid him out of our timeline."

"A doctor." Skye sounded impressed. She picked up her beer and raised it in a silent toast.

"Well, more of a vet most days," Carson joked. "Cane tried to tell me he was a distant cousin, but I have enough of my father's shaman blood in me to hear the winds when they speak to me. They told me he was my son."

"So what brings you here to Sanctuary, Miss...?" Cane asked, picking up his own beer.

"Oh, sorry, I'm Skye Falconi."

"I thought you were a Falconi," Carson frowned. "But we heard your aerie had been wiped out twenty years ago."

Skye shuddered. "It was over twenty-five years ago now. I was on my first solo flight and flew further than I was supposed to. When I got back to the aerie..." Her voice faltered and she looked down at the table.

Carson reached across to pat her hand. "I'm sorry for your loss, Skye. You must have been very young."

She shrugged. "I was twenty-three. I've been flying solo ever since."

"Twenty-three. Wow, you were young." Cane eyed her with respect.

Skye remembered her parents' pride when she shifted at such a young age. Unfortunately, her memories of them always returned to the last ones.

Her mother's voice screaming in her head.

"Don't come home."

"Beware of the Falcons."

Then the awful silence as every call she sent out to her parents went unanswered.

When she dared to creep back home, the place had been painted red with blood. She couldn't forget the horror of seeing her father's lifeless hand stretching out to touch her mother's, as they lay amongst the wreckage of their home and the bodies of their family.

"How have you managed since then, Skye? Your parents would have just started your training." Carson asked, interrupting her darkest memories. "I was nearly thirty when my father brought me to Sanctuary so I could get the help I needed. I know how hard it is to try to learn on your own."

"I managed. I got a little help from a lone wolf in Malibu, but she wasn't very skilled. Mostly I've taught myself and stayed away from people." Skye grinned wryly down at the beer glass in front of her. "I finally mastered manifesting clothes after a few embarrassing changes when my clothes didn't reappear with me. There's so much I don't know, though." Skye lifted her head to look at Carson with speculative interest. "Do you think you could help me?"

"Of course we'll help! Won't we, Dad?" Cane answered, pleased for an excuse to remain in touch with the fascinating Falconswan.

"Absolutely, but how did you know where to find us?"

"It was really odd," Skye shifted in her chair. "I met a man on the beach at Malibu one day, and he told me to come to New Orleans. I don't know why I listened to him, but I made my way here." She grimaced. "It was a long flight."

"You flew." Cane looked surprised. "But—" He stopped when Carson kicked him under the table.

"A man?" Carson queried. "Not a Were?"

"No, he was definitely not a Were." Skye shrugged before turning to glare at Cane. "How was I supposed to get here without flying? Take a bus? No one has been able to show me how to translocate so I couldn't just flash here." She sniffed and turned back to Carson.

Cane struggled to hide a grin at her spirited response.

"Well, we can certainly help you there," Carson smiled. "Hawks often have trouble with translocation. I didn't have a lot of training while I was growing up, but I'm sure I'll be able to teach you."

Cane winced at his father's offer. "As I recall, Mom did most of my training. Maybe I should teach Skye."

"Oh, that would be absolutely wonderful," Skye beamed, unable to stay annoyed with him. "I bet that's why the other man told me to come to Sanctuary."

"The man in California?" Cane asked.

"No, the man I ran into this morning."

Carson's eyebrows lifted in amazement. "Two different men guided you here?" He exchanged looks with his son.

Skye had been playing with her glass, making wet circles on the tabletop as they spoke. Releasing it, she leaned back and looked up.

Gasping, she pointed up at the balcony where a man stood leaning on the rail. He was wearing a garish Hawaiian shirt over what looked like a wet suit. He had dark hair and a neat goatee. "That's the man from Malibu," she whispered, as the man stared back at her.

Carson and Cane both looked to where she was pointing and gaped. "Savitar," Cane whispered.

Savitar smirked at the two men before turning away.

"Savitar told you to come to New Orleans?" Carson turned back to exchange an amazed look with Cane.

"If that's his name," Skye shrugged. "He didn't introduce himself, just told me to come to New Orleans. The other man told me to come to Sanctuary." She looked at them both. "I don't know why I did what either of them said. It just seemed like I had to."

"I don't doubt that," Carson said. "I don't want to think about what would have happened if you hadn't."

Quinn approached the table looking more than a little shaken. He deposited three more beers onto the table. "Compliments of Savitar. He just head-popped me." The bear shuddered at the memory of Savitar's order beaming directly into his brain.

Carson drained what was left in his first glass in one gulp. "Now I know why it's so quiet in here tonight."

Quinn nodded grimly before rushing off.

"This is quiet?" Skye's eyebrows shot up as she looked around at the crowded bar.

Carson grinned at her shock. "Sanctuary is normally louder and rowdier than this. The humans are acting normal, but Savitar's presence explains why everyone else is behaving themselves."

He looked around and saw that the Weres present were split between those hunching themselves over their drinks trying to blend in with the furniture, and those stealing horrified glances up at the balcony. Even the other non-humans in the bar were acting subdued. "I don't think we've had one real argument in here tonight."

"Who is Savitar? I don't recognise him as a Were." Skye looked at Cane.

"Savitar is... well he just is." Cane mumbled.

Carson smiled at his son's stumbling reply. "Savitar is one of a kind. He oversees the Omegrion, the Weres' governing council, and monitors limani like Sanctuary. His word is law, and his temper is legendary. No one defies Savitar and lives to tell of it." Cane nodded in agreement.

"He rarely interferes with individuals." Carson continued as he looked kindly at Skye, "Which explains why we were so surprised when you said he sent you to New Orleans."

"But why would he send me here? To—what did you call it? A lemony?" She waved her hands to indicate the bar around them.

"We may never know why you were sent here, Skye," Carson smiled "A limani is literally a sanctuary for all Were-kind. It gives us a safe place to meet on neutral ground. All are welcome and no fighting is allowed. Well, no fighting between Weres anyway."

Skye listened to Carson's explanation, but her attention was again drawn to his son. From under half-closed lids, she studied the breadth of his shoulders and the strength of his arms. There was something about Cane that intrigued her. No sooner did she manage to look away, to glance around the room, or to look at Carson, than she found herself looking back at Cane. It was hypnotic the way he kept staring at her.

She was vain enough to be glad she had chosen a gold-coloured top when she changed her clothes earlier. She knew the colour brightened the golden flecks in her eyes and added warmth to her pale skin.

"I'm glad he did send you here." Cane smiled warmly at Skye. "Would you like to dance with me?" He pointed to the space in front of the stage.

Skye blushed. "I don't know how. Don't forget I've avoided people for twenty-five years."

"It's easy," Cane laughed and pointed as he stood up. "Look at Kyle over there. He's lumbering around like the bear he is. You just have to move to the music. Come on."

Skye studied the young Bearswain capering around the floor, dancing with three young human women. Taking a breath, she stood and reached out to take the hand Cane was holding out to her.

As their hands touched, a spark leapt between them. The humans at nearby tables all assumed it was the flash of a camera, as it highlighted them both.

An electric surge raced between Skye and Cane as if a circuit had suddenly been closed. The hair on their heads flashed to feathers and back to hair, too quickly for any mortal eye to see. Pulling her hand free, Skye dropped back into her chair.

Carson sputtered over his beer. His attention caught by the flash of light, he had looked up in time to see the feather shift. Amused by their shocked expressions, he grinned at them. "Well, isn't this interesting."

"What the hell was that?" Skye rubbed at her hand, expecting to see a mark there. She turned to look up at Cane.

Carson nudged his son. "Don't stare, Cane. You were going to dance with your mate."

"Mate," whispered Skye.

"Potentially, anyway. An ancestor of ours did a favour for Athena many years ago. She couldn't challenge the Fates about Were-mates, but as a thank-you, she graced the hawks with the shivering." He shrugged. "It's how we recognise a potential mate without having to have sex first. Makes our species a lot more discriminating than the poor wolves, or cats."

Carson smiled at Skye. "It's your choice little one, but I would be delighted to welcome you to our aerie."

"Mate," whispered Cane, staring at Skye as if she were the Mona Lisa, Venus De Milo, and Aphrodite, all rolled into one and coated in 24-carat gold.

"*Potential* mate, Cane. It's up to you to woo her. Now, go and dance." He waved them towards the dance floor.

Skye looked at Cane's hand as he held it out to her once more. She seemed scared to touch it. "The shivering only happens once, Skye. We don't have to go any further until you are ready." He looked into her eyes as their hands met again. "Mating marks don't appear until after we make love, and then we will have three weeks to complete the ritual." He glanced down at her tiny hand wrapped in his much larger one and smiled wryly as he pulled her back to her feet. "If you choose to accept me, that is."

Skye flushed bright red and looked away from him. "After we... but you're an Eagle."

"I suppose there's a lot your parents never got to teach you, Skye." He pointed at his father. "Dad's mother was an Arcadian Eagle, but his father was human. Then there's our friend Wren, a Tigard, whose father was a Tiger and his mother a Snow Leopard."

Carson interrupted to nod his head towards the bar, where Aimee had been joined by a tall dark Were. "Aimee's an Arcadian Bear, but her mate Fang is a Katagarian Wolf. Apparently, there are no limits to what the Fates decree. It is entirely up to us once the match is made."

"Well, it's really up to you." Cane smiled at her.

"Fair warning though, I'll do anything I can to convince you to accept me."

As he looked at Skye, Cane felt the blood heat in his veins as lust cascaded through him. Jumbled thoughts raced through his head as he considered ways to get her alone. Maybe he could use the soundproof room off the bar that the bears used as a convenient place for trysts. Or there was the room he was staying at in Peltier house. He could flash them both there and let the bears deal with mind wiping any mortals who noticed, or—

Cane. Carson's voice seemed to echo in his head as yelled his thoughts at him. Cane saw that Carson was looking at his crotch where a growing bulge was proof of his arousal. *Remember how young Skye is. She's been running scared for years and doesn't need you pushing for more than she is ready to give.*

Cane struggled to regain control of himself. He slipped his free hand under Skye's chin and tilted her face up to look into her eyes. He saw how shyly she struggled to meet his gaze. He also saw the red flush of embarrassment still warming her cheeks, and silently sighed.

He tugged on the hand he still held. "Dance with me." Leading her to the dance floor, he took her into his arms.

Skye shuddered at the feel of his arms around her. She felt was warm for the first time since her family had been slaughtered.

She tentatively rested her head against his hard chest. Skye was so short that her head tucked neatly under Cane's chin, and she couldn't resist nuzzling the vee of skin exposed by his collar. The scent of his skin was intoxicating and seemed to weave around her thoughts until it was all she could do to stop herself from licking him.

Cane began to move them to the music, bending his head until he could drop a kiss onto her hair. "It's just a dance, Skye. Everything else can wait."

Suddenly the music stopped. The opening notes of a different song began to play.

Cane groaned and glared at Kyle who was now standing by the jukebox. "No. Our first dance can't be *Sweet Home, Alabama*. We have to have our own song."

"What's wrong?" Skye asked as she looked up at him in confusion.

"The Bears play it to warn everyone that Ash is here. It gives anyone who wants to avoid him a chance to leave." He pointed to the rear of the bar where a few people were slipping through a back door.

"Ash?"

"Acheron, the leader of the Dark Hunters."

"I've heard of Dark Hunters, but I don't know if I've ever met one." Skye turned in his arms and looked around the room with interest. "Which one is..." Her voice trailed off.

"Skye?"

"Cane, is he the tall man heading for the balcony stairs?"

Cane looked around. "Yep, that's Ash. Why?"

Skye looked at Cane, before turning back to look at the tall, black-clad figure climbing the stairs. "Because that's the man I ran into this morning, the one who told me to come to Sanctuary."

Cane stared at her.

ACHERON CROSSED the balcony to stand by Savitar's side.

"Hey, Grom." Savitar handed him a beer. "You owe me big time for this one. My reputation is going to be worth squat if it gets around that I helped you play matchmaker."

Ash snorted. "Nope, not buying it. I know you've missed Skye's father at the Omegrion table."

Savitar's answering grin was wicked. "I look forward to the look on that Arcadian Falcon's face when he realises who Skye is. Bastard thought he had wiped Skylar Falconi's entire aerie out and got away with it. Damn his feathery ass." Savitar took a long drink from the beer he held and sighed. "And Arcadians think the Katagarians are animals." He shook his head at their folly. "The Omegrion wanted proof of what happened. Skye can provide it."

He frowned. "Meetings have been so boring lately that I haven't had to punish anyone for months. This should stir things up a bit."

"Be careful what you wish for." Ash took a drink from the glass he held. "So, are you going to tell Skye?"

"Nah, I'm going back to the ocean, there's some gnarly waves due to hit Hawaii about now. She'll find out soon enough." Savitar looked over at this friend. "At this point they don't even know that Skye will accept Cane as her mate, so I'll give them a few weeks to adjust."

Ash nodded. "We've certainly had some interesting matings over the last few years." He tilted his head towards the bar where Aimee was trying to fend off the affectionate embrace of her mate Fang.

Savitar shuddered. "If you and those harpies the Fates would stop messing with the natural order of things, I'd be a happy man. A bear mated with a wolf makes no sense at all." Savitar shook his head before nudging Ash with his elbow. "What the hell is Simi going to call the offspring of a Falcon and an Eagle? A Feagle?"

"Blame the Fates for future Feagles," Ash smiled and touched his forearm where his companion Simi rested in her tattoo form. "As for Aimee and Fang, it makes sense to them. You know I can't fight free will."

Savitar groaned and thumped Ash on the shoulder. "On that note..." He disappeared and left Ash to enjoy the rest of his beer alone.

"Well, Skye," Ash mused as he emptied his glass. "It's up to you now. You think you came here to find help with your magic, or a sanctuary where you could rest. What you found was a chance at what you really need."

"Family is more precious than gold, or magic." He smiled wryly. "If you can only find the courage to reach for it."

As Ash watched the pair on the dance floor below him, he saw Cane lower his head to Skye's. He saw the shy way she turned her face up to meet Cane's kiss.

Still smiling, Ash flashed out of Sanctuary and back to his home, where his own family waited.

A FOX WITH NEW FUR

KIM MAY

A fox can change its fur, but not its habits.
    Megumi's grandfather had quoted that saying all throughout her childhood. She was just a kit back then, so of course she hadn't listened to him. Now she wished that she had.

Megumi had ditched her kimono with her family crest in favor of jeans, a tight-fitting black t-shirt, and sneakers. An illusion hid her fox tail and ears from view, since she was too young to completely shift into human form. Megumi kept her fluffy black tail pressed firmly against her back. Being invisible didn't mean that it took up less space. Her long black hair fell to the middle of her back and hid the seam between illusion and reality.

Mardi Gras was in a few days, and tourists flooded the streets of the French Quarter. The cacophony of the throng was deafening. The Oni that chased her across Japan had found her again when she fled to the US. With all of the noise around her, she couldn't tell if that foul demon had found her again. Her pulse raced and she had to breathe slow and deep to calm herself. Because of her sensitive nose, the combined odors of sweat, booze, and sex were nauseating. It made her want to run, but she forced herself to keep walking, keep maintaining a calm façade. The only good thing about the scents around her was that they should be enough to bury her scent. However, there was one more thing she could do to hopefully lose him for good.

Megumi turned onto Ursulines Avenue and headed for a biker bar a few blocks away. The raucous crowd pressed against her as she made her way to Sanctuary. She'd never been there before, but their reputation was well known amongst shifters of all types. Most importantly the scent of bear, mossy pine with the freshness of a mountain stream, permeated the building. It made the building feel like an extension of the forest, like home. If she spent a few hours there, long enough for her clothing to pick up their aroma, it should mask her long enough for her to leave the city with the demon being none the wiser.

After what felt like an hour, the building finally came into sight. The exterior was covered in beautiful rust-colored brick. There was a line of black motorcycles parked outside. A tall, burly man stood at the door. He had long, wavy blond hair, blue eyes, and a bow and arrow tattoo on his arm. The energy rolling off him in massive waves made it clear to her that he wasn't human. Despite that, he posed no threat. Megumi felt no anger or even impatience coming from him. She discreetly sniffed the air as she walked past him. Her nose was flooded with the smell of bear. He was a Peltier, then. Megumi joined the line to get in. The bear noticed her right away and beckoned her to the front.

A small group of co-eds wearing colorful sashes that said "wedding party" complained. One of them, a bottle blonde carrying a pair of bright pink high heels, reached out with her free hand, and tried to pull Megumi back.

"Get back in line. We were here first," the blonde said. Her glare might have scared a few faint souls, but Megumi had seen storms with more fury.

Megumi shook her off and walked to the front of the line. A fierce glare from the bouncer put an end to their protests. The bottle blonde got back in line but continued to glare at Megumi.

"I haven't seen a foxy lady like you here before," the bouncer said.

"I just got into town." Megumi was surprised. Had others of her kind been here before, or was his nose really that good?

"You know the rules?"

"Don't start no shit and there won't be no shit."

He nodded. "And if you don't want to be bothered, then we'll make sure you're not bothered." He waved her in. "Enjoy."

Megumi nodded in thanks.

The inside of the bar was two stories tall. The main part of the bar was open air with plenty of booths and standing tables for their patrons. On the left there was a row of pool tables and a beautiful pine staircase that led to the balcony above. There was a stage directly across from the saloon door she just walked through, and a long, polished bar took up the right wall.

The bar was packed. The band playing tonight was between sets and everyone was talking over each other, so it was probably louder than it was during their set. The bar smelled of alcohol, food, and at least five different types of shifters. Some of the shifters' scents she couldn't identify, they were so foreign to her. There were also strange clusters of divine energy radiating from the balcony. It wasn't likely anyone from her pantheon, so she didn't give them another thought. As long as she didn't cause a scene, they would never know she was here.

Megumi wound her way through the crowd and found a vacant spot at the bar. The bartender was a clean-cut male with short dark hair. He smelled of bear, but he wasn't a relation to the Peltier at the door. There was a subtle difference in the earthiness of his scent—more fresh pine and less moss.

The bartender wiped down a spot with a towel. "What'll it be?"

"Gin."

"You want that with or without the human hair?"

It took her a moment to parse that he meant did she want her drink human strength or shifter strength.

"With. I need to keep my head clear."

He poured her a human-sized portion and left her to her thoughts. Megumi had barely started sipping it when the fine hairs on the back of her neck stood on end. Her instincts screamed for her to run, to hide. She tamped them down before her fear spread to all the shifters in the building.

She glanced over at the door. A group of tourists had walked in but the man standing behind them, scanning the crowd, made her hands tremble.

He had a muscular build and was well over six feet tall. He wore a black silk button-up shirt with the top four buttons undone and the sleeves rolled up. The leather pants he wore were a patchwork of colors— and most of it wasn't of animal origin.

His hair was dyed bright red, and every inch of ex- posed skin below his neck was covered in blue-grey

tattoos. A thin tendril of smoke rose from the lit cigarette tucked into the corner of his mouth.

Somehow Hayato Kanda had found her again.

Megumi's drink fell from her hand. She whipped
around, hoping to catch it, but the glass wasn't falling
anymore. The bartender caught it the instant it left
her grasp.

"Something wrong?"

Megumi froze, paralyzed by embarrassment and
fear. She wanted to tell him. They had a right to know
what was at risk, but she also didn't want to get them involved in her problem. Megumi opened her mouth, but
no words came out. She honestly hadn't expected Kanda
to get this far. She could have sworn that she'd lost him
in the bayou. This was impossible. Megumi clenched
her fist and slammed it against the bar. Her hand stung
from the impact. How didn't matter at this point. Kanda
was here, and he was now everyone's problem.

"Who is it?" His stern expression made it clear that
he wasn't going to let the matter drop.

Megumi sighed. "The tattooed man by the door."

The bartender sniffed the air. "He some kind of
demon?"

She nodded. "Oni. He's been hunting me."

"What did you do to piss him off?"

"I rejected him."

"Seriously?"

Megumi reclaimed her drink and took another sip.
"He's yakuza. One day he saw me walking down the
street and he decided that he had to have me. I said
no. When he persisted, I fought back, but he didn't get
the hint. That's when I broke his neck. His rage and
crimes were sufficient to instantly turn him into a demon. and he's been stalking me ever since."

If he ever caught her... Megumi shivered. Whether it was blood or sex, Oni couldn't be sated. Ever. Death would be a mercy if he caught her.

"Get your tail upstairs. We'll handle him."

"No, you can't." Megumi shook her head. They had no clue.

"Yes, we can. This is what we do."

Megumi leaned across the bar and whispered. "Rules mean nothing to him. If you stand in his way, he'll shift into demon form and tear this place down brick by brick."

"In case you didn't notice, we're not small," he said with a growl.

"Neither is he. His demon form is the size of a parade float."

"Good." The bartender popped his knuckles. "That'll make it more fun."

Megumi rolled her eyes. "I'm surprised your race has lived this long."

The bartender grinned. "What doesn't kill you gives you bragging rights."

Megumi buried her head in her hands. Was she cursed? All her plans were going wrong, and now she was trying to talk sense into a homicidal Arcadian. At this rate she'd never live long enough to earn her second tail.

"Look," the bartender said. "I appreciate the warning," he continued, "but you need to let us handle this." There was a tension in his voice that wasn't there before. He was either itching for a fight, or he was tired of her objections.

It was tempting to sit back and let them bounce him. Kanda terrified her. It was more than his appearance. It was his lack of regard for her feelings. It didn't matter how many times she said no, what illusion she wore, or how many times she ran. He would find her. Death hadn't put an end to his harassment, so killing him again wasn't likely to work either. Knowing her ill luck, he'd probably be reborn again, only this time in a more dangerous form.

She could hide here as planned, safe and protected, but Sanctuary couldn't shelter her forever. Sooner or later, she'd have to walk through those saloon doors. When she did, Kanda would be waiting for her. Megumi had no doubt about that. If she didn't stop Kanda here and now, she would never be free.

At least she didn't have to do this alone. Whatever she tried, she'd have a team of bears by her side—whether she liked it or not. "At least let me help."

"Were you dropped on your head as a kit?"

"Possibly." Megumi locked gazes with him. "I'm terrified. But most of all I'm tired of running. I need to prove to myself that I'm not a coward."

He considered her for a moment before nodding.

Megumi smiled faintly. She was still afraid of Kanda, but she felt confident that she'd made the right decision. Every shifter reached a point when they had to conquer their animal instincts. It sucked that her moment was in a place and time without another fox to help her through it. At least the bar staff she'd met so far were understanding. She was already feeling better about the idea of them being alongside her.

Megumi looked over her shoulder again. Just knowing he was a few feet closer sent a chill down her spine. He hadn't spotted her yet, but his aura was brushing against hers. She tightened her illusion around her.

I need a battle plan, and fast.

Megumi stared at her distorted reflection in the bottles behind the bar. What could she do? She wasn't much of a fighter. The only things she excelled at were casting illusions and creating pocket dimensions. That wasn't much to work with. How in the name of Amaterasu was she going to stop Kanda?

If they were still in Japan, she could lure him to a Shinto temple with a holy tree that she could trap him in. That wasn't an option here in New Orleans. Even if there were a comparable holy site, there was so much magic and superstition in the air that it would backfire if she couldn't surround the entire site in a pocket dimension. The hint of fear she saw in her eyes, reflected to her in a square bottle of whiskey, wasn't helping.

Wait a second. An empty bottle...

Megumi downed the rest of her gin.

"Is there an alley he can be led to? I need about ten cubic feet of empty air and that bottle of booze."

The bartender raised an eyebrow. "Yeah, there's an alley. I don't know what you're planning, but we can get him there, no problem." He picked up the bottle of whiskey. It had a shot worth that swirled at the bottom as he brought it over to her. "If it's liquid courage you're looking for, we've got stronger stuff."

"I need the bottle, not the booze," Megumi said. "I'm going to try to trap him inside."

The bartender poured the remnants into a shot glass. "I hate to tell ya, but he's not going to fit."

Megumi changed the position of his hands, so he held the bottle on its side. "Yes, he will. Once he's outside the bar, I'm going to warp space, so the bottle is large enough." She tapped on the bottle's mouth. Megumi then traced a path along the neck of the bottle and halfway downside with her finger. "Then I'll be the bait that lures him inside. Before you object yes, I know it's dangerous and I'm insane for considering it, but can you think of a better way to lure him inside before he suspects?"

He glared at her but didn't voice any objections.

"Once he's inside, I'll seal the opening so he can't get out." Megumi downed the shot of whiskey.

"Didn't need the liquid courage?"

Megumi shrugged. "I didn't want a shot of one of Tennessee's finest to go to waste."

The bartender took the empty glass from her. Megumi got the impression that he did it more out of habit than to cut her off.

"Don't worry. This will work," Megumi said. *It has to work! I don't have any other ideas.*

He still looked skeptical, but he handed her the bottle anyway.

"You'll see," she said.

The bartender whistled. Most of the human patrons couldn't hear it above the noise. The few near them that did hear it turned back to their drinks and conversations a second later. A blond man leaning against the wall by the door to the kitchen looked up and made his way to them. He had a slight limp that favored his right leg. He also looked identical to the bouncer at the door.

"Cherif, can you take over for a few? I need to give a guy an eviction notice."

He nodded. "Sure, Colt."

Megumi watched Colt walk around the bar and make his way through the crowd to Kanda. Megumi knew the moment Kanda spotted Colt. His shoulders tensed and the smoke coming from the cigarette doubled. Oh no, he's going to shift. It's too soon. There were so many humans around. Someone was going to get killed if they didn't get Kanda out of here immediately.

Megumi headed for the front door but made sure that she bumped into people along the way. She shouted her apologies to each human she collided with. After she apologized to the fourth person, she and Kanda locked eyes.

Megumi ran for the door, not caring whom she elbowed in the process. The bouncer that let her in called after her as she passed him. Megumi didn't slow down. She dashed around the building and into the alley. Kanda would be here in seconds, so her preparations needed to be perfect. If it was the slightest bit off, he'd catch on and this plan would never work.

She removed the pour spout and threw the whiskey bottle in front of her. Megumi filled it and the air in the alley with power. The bottle expanded and grew. The neck and mouth of the bottle was ten feet tall while the rest of the bottle was as big as Sanctuary. Yet despite its massive size the bottle only took up a miniscule fraction of that. She left a Kanda-sized doorway of sorts. Hopefully Kanda hadn't shifted. If he had, she'd have to take drastic measures. Megumi hid the bottle behind another illusion, so it blended seamlessly with the rest of the alley. Only the slightest shimmer hinted that something else was there.

Kanda ran into the alley with Colt and the bouncer on his heels. She raised an illusion behind them with the wave of a hand. To the humans passing by it would look like a brick wall connected Sanctuary with the next building. It wouldn't muffle sounds, but at least it would keep anyone from seeing things that they shouldn't.

"You're not escaping this time," Kanda growled.

That's exactly what she wanted to do. All her instincts screamed at her to run, to find a deep dark hole to hide in. Megumi forced her fears aside. She'd made up her mind and it was too late to change it.

"I'm not running anymore, Kanda," Megumi said. "Come and get me."

Smoke poured from his mouth. His chest expanded, ripping his shirt to shreds as he grew a foot in the space of a heartbeat. His pants parted at the sides, allowing his thighs to double in thickness.

Colt and the bouncer flanked Kanda. They didn't attack him, but the intensity of the glares they gave Kanda made her anxious.

"As much as I want to see his ass get beat," Megumi said, "that's not the objective right now. I need a little more time."

Kanda laughed. "Whatever you're planning, little fox, won't work. You're mine."

"I will never be yours." Megumi said. "You disgust me."

Megumi ran farther into the alley and straight into the mouth of the bottle. She looked behind her and saw Kanda following. Fire glimmered in his eyes.

"You want me?" She shouted at Kanda in Japanese. "Come get me, bastard!"

Kanda charged after her, straight into the bottle's mouth. Megumi ran farther in. She felt a tingle on the back of her neck. Megumi jumped, tucking her feet under her. His outstretched clawed hand grazed the soles of her sneakers. Megumi felt his black nails scraping the rubber soles. Kanda roared in fury as she sailed over his head.

Below her she saw Colt and the bouncer. Shit! They must have chased Kanda into the bottle. She wouldn't be able to seal it until they were all safely outside of this pocket dimension. Her feet were fast enough to get out before Kanda could reach the mouth. Unfortunately, she had no idea if Colt and Dev were, and teleportation wouldn't work in pocket dimensions. Teleportation only worked if you had physical locations for the origin point and destination. Pocket dimensions existed in the space between.

"Dev! Take care of her." Colt shouted.

Colt mule-kicked Kanda in the back, sending him sprawling to the floor. Kanda landed with enough force that it shook the bottle. Colt landed on his feet. He was surprisingly nimble for a bear.

Megumi landed softly in a crouch. Dev placed himself between her and Kanda. Adrenaline surged through her, urging her to kick the demon's face in, but she forced herself to stay put. The last thing she needed to do was get in Colt's way. Dev watched Kanda and Colt intently. There was an eagerness about him. He clearly wanted to join in the fight but held himself back. She caught Dev and Colt casting expectant looks her way.

They're treating me like a cub on their first hunt.

As much as her pride bristled at the thought, she had to concede that they were right to act that way. They were older and more experienced, while she was still cutting her teeth. Megumi took the initiative in the bar, and now she had to follow through and prove she wasn't a frightened kit anymore.

Kanda pushed himself to his feet. Smoke curled from his nostrils. Colt punched Kanda in the head before he fully rose. He kept punching until blood trickled from the demon's nose.

Kanda laughed. "That the best you got?"

Colt growled. The deep rumble reverberated inside the bottle. Megumi could feel it in her bones. It made her shiver.

Kanda lunged at Colt. Colt sidestepped to dodge

the demon. Instead of stopping like she expected, Kanda continued charging... straight for Megumi. Dev pushed her back and tackled Kanda to the floor. Dev sat on his chest and punched him in the head. Kanda brought his hand back. His hand was flat like a blade, with his razor-sharp claws pointed at Dev's back.

Megumi shifted into her fox form. She leaped forward and clamped her jaws on Kanda's wrist. Kanda screeched and threw her across the floor. Megumi released his wrist so she wouldn't lose any teeth. Kanda threw her with enough force that she had to shift back into her clothed human form. Her sneakers gripped the glass better than her paws, helping her skid to a stop moments before she crashed into the side.

Blood trailed down Kanda's arm in a thick stream. Dev rose. He picked up Kanda by his neck and threw him to the far end of the bottle. Kanda never reached the end because Colt leaped into his flight path and clotheslined Kanda. The demon plummeted to the floor. Megumi frowned. She really wanted to see him hit the glass like a bug on a windshield.

Megumi shifted back into a fox. She ran for Kanda. A moment before she reached him, she spun around. Her tail struck Kanda in the side like a club. The impact sent him sliding across the bottom of the bottle. He hit the glass with a satisfying crunch. Megumi shifted back to human form.

"How the hell can you shift that much?" Dev asked.

"Kitsune aren't restricted the way Katagaria and Arcadians are," Megumi said.

Kanda pushed to his feet. Despite the blood loss and taking so many hits, he didn't look like he was close to being done. If anything, he looked more determined to draw blood—specifically Megumi's.

Kanda charged her again. Megumi dropped into a crouch. Colt and Dev stepped forward and body-blocked Kanda. Dev slipped behind Kanda while Colt threw punch after punch to keep the Oni's attention focused on him. The bears assaulted him from both sides, but Kanda dodged every punch and kick.

Why won't Kanda stay down? If it weren't for him, she'd be at home right now, racing her cousins through a bamboo forest. That selfish bastard had ruined her peaceful life!

Hatred filled Megumi until her tail burned from it. A flickering light in her periphery caught her attention. She looked and found the tip of her tail surrounded with blue flames that swirled and danced around her black fur. She shaped the flames into a sphere that balanced on the tip of her tail. Megumi waited for an opening.

Colt grabbed Kanda by the arm and jerked him forward. At the same time Colt brought his knee up, breaking Kanda's nose with a sickening crunch.

Megumi flicked her tail, throwing the fireball at Kanda. The fireball didn't have enough force behind it to knock him over. Fortunately, it didn't need to. The flame latched onto his hair and the tattered remnants of his shirt, burning him with fierce intensity.

Kanda panicked. He howled and rolled on the floor. The foxfire didn't need air to exist, so it didn't matter what Kanda tried. As long as her hatred for him burned, the fire couldn't be smothered. Kanda didn't know that though. He kept trying to put out the flames, which created the opening she needed.

"Get out now," Megumi shouted at Colt and Dev. She ran for the bottle's mouth. The opening to the pocket dimension would automatically close behind her regardless of whether Colt and Dev were outside or not. "Hurry! I have to be the last one out!"

Megumi stood by the exit, waiting for Dev and Colt. Dev ran through the bottle's neck and back into the alley. Colt was a little slower. He kept looking over his shoulder at Kanda, making sure he wasn't going to pursue.

"Move your tail, bear," Megumi growled. "I can't keep this open all day."

Colt moved past her in a blur. Megumi dashed through the bottle's neck. The instant her foot touched asphalt there was a pop. The warping field on the bottle snapped. The bottle shrank back to normal size, and Kanda shrank with it. Megumi shoved the pour spout back into the bottle. Kanda should be too small to fit through the spout, but to be sure she shrank the spout's tip until not even a needle could pass through it.

Megumi picked up the bottle. Kanda pounded on the glass walls of his prison, his back still burning. He shouted something at her that she couldn't hear through the glass.

"What was that, Kandakun? You're not going to be following me anymore? I'm heartbroken," she said with feigned horror. Kanda continued to pound on the glass. The black smoke that flowed from his mouth filled the bottle. Within a few minutes it was too hazy inside to see him clearly.

Megumi spun in a circle and laughed. It felt amazing to finally be free.

"What are you going to do with him now?" Colt asked. There was an intricate tattoo on his face that wasn't there when they were in the bar. *He's a Sentinel? That explains a few things.*

"I have no idea. I didn't think that far ahead."

Dev took the bottle from her. "I'll see if Acheron will take care of it. If anyone knows what to do with a homicidal demon, it's him."

"Too bad he's not in a barrel," Colt said. "Then we'd have the Devil's cut."

Dev groaned. He punched Colt in the arm. Megumi laughed till her sides ached. They walked back to Ursulines. The fight must have taken more out of her than she thought. It felt like she was dragging a ten-pound weight behind her.

Colt looked at her and smiled. "Congratulations on leveling up."

Megumi twisted around and saw that there were two tails behind her. No wonder she felt like there was extra weight behind her. Her second tail was black and bushy like her first. She squealed in delight as she twirled to get a better look at her brand-new tail.

"I would have been happy being free of Kanda. Getting foxfire and my second tail because of it is incredible."

She tucked both against her back and hid them with a fresh illusion. Megumi dismissed the illusion on the alley. With renewed vigor she followed the guys back to the bar.

"I hope you have some *sake*. It seems I have a lot to celebrate!"

THANK YOU...

WE HOPE YOU'VE ENJOYED THIS DARK
HUNTER ANTHOLOGY.

Lightning Source UK Ltd.
Milton Keynes UK
UKHW040730110222
398424UK00003B/55